OFF TO WAR

SARA R. TURNQUIST

MOUNTAIN
SUMMIT PRESS

If you would like to stay up-to-date on this and other series from Sara and receive a free ebook, sign up for her newsletter:

https://saraturnquist.com/list

*For my Mother, who first instilled in me a
love of the written word. And who has
read everything I have written.*

CHAPTER ONE
NEWS

The war was all anyone could talk about these days and Elizabeth was tired of hearing about it. Especially since the whole thing was altogether ridiculous. The South didn't have an ethical leg to stand on. Who in his right mind would think it just to own another person, to sell another person, to beat another human being, to separate someone from his or her family? It was obvious the Union had the moral high ground. And then for the Southern states to just leave? Secede from the Union indeed! Unimaginable! Yet it was happening. And now Americans were killing Americans. It was unthinkable.

Turning to John, she hoped she might engage him in less ghastly conversation. But to her surprise, she found him rather fixed on the exchange. Strange, she had never known him to be so interested in the goings-on of war. Then again, he was always looking for stimulating conversation. So, she was consigned to be a party, albeit a silent party, to all this talk of war.

Tucking an errant, blonde curl back into place, she noticed a loose pin in her hair. With gentle fingers, she secured it once again. A glance in her mother's direction warned her that her ministrations had been noticed. Placing her hands in her lap, she refocused her attention on her and John's fathers as they continued their discussion.

After what seemed like hours, the dessert plates were taken and the men stood, preparing to retire to the men's lounge. Only John remained by his seat as he rose.

"If you will excuse me, Dr. Thompson, Father, I hoped I might take Elizabeth for a stroll."

Elizabeth's eyes shot to John's face. What an unexpected indulgence! How long had it been since they had taken an evening stroll? Several weeks? She forced herself to remain in her seat and keep her hands in her lap, lest she betray her excitement. One glance at her mother's sharp gaze reinforced her need to retain a ladylike posture.

Dr. Thompson exchanged a look with John's father, Dr. Taylor. A smile passed between them.

Elizabeth's father nodded before stepping away from the table.

"Please take an outer covering, Elizabeth," her mother insisted. "It's still rather chilly out."

"Yes, Mother." Elizabeth stood, careful to slow her movements.

John offered his arm, a warm smile spread across his features.

It did melt something in Elizabeth, perhaps the iciness of the ceremony upon which she stood. For as she took his arm, she allowed her exterior to crack and returned his grin. Maybe with her back to her mother, she hadn't noticed.

Moments later, draped in her cape, and without further ado, Elizabeth and John were off. They stepped out of the house and onto the sidewalk. Elizabeth took a deep breath, glad to be free of their parents and of having to stand on any form of ceremony save one. Amanda, one of the housemaids, followed along, serving as their chaperone. But it wasn't the same as having her mother looking over her shoulder. For all intents and purposes, it was just the two of them.

Glancing over at John, she drew closer to him, wrapping her arm even tighter around his. He offered her another smile, placing his free hand on hers that captured his arm. Her heart fluttered being so close to him.

Closing her eyes, Elizabeth clasped the cross that John had gifted her one long-ago Christmas. He was everything to her: best friend, confidante, beau, and, unofficially, fiancé. The features of his face, his dark brown eyes, square jaw, chiseled nose and brow, and brown hair, were as familiar to her as her own reflection.

Elizabeth allowed her mind to wander back to their conversations of late. She and John had talked and dreamed about marriage, but nothing had been set in stone. This was not for fear of their parents' reactions. Quite the contrary. Their parents would be all too happy to hear of their plans. For now, it was their secret. It was, perhaps, a poorly kept secret. She would wager almost anything their parents expected their intentions to marry.

Together they strolled down the street, Amanda trailing behind, enjoying the fine weather and beautiful scenery, making small talk. It wasn't long before John turned toward the park. As always, Elizabeth enjoyed the easiness of these moments. They covered benign topics such as the weather and the goings-on of their families and mutual friends.

Once they entered the park, John found a bench for them to settle on. Amanda chose one far enough away to afford them some level of privacy, yet close enough to maintain a proper chaperonage. John helped Elizabeth arrange her cape so she was covered and warm. It was an unnecessary worry. With him beside her, the coolness of the evening was the last thing on her mind.

A silence fell between them.

"How were your rounds today?" she offered into the quiet that had befallen them.

John had just completed medical school and was interning at the nearby hospital.

"Fine," he replied, not offering anything further.

Such a simple response was quite unusual. He always had a couple of cases to discuss with her. When they were younger, they poured over their fathers' textbooks together. And she had done her share of helping him study during his tenure in medical school. It had become a game of sorts for him to detail the cases he had seen that day and let her attempt to diagnose the patients. Yet this evening he remained silent. Why? Whatever was on his mind weighed heavily.

"Do you want to talk about it?" She tested the waters.

He stared off into the distance. "We visited a wing of the hospital that cares for wounded soldiers."

"Oh." Her voice was just above a whisper. *How horrible.*

"It was unlike anything I had ever seen before...bodies mangled..." He shook his head. She knew he didn't want to impress any more imagery on her.

"I can't imagine what that must have been like for..." She reached out to touch his arm.

He interrupted her, his words rushing from him. "And so today I enlisted in the Northern regiment." His eyes held hers. They were serious.

Her heart dropped. What could she say? How could he make such a decision without talking to her first?

He stood and stepped away from her before turning back to face her. "I know. I know. I should have said something to you first. It was terrible, Lizzie, the pain, the death. What those men needed was more help on the front lines. That could have saved limbs. That could have saved lives. How could I not offer my skills to help so many?"

"I understand." How could she be so calm? It seemed as if she watched herself from outside her body. Then her voice began to break. "But I can't...I don't...that is...I..."

"It's all right." He sat down and pulled her into his embrace.

"What of our plans?" she managed through tears.

"I still want to marry you." He pulled back and cupped her face. "So much."

"Then let's get married now, before you go." The words fell out of her mouth almost before she thought them. A tingle shot through her. *What did she just say? Get married in the next few days?*

John cocked his head as he studied her features.

Elizabeth knew that look. She couldn't hide her trepidation from him. He would know she didn't want to throw a wedding together in a few days any more than he did, rush through a honeymoon, and then spend their first married year separated for who knew how long.

"That would make me happy. Truly happy," he said. "But I won't make you a war bride. And I won't risk making you a young widow."

Why would he say that? She reached up, placing her fingertips on his lips. "Don't talk like that."

He captured her hand in his. "It's a real possibility."

There seemed to be a hole forming in her chest where her heart had dropped. It ached. She threw herself into his arms. "I won't think like that. I can't!"

Elizabeth remained in his embrace for a few moments. *What must Amanda think?* It didn't matter. After some moments, John pulled back only far enough to look at her. He hooked his finger under her chin to tilt her head toward him.

"Remember, I love you," his voice was firm and confident.

"Always and forever?" She sniffed.

"Always and forever." He pressed a kiss to her lips.

Abigail Thompson sat in her favorite chair in the family parlor, working a cross-stitch that would become a decorative pillow. She enjoyed this craft as it gave her ample time to work things out in her mind as she worked the thread with her hands. If only everything could work out as easy and clean as her designs did! Her mind wandered amidst the ornate décor of her parlor, but her thoughts dwelt on how weary she had grown of watching her daughter mope around the house these last few days.

Since the night of John's big announcement, Elizabeth moved about her days as if she were thousands of miles away. Always sad, always downhearted. Abigail could only imagine the pain her daughter went through knowing her best friend and beau would soon be off to the war, perhaps never to return. It could not be an easy prospect to face. Indeed, they were all shaken by the news.

She admired John's decision to fight for his country, to stand for the principles for which the Union stood. Still, she couldn't agree with his decision to leave. As he neared the end of his internship, the prospect of his future lay before him. There was so much good he could do right here in Boston. So many people here needed him. Including Elizabeth.

Gentle footfalls neared the parlor. Abigail paused her work. Whoever dared disturb her solitude stopped just behind her chair. She turned as Amanda came around to face her.

"Excuse me, ma'am. I have the menu for this evening."

Abigail set her cross-stitch in her lap and, smiling up at the girl, encouraged her to continue. "All right."

"Roast, potatoes, carrots, green beans, yeast rolls, and custard dessert," Amanda recited.

"Everything sounds fine indeed."

Amanda curtsied and took her leave.

Every night since John made known his intentions to join the Northern army, the Thompsons and Taylors had dined together. John insisted on spending every available moment with Elizabeth. Even now, she was due back from the hospital. She spent her midday there to take lunch with him. Of late, their lunches had become more drawn out. It was doubtful that any of John's supervisors minded, considering the circumstances.

But no matter how long they were together, Elizabeth always returned in a sullen mood. Whatever did they talk about? What did one talk about when you were off to war in a handful of days?

Just then, the front door creaked. Had she returned finally?

"Elizabeth!" Abigail called out.

"Yes, Mother?" she heard from the direction of the foyer.

"Would you join me in the parlor?"

"Of course." Elizabeth let out a deep sigh. She sounded so tired. No — weary, fatigued.

Moments later, Elizabeth came into the parlor, countenance as downcast as ever.

Abigail's heart broke for her daughter. "Please, sit with me for a while."

Elizabeth nodded, taking a seat on the settee near her mother's chair. Folding her hands in her lap, Elizabeth looked at the floor. Was she truly as disinterested in her mother's words as she seemed? It was clear all she wanted to do was escape to her room.

Abigail put her cross-stitch to the side. "Tell me. How was he today?"

Elizabeth's gaze wandered toward the window. "Just as he always is...excited about the difference he's going to make." Was it Abigail's imagination, or was there a hint of exasperation in Elizabeth's voice?

"Perhaps he will make a difference. I'm sure he will save lives."

Elizabeth became quiet and turned her attention to her hands, still in her lap.

"But it doesn't help your heart to hear that, does it, darling?"

Elizabeth shook her head and fresh tears appeared at the corners of her eyes.

Abigail reached out and took her daughter's hand. "Do not fear for him so, Lizzie. I understand that the doctors are kept far from the front lines in the camps where they can do the most good. He will be out of harm's way." She watched for even a glimmer of hope that she had assuaged Elizabeth's fears in the slightest.

"John said as much, too. But I don't know if I can take it. Not knowing day to day if he is well. If he is alive, or..." The sentence was choked off by Elizabeth's sniffles.

"I know, darling, I know." Was her voice tender enough? Or was she still the distant mother she had become with Elizabeth?

"If only I could go with him..." Elizabeth started.

"Shhh!" Abigail patted her hand. "Darling, you know that's not possible. Women of our station do not say such things. We will support him in the ways we can. You can join a booster or write letters."

Elizabeth nodded, but said nothing further.

Did Elizabeth think that Abigail didn't understand? She did. Elizabeth wanted to go with him. But that wasn't possible. Taking another long look at her daughter, she confirmed that Elizabeth's tears had dried, replaced by a look of determination. There now, they would work together to support the cause. And that would be the end of it.

Henry Moore stood in his family's parlor, hanging his head, not able to brace himself against the tidings he had just received. It couldn't be so. He looked over at his wife, Martha. She had shut her eyes against the news their seventeen-year-old son brought. The color drained from her face and she reached for the arm of the closest chair. Was she going to faint?

Reaching out, he helped ease her into the chair and left his hand on her shoulder. Perhaps that would give her some comfort.

If only time would stop so they did not have to endure the pain of what lay ahead. The parlor whirled for several seconds. This room, filled with happy memories of family times spent together, would now forever be scarred with the memory of this exchange.

Their son, his bright-eyed boy Jacob, barely a man, had enlisted to go to war. Oh, he was old enough to be recognized by the state as a man, old enough to serve. So they could do nothing but let the fears come, and Martha, it seemed, did nothing to stop them.

How could he do this to his hapless parents? He was too young to understand the ramifications of what he had done. But, of course, the Union army didn't see things that way. No, he was nothing more than one more soldier added to their roster today. That was the price of war.

Henry and Martha's older son, Benjamin, had already gone off to war months ago. At that time, they had been proud of his bravery and respected that he wanted to fight for his country. But he was a grown man! And they had been naïve to the burden of having a son at war. Every day after had been a lesson. Since the last time Henry saw his face, he feared for Benjamin's safety every minute of every day. But at least he'd had Jacob at home. Until now.

"Mother, I promise, I'll make you proud. Just like Benjamin!"

Martha shook her head.

So that was it. He had seen how pleased they were when Benjamin signed on. Had he been counting down the days until his enlist date? Did he think this was what they hoped for? This was the last thing Henry wanted.

"You don't understand, Jacob, I can't..."

Henry's grip tightened on Martha's shoulder, cutting her off. This was not the way to handle things.

"We are proud of you, son. You've done us both proud," Henry said, doing his best to keep his voice steady. "I think your mother is just surprised. We both are."

"I know I should have said something first, but I wanted to surprise you," Jacob said.

"You certainly did that." Henry smiled at Jacob.

Underneath it all, he hoped Martha would understand. He did not want to sound cold and heartless to her pain. No, he understood what she was going through. But the deed was done. And now Jacob needed their support.

How could she give that? One look in his wife's face and he knew. All she wanted to do was scream. But she would have to lean on her husband's wisdom no matter how her heart cried out against it. At this point, there was no going back.

"Do you think they'll put me in Benjamin's regiment?" Jacob asked, his voice hopeful.

"No. Not likely," Henry said, his voice even.

Jacob's features dropped. Had that not occurred to him?

"But I'll get to wear a uniform and carry a gun?"

Henry nodded. "Yes, you will."

Henry's stomach churned. The thought of his young son who used to play with wooden guns carrying a real weapon into a fight...it made him nauseated. He turned away lest Jacob see his sickened expression. Jacob was so eager. And he hadn't a clue. War was a game to him. The reality had not yet set in.

What could he say to help Jacob realize? He needed to give his son some words.

Looking up at her son, Martha motioned for him to come closer to her.

He did so, crouching in front of her so they were eye-to-eye.

"Just promise me one thing, Jacob," she said, taking his face in her hands.

"What, Mother?" his eyebrows went up.

"That you won't go rushing into any fight. That you will stay back and watch out for yourself."

His brows furrowed, but he nodded all the same.

Even if he didn't understand now, Henry hoped that at that critical moment, he would remember and heed her advice.

And so, Martha smiled at him and leaned forward to kiss the side of his face.

He accepted her affection, smiling back at her.

And Henry's heart beat strong once again.

The doorbell rang, disturbing the Thompson family's lunch. In the dining room, Elizabeth exchanged looks with her parents and brother as their conversation came to a halt. Who could it be? No one gave any indication they expected a guest. All they could do was wait until a servant came to announce the unexpected visitor.

Each member of the family set their silverware down, dabbing at their mouths, each readying him or herself to receive the guest. They didn't have to wait long until the butler appeared at the doorway.

"Mr. John Taylor is here to see Miss Elizabeth."

Elizabeth's heart tumbled. Why would John be here? He was much too early. Because he would be shipping out tomorrow, they had agreed he should spend the day with his parents. He and Elizabeth had planned to meet later in the afternoon. Had something happened? Fighting a wave of dread that rose from within her stomach, Elizabeth waited for her mother to excuse her.

"Go ahead." Abigail motioned for her to follow the butler to the parlor.

Elizabeth stood and fell in step behind the tall man who looked after their home.

The parlor, adjacent to the dining room, was a short walk away. But today the hall stretched for miles as Elizabeth anticipated what news John might bring.

Stepping through the doorway, Elizabeth was unable to catch her breath for a moment. John stood tall and proud in his Union uniform. A question bubbled to the surface, but her emotions overtook her and she could not form it into words.

John nodded to the butler before the man quit the room, leaving the door open and positioning himself on the other side as a chaperone. Only then did John speak.

He moved toward her, placing his hands on her arms. "We're shipping out tonight, Lizzie."

She held back from his embrace, moving a hand across her face in disbelief. "What? But you are supposed to leave tomorrow."

"I know. Things have been expedited. I have been informed that our train leaves tonight."

The room began to spin and Elizabeth's knees became weak.

John pulled her into his arms, but she couldn't gather her thoughts enough to embrace him.

Tonight? She wasn't ready! Her plans were not fully set in place yet...

"I know it's a little sudden, Lizzie. But we knew this was going to happen. It's just a little sooner is all." He pulled back to look at her and brushed away the tears she didn't know she had shed.

"I...I can't..." she tried.

"Can't what, Lizzie?" His voice was soft as he tucked that errant curl behind her ear. The touch of his fingers on her skin was gentle, soothing.

"I can't say good-bye." How could she? She could hardly form a coherent thought.

He wrapped his arms around her again. This time she clung to him and sobbed. It didn't seem possible, but he held her even tighter.

"It will be all right," he soothed.

She trembled.

He leaned back, only far enough to capture her lips with his. When the kiss broke off, he held her to himself again.

"I need you to be strong for me now, Lizzie."

She wanted to. Breathing deeply, she attempted to rein in her emotions.

All the while, he continued to rub her arms, her shoulders, pressing kisses to her forehead and her hair.

Why did he have to be so wonderful? Tears threatened to break through again, but she held them back.

Once she calmed, he used his finger to tilt her chin so she looked up at him. "Can you be strong for my parents?"

She knew what he meant. He spoke not only of today, but also if something were to happen to him. "Yes," she lied.

"I know you can, even if you don't," he assured her, cupping her face.

She hung her head, fighting more tears.

"Write to me?" He hooked her chin with his finger so she had to look at him.

"Every day."

"Wait for me?" he asked, his voice as tender as she'd ever heard it.

"Forever."

John's face broke out in a slow smile at that.

Elizabeth allowed herself to get lost in his eyes. They belonged together. In that moment, she knew...that's why he wasn't afraid. He would return to her because he had to.

His lips met hers again in a gentle kiss. She returned his kiss with everything she had, longing to communicate all of her love, all of her hopes and dreams in that one kiss.

When John broke contact, her head still spun.

"I must go." He blinked, moving toward the door, his step wavering. Was the room spinning for him, too? "I carry you with me, Lizzie. Always and forever, remember?"

"Always and forever." She fought down a fresh wave of emotion, refusing to cry in front of him again.

He reached over and pulled her to him for another quick kiss. Then he was gone, and she was alone.

Elizabeth fell to the floor, sobbing. From the depths of her heart rose a determination to see her plan through. If his leaving was accelerated, so was her plan. She had to get things in motion. Wiping at her tears, she got up. There was much to do.

Charlotte sat at her small desk writing letters. She had been on a campaign since John enlisted, trying to secure more support for the troops and for the wounded soldiers in the hospital. She was proud of her work on behalf of the soldiers who couldn't help themselves, but it wasn't for their sake she made such tireless efforts.

The floorboard creaked behind her.

Charlotte looked up from her work. Franklin stood in the doorway to the parlor.

"Good afternoon, darling. You are home early. Is everything all right?"

His features unchanging, he closed the distance between them. Now over her, he leaned down to place a kiss on her forehead. "Our son has news for us."

The pen slipped from Charlotte's fingers. Could her heart take the news?

Franklin stepped to a settee nearby and patted the seat next to him. "Come, my dear. Come sit by me."

Her movements were slow as she turned in her chair and watched him. What tidings were these he brought? Did he know this news that John would bring? Should she stay where she was? What good would come of that? After some moments, she rose and took the steps to where her husband sat.

"Let us just sit together for a while." Franklin wrapped an arm around her.

Her brows furrowed as she searched his eyes. Why was his behavior so suspicious? It wasn't as if they had a loveless marriage, but he did not make a habit of coming home early to sit on the couch with her.

He sighed. Taking her left hand in his, he softened his tone. "How are Rose's studies?"

"Quite well. She is in her room even now, busy with schoolwork. Shall I have her come down?" Charlotte shifted to stand.

"No." He moved his hands over her arms, stilling her.

They sat in silence for a few moments. What did he know? Was it bad? Charlotte couldn't help the sense of foreboding that fell upon the room.

"What is this news from John?" Charlotte blurted out after several seconds as she turned to face him again, her eyes wide and her breathing ragged.

Franklin sighed again. He gazed into her eyes but he seemed hesitant to share. Still, he spoke. "John is coming home soon. He stopped by the practice before lunch and had a discussion with me."

"And?" Her voice rose.

"Charlotte, he is shipping out tonight."

"Tonight?" All the heat drained from her, and her body became weak.

"Yes, tonight." Franklin placed gentle hands on her arms. "I know it's not ideal, but we need to be supportive. He's coming here from the Thompson's home where he will have bid farewell to Elizabeth. You know how hard that will have been. We cannot make this more difficult."

She nodded. Tonight. Her son, her John, was going off to war tonight. How was she going to say farewell to him? What would it be like to hold him for perhaps the last time? Her thoughts began to run away with her. This would not do.

Charlotte took a deep breath, this one more even. Then, when she looked at her husband, her mind was set, determined. No matter what happened, she would face this situation with grace. Even if Franklin had to hold her while she cried tonight, she would be strong for John right now.

A slight smile graced Franklin's features. He kissed the side of her face. "If you're ready, we need to go upstairs and tell Rose."

Charlotte nodded, giving his arms a squeeze. "I'm ready."

And in that moment she was. Ready for anything.

Would the Moore family ever be the same? If they had been splintered when Benjamin went off to war, as Mother said, would they now be hopelessly split as Father and Jacob left home and headed toward the train station? Mother had not been able to leave her room since news of the early departure reached their home. Had it just become too much for her to say farewell to him?

And so, Father decided he and Jacob would slip out this evening while she napped. Try as he might, Father had not been able to disguise how this whole thing had affected his mother. How could

Jacob not know why she kept to her room? How could he not hear her as she cried at night?

"Please help her understand, Father," Jacob said as Father closed the door behind him.

"I will do my best. She will come to understand in time."

Jacob nodded, his heart aching.

"Let's get you to the train." Father turned in the direction of the station, putting a hand on Jacob's shoulder, clad in Union blue.

He certainly looked rather distinguished in his uniform, perhaps even a bit older. Father even told Jacob as much when he'd first put it on. But he felt a hesitation on this night. He no longer felt the confidence he once had. Yet he obeyed his father and picked up step with him.

They walked much of the distance in silence. Did Father, too, struggle with his own thoughts and emotions about what would happen once they arrived at their destination? Jacob did. How would they say good-bye? What would it be like to walk away from his father for perhaps the last time?

"Did you pack enough paper to write us?" Father broke the silence.

Jacob nodded. "I'll write often and tell you all about what's happening."

Benjamin's letters had become something the family enjoyed together these last couple of months. Jacob envisioned his parents and Susan huddled around the parlor's fireplace as Father's booming voice recited his letters from the front. As he imagined this scenario, he remembered the numerous letters from Benjamin that Father read in just this fashion.

However, this time, instead of focusing on the letter's contents, he let his mind's eye take in the people in the room. He saw, for the first time, his mother's reaction to these letters – relief that they had another letter, fear for her son's safety, helplessness. How had he never noticed these things before? Had he been so caught up in the grandness of what Benjamin was doing to see her response?

And so Jacob determined that he would write without fail, but also that he would guard his words to give his mother comfort and not cause unnecessary worry.

"Will you write to me and tell me of Benjamin?" Jacob turned toward his father. As difficult as it was to see in the dimness of the evening, he thought he caught the shimmer of moisture in Father's eye. Had he?

"Of course," came Father's strong, deep voice. "We'll send word of your brother as often as we have it." Father flashed him a half smile.

Jacob could not think of anything else to say the remainder of the walk to the station. So they passed the time in silent companionship.

When they arrived, they met with ordered chaos. Supplies were loaded and soldiers said their farewells to all manner of family. Women who joined the regiment as part of the Sanitary Commission, as well as a myriad of other passengers, milled about, saying their goodbyes and placing their luggage amidst the soldiers' things.

Jacob's gaze wandered across the platform at the many family farewells. There was no shortage of tears. His heart ached to not have a final moment with his mother, but he told himself to be glad she had not come. He had no desire to cry in front of the members of his unit. And his mother's tears would inevitably lead to his own.

Father clapped a hand on Jacob's shoulder, turning toward him. "This may well be the worst part of it," his father said, his voice soft and low.

Jacob nodded, a lump forming in his throat. How was he to do this?

"I wish I had some great words of wisdom to impart to you." Father looked toward the ground. The shaking in Henry's voice was almost imperceptible. Almost. After some moments Father met his eyes again. "You are your own man now, and we are so proud of who you have become."

"Thanks, Father." Jacob attempted to swallow past the lump. It was not easy.

Then Father's eyes became serious as he laid a firm hand on Jacob's other shoulder. "Be mindful of yourself, son. Be careful. Come home."

Jacob nodded, and with a confidence he didn't quite feel, said, "I will, Father."

Father pulled Jacob forward into his embrace, and Jacob allowed himself to stay for just a moment. How long would it be until he would be with his father again? But it was over all too soon when Father clapped his shoulder again and pulled back.

Offering Jacob a small smile, Father's lips quivered, but he didn't speak as he indicated with a wave of his hand that Jacob should check in with his commanding officer.

Reaching for his bag, Jacob then turned and moved away from his father. A prickling sensation pinched at him behind his eyes. He would not cry.

"Jacob! Jacob!"

He whirled around, eyes scanning for the source of the familiar voice. At last, he spotted his mother running through the station, barreling straight for him. Father reached out to stop her, but Jacob moved around him. He and his mother crashed into each other.

"Jacob, how dare you try to sneak out like that?" his mother's sobbing voice admonished him. The tears rolling down her face wet his neck, and the tears forming in his own eyes wet his face. But in that moment, it didn't matter who saw him crying.

"I'm sorry, Mother, I didn't want to...I thought...I shouldn't have." He buried his face in her shoulder.

"It's all right." She stroked his back.

He rested for a few moments more in her embrace. Strong arms encircled both of them. Father's. If only Jacob could stay in this perfect peaceful cocoon. But after some time, his father pulled back, tugging on Mother to do the same. She wiped Jacob's tears away as she did so.

"I love you, Jacob. Take care of yourself," she said, choking back more tears.

"I will, Mother. I promise."

She nodded, straightening his jacket.

"You are so handsome in your uniform." She offered him a smile.

One side of his mouth curved upward.

"I'm certain your commander is waiting," his father interjected.

With slow movements, Jacob took a step back from his parents, gathered his bag once more, and, turning, walked toward his commander. After he had taken few steps, however, he turned and saluted his parents, wanting to show them all the love and respect he felt for them in that moment.

Smiling, they dipped their heads.

With that, he turned toward his commander and did not look back.

CHAPTER TWO

SHIPPING OUT

Night fell upon the grand house the Thompson family called home. All within lay in the comfort of their beds, in peaceful slumber. All but one. Elizabeth strained her ears, listening for any sounds outside the walls of her bedroom. The time had come to put her plan into motion. It pained her to leave like this, sneaking off under the cover of night. But her parents would never let her go if they had any idea. Still, she could not sit idly by if John was in harm's way. She had to be with him...somehow.

Grabbing her bag, she packed the few things she needed: clothes, shoes, paper, and writing tools. How was she to know what she would need for such a journey? But one thing was clear – her current wardrobe would not do. There weren't many simple dresses in her collection, so she had bartered for some from a young maid in the house she supposed to be about her size.

Slipping into one of the simple frocks, she thanked God for the provision of the darker blue fabric. Perhaps it would make her disappearance into the night easier. She adjusted the skirt into place. The dress was a bit loose in the waist and bust, but it would do.

A knot twisted in her stomach as she set out the letter for her parents. It wasn't fair.

They would shake their heads despite her best explanations. And they would try to find her and bring her back. She prayed they wouldn't be able to. Gathering the money she had collected over the last few days, she frowned. There wasn't much. Would it be enough to buy her passage closer to the front lines? It would have to do.

Moving through the house with soft footfalls, she made her way to the kitchen. What foodstuffs could she carry in her satchel? Some bread, a small bit of cheese, and a few apples. Not much. But it would sustain her for a little while.

What more was there to prepare? Maneuvering toward the servants' entrance, she steeled herself. This was it. Her moment of truth. Did she have the courage? An image of her mother's face came to her. Yes, she would be devastated. Her father would be sad. Would her younger brother even understand? But John... She did this for John. Placing a hand on the latch, she opened the door and slipped into the night.

As she came back around to the front of the only place she'd called home, Elizabeth stopped to soak it in. Would she ever return? That evening when she hugged her parents goodnight, she'd fought the urge to linger in their embraces. Would she ever see them again?

Yet even as she gazed at the only home she'd ever known, she couldn't look upon the house without thinking of John and times spent here. In her mind's eye, she saw him as a younger boy standing outside her window on the street throwing pebbles at her window to get her attention. John. She had to be with him. Her resolve deepened and she moved in the direction of the train station to face her destiny.

John meandered through the train, looking for an empty seat. He spotted one next to a young man. Was he truly old enough to have enlisted? The boy's eyes darted between him and the window. He rubbed his hands on his pants as he shifted in his seat. Their destination and what they would face when they arrived may forever connect them, but this young man's demeanor could not be more different.

"This seat taken?" John put on his most charming smile.

"No, sir," the young boy responded, his voice shaking.

John settled into the seat and took his hat off. Perhaps if he relaxed it would calm the boy. He stuck out his hand. "John Taylor."

The boy shook it. "Jacob Moore." Even his hand trembled.

John searched for something encouraging to say. What was there to say to a boy so young that John himself couldn't fathom any reason he should be here?

At last, he found some words. "You're doing your country proud, you know."

Jacob shook his head. But he still had a hollow, haunted look in his eyes.

Facing forward, John took a moment to think. The silence between them became thick and uncomfortable. He felt the need to get a conversation going.

"I'm a doctor. I signed up because I wanted to make a difference. Thought I could do a lot of good for the soldiers getting wounded if they could get good medical attention sooner. What about you? What made you enlist?"

"M-my older b-brother enlisted a couple of months ago," Jacob struggled through his simple explanation.

A brother. Perhaps they could talk about him. "What's his name?"

"Benjamin." Jacob's voice was already stronger. Talking did seem to calm him somewhat.

"Did he send a lot of letters from the front?"

"Yeah! They were incredible. The stuff he wrote about was amazing, and I wanted to be right there beside him." The young man's eyes brightened.

"Oh?"

Jacob nodded. "When we were kids, we did everything together."

"That sounds great." John could only imagine the antics of two young boys. He had always wanted a brother.

"It was. We would play pirates, or cops and robbers, or army. We've always been there for each other. Do you have brothers?" Jacob's eyebrows rose.

"No, I have a younger sister. But she never wanted to play any of those games. She just wanted to play princess." John laughed a little.

"I have a sister, too. I know what you mean." Jacob's gaze turned forward and John feared the conversation might dwindle.

"I think girls get better as they get older." John stretched out his legs as much as the tightly spaced seats would allow.

"Yeah?" Jacob quirked an eyebrow.

John stifled a laugh. "Sure. Don't you have a girl back home? Someone you care about in a special way?"

"I don't know." Jacob's words came out slow and hesitant. His tone betrayed that he didn't, but his eyes shone his interest. After all, what boy of age wasn't?

"I do." John laid his head back on his seat. "Her name is Elizabeth and she is the most beautiful woman I've ever seen."

"That is special. Does she like you back?" Jacob tilted his head.

John leaned toward him as if he were about to share a deep secret. "Oh, it's more than that, Jacob. We're in love."

"How do you know?"

John paused. This was a deep subject to get into with someone you just met. But it would keep Jacob's mind off what awaited them on the other side of this train ride. What could it hurt to share with this young man what he knew of love?

"When you're in love, you want to spend all your time with that person. You get a happy feeling inside when you think about her. It's hard to explain. Trust me, you'll just know."

Jacob remained quiet.

"Being in love isn't always easy, though. Because the women we love won't always understand the decisions we have to make. We just have to hope they have the courage to support us."

John's gaze drifted toward the window and became lost somewhere off in the distance. Elizabeth had tried so hard to understand. But in the end, had she been able to? Their farewell ran across his memory. Her face, her eyes, her lips were so vivid he could almost reach out and touch them. Would these images haunt him over the weeks to come? It had been but a handful of hours yet, and already, he couldn't deny that he missed her terribly.

A sharp blast from the train's steam whistle pierced the air. The train jerked and began its forward momentum. Elizabeth grasped for a handhold. Her body thrown off balance, she knocked into another young woman who had been sliding past her.

"Pardon me!" Elizabeth apologized, mortified at her clumsiness.

"It's all right." The woman struggled to right herself amidst the rocking motion. "There's not much room to move around in here."

"No, not at all." Elizabeth glanced from side to side and frowned. Would she find a seat? It did not look promising.

A hand fell on her shoulder. She jerked from the contact then stilled herself. There was likely to be plenty of that in such close quarters. Turning her head toward the intrusion, she spotted the same young woman standing behind her.

"Do you have a seat?"

Elizabeth shook her head.

"There's one available in my car. You are welcome to join me."

She wanted to throw her arms around the stranger, but stopped herself and smiled her thanks instead. Nodding, Elizabeth then followed the young woman into the next car. Toward the end of the car, there was an unoccupied bench. Two middle-aged women sat facing the vacant seats, both dozing. The young woman moved toward the bench and indicated for Elizabeth to sit beside her.

"I'm Melanie." She extended her hand.

Elizabeth shook it. "Elizabeth."

"This is Louisa and May. Both of their husbands are on this train. Enlisted. Myself, I'm not married. I'm just looking for some way to assist with the war effort. I thought I'd come along and do laundry and mending and cooking and whatever else the men needed. Why, I'd fight if they'd let me."

Elizabeth nodded, trying to take it all in. She had a lot of respect for Melanie's passion even if she didn't share it. Take up a weapon? Unimaginable.

"You?" Melanie's eyes were bright and earnest.

"Same as you." Elizabeth plastered a smile on her face. She had not been prepared to answer questions about her presence. "I'm ready to help out wherever I can."

"That makes us kindred spirits," Melanie said, her voice elated. "Which is just as well. We'll be seeing a lot of each other, I'm sure." Melanie smiled at her.

Elizabeth didn't know about kindred spirits. Melanie seemed a little chatty for her liking.

"I don't mean to interrupt your tea party," Louisa spoke up, opening one eye. "But we will have a long day tomorrow. I advise we all get some sleep if we can."

Melanie and Elizabeth apologized, sharing another smile, and Melanie quieted down.

Elizabeth leaned her head back and gazed out the window, watching Boston fade out of view. She still couldn't believe she had done it – left her home and everything she had known to join a Union camp's Sanitary Commission. Not just any Union camp – John's camp.

How was she going to keep John from finding out? As much as she needed to be near him, she had no doubt he would have her sent home if he found her, out of fear for her safety. That was the last thing on her mind. She cared little for her own well being as long as she could be near her beloved.

Women that traveled with the troops were either wives coming to help out with the cooking and laundering or nurses for the most part. Elizabeth would have to stay away from the hospital and blend in with the wives as much as she could. Which appeared to be Melanie's plan.

The rocking of the train and the lateness of the hour began to work on Elizabeth, causing her eyelids to feel heavy. In a matter of minutes, she was sound asleep, dreaming of what the next day might bring.

Morning had barely broken. Throughout the house, servants moved about their tasks. But Abigail's corner of the world was quiet and calm, just as she preferred for this hour of the day. She sat at her vanity, watching in the mirror as her maidservant worked to put curls in her hair. What would the day bring? Examining her nails, she sighed. Her days had become so much the same of late. Was the life of a lady of leisure to be so boring?

But today would be different. John had gone. Elizabeth would need her. Abigail gazed at herself in the mirror. A purpose for her day, for her being. One of her children needed her. It had been so long since she felt needed.

Her door flung open. *Who? What?* She spun toward the intrusion, her head jerked by the iron still in her hair.

Elizabeth's maidservant rushed into the room without knocking.

Abigail scowled at her. What could possibly excuse such behavior?

"Excuse me, Ma'am," the young woman said, curtsying. "But I cannot find Miss Elizabeth."

Abigail's heart dropped. "Can't find her?"

The girl shook her head. "She wasn't in her room this morning. But I found this note." She reached out a shaking hand, which bore an envelope.

Taking the note, Abigail's breath caught when she saw 'Father and Mother' written in Elizabeth's hand. *What could it mean?* She feared the answer. Ripping at the seal, she tore the letter from its enclosure.

Dearest Father and Mother,

By the time you read this letter, I'll be far away...

Her heart froze.

"Get Dr. Thompson!"

Elizabeth's maidservant curtsied once again and moved off after her given task.

Abigail's maidservant moved to make another curl in Abigail's hair, but she waved the woman off. What should she do? Continue reading or wait for her husband? Waiting for Thomas seemed the wiser thing to do. He would keep a level head. Yes, he would know what to do.

Moments later, he appeared at the doorway, his features twisted in concern. Abigail couldn't form the words, so she held the note out to him, her hand trembling.

He read the first few lines and looked up at her, eyes wide.

"Out loud," she managed, her mouth suddenly dry.

Excusing the servants, he then closed the door behind them and sat on the edge of the bed nearby.

"Dearest Father and Mother, by the time you read this letter, I'll be far away. I am sorry tell you this in a letter. It's not fair to you. Please forgive me. But I could not risk that you would stop me. What I am about to do is too important.

"I can no longer imagine continuing on here while John is at war, risking his life every day. The thought that I would wake each day not knowing where he is or if he is alive is too much. I have to find a way to be with him. So, I am joining the women who follow the camps. This is the only way. Do not worry so, Mother, I will be away from the fighting. And I will write often. I love you both. Elizabeth."

How could Elizabeth do this? Abigail's face fell onto her arms on the vanity. "My girl!"

She heard Thomas's movements behind her. Then his hand was on her back. "There, there."

Pushing back from the surface of the vanity, Abigail spun on him, grabbing at his forearms. "You must go after her, Thomas. You must bring her home."

"You know that's not possible. The train left last night, and for where I do not know. She is beyond our reach."

"No," Abigail insisted. Was there no hope? No recourse?

When John first announced that he had enlisted, Abigail sympathized with Charlotte. But she could only imagine what her friend went through. Now she knew all too well the emotions that had coursed through Charlotte on that day. And they overwhelmed Abigail. Her breathing came rapidly, chest heaving. The world around her became hazy.

Searching for solace, she focused on Thomas. He grounded her. His arms moved to surround her, pulling her into an embrace. And the tears that pricked at her eyes came full force, pouring from her. But the moisture on her face was not her own. Thomas's tears mixed with hers. And she knew, he felt it too. Their daughter had gone off to war.

Just as Louisa had said, the next day proved to be arduous and long. The train took them as far south as Charleston. From there, they walked for miles upon miles before setting up camp for the night. It couldn't come soon enough.

And while Elizabeth considered herself to be in excellent physical condition, only a few hours in, her feet hurt. No doubt she had blisters from her impractical shoes. Why hadn't she thought to exchange those when she bartered for plainer dresses? Her lack of foresight left her with no choice but to suffer.

For the sake of the women, the unit commander did pause from time to time. However, the infrequent stops weren't quite long enough for Elizabeth's poorly clad feet. But as the sun dipped closer to the horizon, the unit came to a stop and set up camp for the night.

Elizabeth and Melanie were assigned a tent with two nurses. How were they to manage that? It was an unnecessary worry. Their tent mates, Sarah and Lily, had far more experience assembling tents. Once the tent was miraculously standing, the girls set out their sleeping mats. The tent only had room for their four sleeping mats to squeeze in, but Elizabeth was thankful for beds and shelter all the same.

After laying out her mat, Elizabeth collapsed on the thinly padded surface. Could she just lie here for the remainder of the day? She shook her head. That was not possible. There were other tasks to attend to. Forcing herself into a sitting position, she then pulled one foot close to herself and tried to remove the shoe.

"You're over there grunting and whimpering about something. What's the matter?" Melanie teased from her sprawled out position on her own mat.

"It's these shoes," Elizabeth moaned. "I can't get them off."

"Let me help." Melanie sat up and scooted toward Elizabeth.

Elizabeth's face warmed. How was it that she couldn't even get her shoes off by herself?

"Where did you get such fancy shoes?" Melanie's eyes caught hers.

"It's a long story," Elizabeth looked away, hoping to dissuade Melanie from further questions.

"But, they…"

"It's not important," she snapped, a bit louder than she meant to. "I didn't mean that." She turned to face Melanie again. "I'm just in a lot of pain. Please, help me."

Melanie freed the laces all the way down, and then worked at loosening the leather. She tugged at the shoes with great care. It took some effort due to Elizabeth's swollen feet. But after several seconds, Melanie got them off.

Melanie's breath caught.

"What is it?" What could have startled Melanie so?

"These blisters. My goodness, Elizabeth! You need to see one of the doctors about these."

Looking over her knees, Elizabeth caught sight of her lumpy feet even through her foot dressings.

"No, I'll be fine." The words rushed out. A doctor did need to look at her feet and tend to the blisters, but she couldn't let John find out she was here.

"Let's take off your stockings." Without waiting for consent, Melanie's gentle hands worked to remove them. The angry, red, water-filled blisters on her heels and the pads of her feet were laid bare for them both to see.

Elizabeth reached out to touch one, but drew back.

Movement at the tent opening drew Elizabeth's attention. Sarah walked in and toward her bag. Melanie beckoned her over to where Elizabeth sat.

"Sarah, I'm trying to convince Elizabeth that the doctor needs to take a look at her feet. What do you think?"

The nurse glanced at Elizabeth's feet and made a small sound. Then she made her way back into the thick of camp before Elizabeth could protest. What was she going to do? Would she return in short order with a doctor?

Elizabeth fell back on the mat, throwing an arm over her face. Her well-laid plan was over before it had begun. All of this...for nothing. John would be here in a matter of moments and he would send her back home.

Two sets of footsteps crunched in the grassy area nearby. A whisk of a breeze flew through as the tent flap opened again. Still, Elizabeth refused to look up into John's face.

"What seems to be the problem here?" a male voice said, but it wasn't John.

Jerking back to her sitting position, Elizabeth sought with her eyes to confirm what her ears told her. The kind blue eyes she stared into were decidedly not John's. Had she joined the wrong unit?

"I have, um, that is...there are some, um...I've got blisters," she managed.

"Is that all?" The man watched her, smiling, and a little laugh escaped from deep in his throat. He was older than John, but not quite her father's age. And he seemed rather amused at her tongue-tied state. Getting down on one knee, he reached for her feet.

"I'm Dr. Smith. We'll be seeing a lot of each other. There are two other doctors in the unit—Dr. Taylor and Dr. Young. You'll meet both of them in time." As he spoke, he examined her blisters. "And I'm afraid I'm going to have to lance these."

Elizabeth nodded. She had known as much to be true.

"Sarah, I need some clean bandages and a sterile needle."

The young nurse moved off to fetch the supplies the doctor ordered while Dr. Smith's eyes wandered around their tent. What was he looking for? Salt and pepper eyebrows shot up when he spied her shoes. His eyes met hers again. Did he know she was playacting? That she was from an upper class home? Did her shoes give her away? She opened her mouth to weave some excuse, but closed it again.

"I hope you have other shoes for the journey tomorrow. There will be more walking, and I can't guarantee it will be any easier in those. In fact, I doubt your swollen feet will fit into them."

Elizabeth shook her head, looking down. She hadn't planned well at all.

"No matter," Dr. Smith said, his voice kind and gentle. "I'm sure we can find a spare pair of soldier's boots. You'll need a larger size shoe with the bandages anyway."

Elizabeth nodded, meeting his gaze.

They both turned as Sarah shuffled back into the tent with the things Dr. Smith had requested.

Taking the needle in one hand, he clamped a hand around Elizabeth's ankle. "You shouldn't feel much, Miss. But even if you do, you must remain as still as you can."

Nodding, Elizabeth braced herself. But, true to his word, she didn't feel much of the pinpricks. Then he cleaned the wounds and began wrapping her feet.

"I'll find you some suitable boots," he said, as he tied off the last bandage. "I need you to stay off your feet the rest of the evening, understand?"

"Yes, Dr. Smith."

He stood, turning to leave.

"Dr. Smith," she called after him. Would he tell anyone about her?

He turned back toward her.

"Thank you," she said in a meek voice.

"Of course. Anything for a woman so brave she would leave all behind to join this ragtag bunch."

Elizabeth nodded. They understood each other. He would not disclose her identity to anyone.

As he left the tent, she lay back on her mat and stretched out her tired legs so she could rest her bandaged feet on her folded jacket. The bed mat, a far cry from the down feather pillows and soft mattress she had back home, was little more than a thick blanket on the ground. Even so, after the exhaustion of the day, it wasn't long before she slept.

They had covered many miles today. Miles that John felt in his feet and legs. Lying back on his mat, he stretched his limbs out. Tomorrow would bring more walking; he needed to take what respite he could. Closing his eyes, he remembered some of the scenery from the day. The distance they had come was great. Those miles not only wore on his body, but they also put distance between him and the ones he loved most dearly.

An image of Elizabeth floated in his mind's eye. How was it that he had been away from her but what? Not yet two days even? And still she was on his mind whenever he had a spare moment. He thought briefly of Jacob and the things he had told him of love. Yes, he was in love with Elizabeth. Deeply. How, then, could he have left her? For the sake of the war effort. To save lives. Would the war change him? Would the time and distance change her feelings for him? That thought caused his stomach to drop and his heart to pound. She wouldn't...couldn't...could she?

He sat up and shook his head. His hands ached to be doing something. And his mind needed respite from these haunted thoughts. The stack of medical supplies called to him. Rising to his feet, he cleared his mind. Or attempted to. Then he moved toward the supplies and began looking through to ensure nothing was damaged.

Soon after, the tent flap opened. Dr. Smith entered, nodding toward John as he did so. Oh yes, he had gone off to look after one of the women. One of the young nurses had fetched him.

"Nothing needing a second pair of hands, I hope." John looked up from his work.

William offered his colleague a smile as he moved toward his mat. "No, only some bad blisters needing to be lanced."

"That was quite a walk today. Someone have improper footwear?" John asked, his focus now back on his work.

William nodded, sitting. "One of the women."

"Seems about right." Some of these women were just here to play army. They didn't realize what they had signed up for.

"I wouldn't be so quick to judge this young woman." William yawned and stretched.

"What do you mean?" John crouched down to access the lower crates.

William's eyes settled on John, as if trying to wager how much to share. He was quiet for several moments. "She is a woman from a privileged life. From an upper class home."

"What is she doing here?" John jerked upright, his head swimming a little from his drastic movement.

"Choosing to serve her country." William responded, his voice even.

"We have to tell the commanding officer." The words rushed out of John. "Her parents couldn't be aware that she…"

William shook his head, and spoke in a firm voice. "No matter her circumstances at home or how she got here, I'm doing nothing of the sort. I respect what she's doing. It's rather brave, don't you think?"

"But she has no idea the hardships she'll endure out here while…" John started to argue.

"It's her choice to face them."

John fell silent, shrugging his shoulders. William had a point. At least Elizabeth was safely at home, away from such adversity and danger. Perhaps this woman's family and friends would be able to make peace with her decision, but John could not deny how relieved he was that he didn't have to.

Charlotte Taylor rang the doorbell at the Thompson residence. She stepped into the home of her dear friend and relinquished her coat to the butler. No words were spoken between them but he escorted her to the parlor. Was it Charlotte's imagination, or was there a chill about the home? As they approached the doorway to the parlor, Charlotte peered in, unsure of what she might find.

Abigail sat in her favorite chair, eyes drawn out the window, glassed over. Her hands were idle in her lap. And there was no fire in the hearth. Charlotte frowned.

The butler moved past her into the room to announce her presence.

Abigail's eyes did not move from the window until Charlotte's name was upon his lips. Then she turned toward her friend, life returning to her features.

Charlotte closed the distance between them and embraced Abigail.

While Abigail rose and opened her arms to her friend, she seemed rather limp.

"Franklin has told me everything," Charlotte spoke near Abigail's ear.

When they broke apart, Abigail led Charlotte to a nearby couch. The butler had turned to leave, but Charlotte called out to him.

"I would have you call upon a kitchen maid to start this fire."

He turned his head, gave a curt nod, and quit the room.

"What can be the meaning of this? Leaving you in here with no warmth?"

"One of the maids came to stoke the fire perhaps an hour ago. I sent her away. And the fire died."

What could Abigail have been thinking? Or rather not thinking? To sit in her parlor with no heat on such a day?

"Please, Charlotte, do not be cross." Abigail's gaze fell.

"I am not angry." Charlotte became quiet. What a state her friend must be in! What words could she offer her? What could she say that would assuage her wounds?

Abigail's shoulders shook but slightly. And she bit at her lip. Tears would soon follow.

"Oh, Abigail, I scarcely know what to say!" Charlotte confessed, eyebrows furrowed.

"It's all right. I don't know what to say myself." She sniffled, dabbing at her eyes with her handkerchief.

"Elizabeth gave no indication she was planning anything like this?" It was the obvious question but it needed to be asked.

Abigail shook her head. "We knew, of course, that she was unhappy with John's leaving."

"As did we all," Charlotte added, laying a hand on Abigail's arm.

"But who could have imagined this?" Abigail cried. The tears did come then.

"Who indeed, dear friend? And what is to be done?" Would that they could come up with a plan! Something they could do other than sit around and feel sorry for themselves.

"Thomas says he cannot pursue them but he thinks perhaps if we could get a letter to John or to his commanding officer. Perhaps they may see her home."

Nodding, Charlotte forced a smile onto her face. "See now, there is hope. John does not wish her to be in harm's way. Once that letter finds him, John will send her home."

Abigail nodded, but she did not meet Charlotte's eyes.

Charlotte hung her head. She pulled herself to her feet, taking some steps away from the couch. "I must confess I feel as if I am partially to blame. My son..."

"No! I won't hear of it," Abigail said, her voice firm. "Elizabeth is head strong all on her own."

Relieved that Abigail did not blame her for any part of Elizabeth's flight, Charlotte turned back toward her friend and took a deep breath before continuing. "Do you think John knows?"

"Her letter didn't say, but I find it doubtful." Abigail's eyes held Charlotte's

"I, too, doubt it. It's unimaginable that he would have let her go through with it." Charlotte moved across the room again. This time toward the window that overlooked the front of the house.

"That is what I told Thomas," Abigail said, unwavering.

Turning to face her friend, Charlotte said, "Should he discover her in the camp, he will send her back home."

"I know, dear friend. Your son is a good man and he loves my Elizabeth a great deal."

Silence fell between them for some moments. Charlotte's attention was drawn out the front window toward a young couple walking by. That should have been John and Elizabeth on an afternoon stroll, on their way home to announce their engagement.

"I know we haven't spoken of it, but I was surprised they did not make plans to marry before he went off to war," Charlotte wondered out loud.

"I admit I was as well. But I think we're all relieved they didn't add the stress and emotion of a wedding to the mix. Yet it was what I expected when John first made it known he had enlisted." Now focused on something else, Abigail's voice was not so charged with emotion.

"I wonder which of them convinced the other to wait."

"It is a mystery with those two," Abigail sighed.

"Everything always is with them." Charlotte turned back toward Abigail.

"Indeed," Abigail said, looking into her friend's eyes.

As Charlotte watched, Abigail's eyes filled with emotion again. Charlotte rejoined her on the settee, laying a hand on her shoulder. She waited for her friend to speak.

"I now know what torment you have been going through, knowing your child is off to war."

Charlotte nodded, swallowing hard.

"And I understand your obsession with the war effort," Abigail added, meeting her friend's eyes again.

"It's a way to stay connected to him," Charlotte confirmed.

Abigail nodded her understanding. "Do you think you could use another hand to write letters? Or another person to collect donations?"

"Of course!" Charlotte said, excited at the prospect of her friend working alongside her. "We'll be happy to have you."

"Good. Because as long as she's out there, I want her to have everything that she needs."

The next morning, Elizabeth awoke to the sound of a bugle blasting. Time to rise. As promised, a pair of soldier's boots was by her mat. Sitting up, she was tempted to remove the dressings and examine her blisters. It would be best to leave them alone for a day or two and let them heal. So she slid her stockings over the bandages, and with great care, worked her feet into the boots. A perfect fit with the bulky bandages. She silently thanked the kind doctor.

"They work?" Melanie yawned as she sat up.

"Yes," Elizabeth said, lacing them. "They're perfect."

Melanie moved to the tent flap and looked out. "It is too early for all this activity."

"I think we're going to have to get used to that." She tested her weight on her feet. Pain shot through her feet but she could manage.

"I think you're right." Melanie stretched her arms.

Elizabeth glanced over to where Sarah and Lily's mats should have been. Nothing but bare grass flattened where their bodies had been. Early risers. Were they helping the other nurses catalog and pack the medical supplies onto the wagon? She would wager so.

"Let's get these mats rolled and the tent packed. How hard could it be?" Melanie's voice was more confident than Elizabeth would have expected. With the lack of skills Melanie had displayed in erecting the tent, and Elizabeth's own ineptitude in this arena, she was doubtful they could accomplish such a thing.

It was, as she feared, quite difficult. They'd had a lot of help from Sarah and Lilly setting up the tent. And now they were left to their own devices trying to get it down in an orderly fashion. The more they worked with the rough canvas, the more it seemed to fight them. They made a bigger mess than they intended before a kind soldier who happened by offered to help show them how to fold it. With his help, it was done in short order. They thanked the young soldier, who moved on to his next task without further ado.

Melanie watched him go, and Elizabeth wondered if perhaps part of her volunteerism was spurred by her desire to find a husband.

"He's good-looking. Don't you think?" Melanie's eyebrow piqued.

"Yes, but I'm a little more concerned with getting our packs together." Elizabeth tried to pull Melanie back to the task at hand.

"You're no fun." Melanie grabbed for her packs.

"That's fine. You can be enough fun for the both of us." Elizabeth offered her a smile as she picked up her load. She stifled a grunt under the added weight. How was she to manage all of this on her damaged feet?

Melanie made a face but did as she was directed, gathering her things to carry in one place.

A breeze caught Elizabeth's hair, which she had decided to leave down. She turned her face toward it, allowing the calm of the gentle wind to brush over her, carrying her worries away. As she opened her eyes, she was once again faced with the reality of where she was and what lay before her. But something else caught her eye. Someone moved through the camp. Why should this soldier... John!

Still several feet away, he moved toward the wagon. Everything seemed to slow down. She thought to turn away, but he was so focused on his work she doubted he would look in her direction.

Elizabeth drank in the sight of him as if it had been years since she had seen him, not a mere two days. His dark hair, dark to match his eyes, was less kempt than she was used to. His strong, capable hands moved over the boxes and packs with ease, checking and securing everything. Was it just her imagination or was his skin more tanned? Long ago she had memorized the curves of his face, but here she stood studying them anew.

"Look who's all moonstruck now?" Melanie's voice interrupted her thoughts. "Who's caught your eye?" She looked off in the direction Elizabeth had been staring.

At the same moment, John turned his head in her direction.

Elizabeth threw herself down on the ground.

When she looked up, she caught the confused eyes of her companion.

"What has gotten into you?" Melanie asked, concerned.

"I, um...I thought I saw a bee."

"A bee? I didn't see a bee."

Elizabeth returned to her feet. She glanced where John had just been. He was nowhere in sight.

"My mistake," she said, brushing off her skirt.

"Who were you looking at?" Melanie's eyes narrowed.

"No one." Elizabeth attempted to sidestep Melanie, but it was no use. With hands on her hips, she moved into Elizabeth's path.

"Come on, Elizabeth. You were burning holes into someone with that stare. You can't lie to me. Remember, we are kindred spirits."

"I just thought I might have recognized someone from back home." Elizabeth busied herself with her packs.

"An old beau?" Melanie stood right behind Elizabeth, her voice rising. She was not going to let this go.

"Something like that." Elizabeth tried to sound dismissive.

"I feel a good story coming."

"I assure you it's nothing of the kind." Elizabeth turned to face her.

"I'm up for a dull story. Anything to break up this trip," Melanie pleaded, sticking out her bottom lip.

"All right." Elizabeth rolled her eyes. "I'll tell you all about it."

So Elizabeth wove a fabricated tale of a beau that never existed for Melanie's amusement. She used some of the details of her and John's story, but most of the story was good old-fashioned tales. It seemed to entertain Melanie for the portion of the trip she could stretch it out. Then Melanie rewarded her with a story of one of her beaus. It proved to be quite intriguing. And a little disturbing. Melanie was quite a girl.

When the sun was high in the sky, they stopped, and the commander declared that this was where they would set up camp for the time being. Elizabeth took in their surroundings. The camp, situated on the edge of a field, backed up to a forest. To the north, there was a sloped hill from which one could overlook the camp. But to the south, there were rolling slopes for several hundred yards before being cut off by the forest line. Not far into the woods was a stream with fresh water. The tree line wrapped around to provide some cover for the camp while the field offered ample space for tents. A sentry post was set up on the hilltop. It seemed quite a happy situation for their camp.

As much as Elizabeth and Melanie were determined to learn how to put up the tent, Sarah and Lily were half done by the time they found their campsite. Today, however, after Elizabeth and Melanie laid out their mats, they congregated with the other women to set up a makeshift kitchen and laundry. By the time that was done, Elizabeth was ready to head back to her tent and lie down, but Melanie put out a hand and halted her.

"Not just yet, Bright Eyes, now we serve supper to the menfolk."

Elizabeth wanted to give up then and there. Tell everyone who she was and be sent back home to her comfortable life. No, that would not do. This wasn't about her. John. She had to remember she was here for John.

Putting his face before her in her mind, she found the strength to make it through dinner service. Then she stumbled to her tent and collapsed in a heap on her mat. The day was over.

CHAPTER THREE

BATTLE

It didn't take long for the other women to find out Elizabeth didn't know much about cooking or laundering or more than basic stitching. Melanie reported to her that they all found this rather curious, but they appreciated her willingness to learn. And they seemed pleased with how quickly she picked things up.

By the end of the first week, she performed all of the basic tasks with surprising proficiency, even if she was slower than the other women. Everyone became most impressed with her drawing skills. In her free time in the afternoons, she would draw portraits or scenes of the camp.

Melanie continued to feed Elizabeth a running commentary on the men in the unit: who was available, who was married, who was cute, who was plain, who was 'husband material', and who wasn't anything special. Elizabeth's suspicions had been laid to rest. She was certain Melanie would go home with a fiancé.

Elizabeth and Melanie seldom saw their tent mates as the nurses' time was taken up at the hospital, setting it up to receive casualties, only returning to the tent to sleep. Even then, Sarah wasn't much of a conversationalist. Not even at the behest of the ever-chatty Melanie could they get more than rudimentary pleasantries out of her. Was she shy or tired or just not interested in concerning herself with making friends? Lily, on the other hand, would engage in simple conversation, but was always more interested in hearing about Melanie or Elizabeth than talking about herself.

Everyone became more and more certain their unit would find themselves in combat soon. After getting to know some of the soldiers, it broke Elizabeth's heart to think that some of them would leave the camp and not return. At least John would be safe. The doctors would stay in the hospital to receive the sick and wounded, a safe distance from any fighting. Still, that was of little comfort.

"What do you think, Elizabeth?" Melanie asked. They were in their tent, preparing for bed.

Elizabeth hadn't been paying attention as Melanie went through her evening litany of the men she encountered that day.

"I'm sorry, what?" Her face warmed in spite of herself.

"I met the young doctor. What was his name? John. He's handsome. I may have found my match," came Melanie's gleeful voice.

Elizabeth dropped her apron. Her John? Was Melanie talking about her John?

"He has a girl back home," Sarah piped up, startling Melanie. But she recovered well.

"Is that so?" Melanie fingered the edge of her pillow.

"Yes," Lily said, settling herself onto her mat. "I hear they're engaged."

"Well, he didn't marry her before joining up. That says something. War changes people. Maybe I still have a chance. After all, I'm here and she's not." Melanie met Lily's gaze as she eased herself onto her own mat.

Elizabeth drifted back off into her own thoughts. *War changes people.* Was that true? Did war change people? Would it change her?

Would it change John? Would it change the fact that they loved each other? Surely not. What they had was so deep, so real. Elizabeth could not, would not accept that war could change that. Melanie didn't know what she was saying. She didn't know John.

"What do you think, Elizabeth?" Melanie interjected into her thoughts.

Elizabeth had missed Melanie's question again.

"I think it's time to get some shut eye," was all Elizabeth could manage to say.

"I agree!" Lily said, her voice quite loud.

Melanie's eyebrows furrowed and her bottom lip protruded as she crossed her arms.

Sarah leaned over and turned out the lantern, plunging the four women into darkness.

"Melanie," Elizabeth said, as she slid down onto her thin mat, her voice gentle. "I think you need to realize that one day soon some of these men are going into battle and they're not coming back."

"I know that," she said, her voice quiet and soft.

"Then why plan futures with so many of them?"

"Because it keeps me from thinking that way, that there's a clock on their lives."

Elizabeth held her breath as Melanie spoke, her voice so quiet.

"I don't want to treat them that way. I don't want to think about them like that."

Elizabeth glanced in her direction, but was only able to see her silhouette in the night. This was a deeper side of Melanie. Elizabeth never could have guessed that there was something more behind all this boy craze.

"I'm sorry," Elizabeth whispered. "I didn't realize..."

"I know," Melanie said into the darkness. "It's all right. Let's just get some sleep."

"All right." Elizabeth lay down on her pillow and listened to the gentle sounds of the women in her company breathing. But her thoughts were on John and what Melanie had said about war changing people. And it kept her awake long into the night.

Another early rise for the troops. Jacob sighed as he sat up and moved his legs to wake his limbs. This was definitely something Benjamin did not write about. They had been rising well before dawn these last few days. Yawning and stretching, he pulled on his pants first, then his uniform jacket. He had to report soon.

His tent mate was already dressing as well. It wasn't long before they were both regulation, gun in hand, and ready to go. Making their way outside their tent, they reported to the command post, taking their places in the lineup.

All the soldiers stood at attention while the captain walked up and down the line, inspecting the troops. Jacob held his breath as the man passed by. On occasion, the captain would find what he considered a sloppy appearance and yell at the soldier. For the most part, they were a ship-shape unit, if not by nature, by fear of this particular captain. Their captain had a reputation for remembering anyone who dared show up sloppy. Thus far, Jacob had escaped that nightmare.

After inspection, they were released to breakfast. Would it be a warm breakfast? That all depended on what foodstuffs were available. This morning, it was the hardtack bread rations and some cooked bacon.

Jacob ate his food in silence. His mother would make him flapjacks and maple syrup if he had a test or needed cheering up. And he could use a good breakfast like that on days like this. He appreciated the women who had given up so much to come stay at the camp and cook for the soldiers, but they could not compare to his mother's home cooking. Especially the blonde girl they called Elizabeth. Whenever she had been cooking, the men groaned. It just wasn't her strong suit.

Forcing down the last of the hard tack, Jacob saw the captain signal the troops to line up for their morning run. After a quick breakfast each day, they would line up again for maneuvers. This could mean any number of things physical. They would run for some length of time every morning. Sometimes they would have exercises where they had to crawl with their muskets in hand, climb with them, or practiced hand-to-hand combat with their bayonets. And then there was his least favorite – taking apart their muskets and putting them back together.

Jacob moved toward the front of the line for their morning run. He seemed to be one of the faster men in the camp. At least he could keep up his speed throughout the duration of the run.

The captain counted them off and they started moving.

Though he never dared breathe a word of it, he found the morning run invigorating. He enjoyed the fresh air, the scenery, and though he was sure most of the men did not find the run enjoyable, the camaraderie was something to be appreciated.

So they were off, out into the field. Jacob allowed his mind to wander when a couple of other soldiers began shouting at him from behind.

"Hey, you trying to make us look bad?"

"Yeah! What's in your head?"

"Show off!"

He had gotten a bit further ahead of the rest. Should he yield to their teasing? Or bite back at them?

"You're just jealous," Jacob yelled back. That would bug them. After all, it was the same heckling every morning. A handful of them would get together after morning drills and chide each other. It almost seemed like everyone had a certain thing the others would tease about. They ribbed Frank about how he always had a piece left over during musket drills. George would be razzed about his poor time on ground drills. And they hassled Jacob about his running.

"What are you doing? Running from the front lines?" Were

they trying to make him mad? It wasn't working. Jacob turned his head for a second, eyeing which ones managed to keep up with him.

"No, I'm leading a rag tag group of misfits," he howled back. He would show them they weren't getting to him.

A hand landed on his shoulder.

Jacob glanced back. One of them had gotten close enough to touch him.

"So, one of you can actually run!"

Jacob feinted left and right, dodging this other soldier who tried to grab him. It brought back memories of him and Benjamin playing in the backyard when they were boys. He hurled out taunts. The guy behind him started to pant and lose his gain. Slowing down a bit, Jacob turned while still jogging.

"What now? Can't keep it up, Old Man?" He laughed.

The troops seemed as if they were chasing him.

Old Man sprinted faster.

Jacob's eyes widened. Old Man just might get him. He turned back around and picked up the pace. As he did so, the path dipped. His feet caught and he stumbled, hitting the ground hard.

Old Man was so close behind him that he crashed into Jacob as well. They both lost their breath, the wind knocked out of them.

The captain was soon on the scene. "What is wrong with you two? Moore, Johnson!"

Jacob was just then catching his breath and pulling himself to his feet. The fall did not injure him. Old Man didn't look too good though. When he got up, he couldn't put weight on his ankle.

"Moore, you get Johnson back to the infirmary. Move out!"

Jacob extended a hand to help the man. "What's your name?"

"Daniel. Daniel Johnson." The man said, grimacing as he once again tested his weight on the injured ankle.

"Well, Daniel, congratulations on figuring a way out of morning drills." Jacob offered the man a smile. "I just hope the captain doesn't clean your clock for it later."

Daniel chuckled, leaning on Jacob while they limped back to the hospital.

Once there, it wasn't long before the doctor had wrapped Daniel's ankle and told him to take it easy for the next few days. As the doctor walked away, Jacob decided to get one more jab in.

"See, I knew there was a way to slow you down!"

Daniel gave him a cross look and Jacob knew he had made a life-long friend.

Troop movement outside the thin fabric walls of the tent awakened Elizabeth. They would have risen before dawn in order to practice maneuvers. If she strained her ears, she could hear the artillery unit doing the same thing, loading cannons to prepare for battle. Would it be today? Would the men head to the front lines today?

Making slow movements, she sat up and stretched. Heavy breathing nearby alerted her that Melanie still slumbered. Elizabeth was not so blessed to be such a deep sleeper. Sarah and Lily, of course, were already gone.

Elizabeth begrudgingly moved out of the tent and toward the women's common area. How she longed for those cozy mornings when her vanity was but a few steps away from her warm bed and she could freshen up in the privacy of her own bedchamber! Still, she had become accustomed to this new level of modesty, walking about in her nightshift, nodding to the women she passed on the way to the common area.

Once she arrived, she gathered some water to pour into the simple bowl. She splashed some water onto her face, hoping to liven her features and wake her senses. Rinsing her hands as well, she then dumped the water so the bowl would be ready for the next woman who came by.

She was more alert on the trip back to the tent, but not always in better spirits. It was still too early, and she was still in naught but her nightclothes. Upon returning to the tent, she made her way over to her bag and pulled out yet another simple frock she had acquired from the maidservant in her parents' home. Time to get ready for another day.

Home. Ah. Just thinking of her parents' home brought back memories that seemed thousands of miles away. It had been quite an adjustment for her to be wakened by troops or a bugle blowing. At home, she was roused from sleep by a maid coming into her room to open the curtains and help prepare her for the day. She was then helped into her attire and her hair was done for her. Next it was downstairs to a hot breakfast prepared by the family cook. Elizabeth could almost smell the numerous pastries and breakfast meats that she could indulge in each and every day. Then her day would be filled with hobbies and the things she wanted to do, not the menial tasks that filled her days here. Yes, she had taken that life for granted. When she had made the decision to leave, she had known all this would be left behind, but she had neglected to realize what an adjustment it would be.

Once dressed and her hair pinned, she shook Melanie.

"Time to rise and shine," she said in her brightest voice.

A groan was the only response.

"See you at breakfast?" Elizabeth said, not truly asking a question.

Melanie waved from under her blanket. Her new friend was not a morning person.

Elizabeth grabbed her papers and charcoal and stepped out of the tent. She wouldn't have a lot of time to herself. Breakfast would start soon, and then they would be on to the tasks of the day.

Moving a little ways outside camp and up the hill to afford herself a bird's-eye view, she found a spot to settle. This little patch of grass was far enough away from the sentry's post to not give him grief, but far enough up the hill to still have a good view of the camp. So she plopped down, and without ceremony, began to sketch. She had not the chance to capture the morning maneuvers and now was a prime opportunity.

This had become her favorite spot for the view. There were the family tents, the men's tents, her tent, the hospital, the place the women did laundry and cooked. On one side of the camp, the soldiers were marching in lines and on the other, the artillery unit worked with the cannons. The camp already buzzed with activity and she tried to capture it all on paper.

Elizabeth could never have imagined this place would affect her so, but she had already formed relationships with so many of the people she came in contact with. If anything happened to any of them it would devastate her. Yes, Melanie had indeed been right in what she had said. War changed people. This war was already changing this girl who had been born to privilege and never faced any real hardship in her life.

Looking with an artist's eyes, Elizabeth's gaze swept over the camp again as she put the finishing touches on her sketch. Two figures walking on the outskirts of the camp caught her attention. They looked in her direction and waved. She responded in kind, narrowing her eyes to focus them. Who would come to join her in the moments to come? Seconds later, she realized it was John and Dr. Smith. And they were headed straight for her!

Searching for some place to hide, she came up short. There was no where to go. And they had already spotted her. Elizabeth swallowed hard. So this was it. John would finally discover her. It would only be seconds now until they were close enough. She braced herself for his reaction as the two men came ever closer. Any moment her features would be clear enough that he would know.

Boom! The sound of cannon fire filled the air. Elizabeth hit the ground, covering her ears. Had the troops set off a cannon by accident? As she sat upright again, she noted that John and Dr. Smith had crouched and were looking around, perhaps wondering the same thing. She glanced over at the artillery unit. They scurried about, seemingly just as confused.

From her perch on the hillside, she saw a scout flying toward camp from the south. His form appeared out of the forest line moments after the cannon fire.

The two doctors ran toward the camp. Had they spotted the scout as well?

Elizabeth followed suit.

Camp was in utter chaos. Elizabeth tried to make her way to her station to get some information from her direct report, but there were too many people moving about. The troops moved in one direction, like a wave. It was difficult to push against them. At last, she spotted Melanie.

"Mel!" She called out, "Mel!"

Melanie jerked her head in Elizabeth's direction and grabbed for her hand. Together they pushed through the crowd and found a space next to a tent out of the rush.

"What's going on?" Elizabeth panted with effort.

"It's the Confederates. They're here!"

Elizabeth's heart stopped. What would happen to them all? To John?

"The troops are marching out to meet them," Melanie continued.

Elizabeth nodded, feeling numb. "What can we do?" Her voice shook.

"Pray. Pray and get to your station!" Melanie squeezed Elizabeth's hand once more before heading back out into the throngs of people.

Was this truly her friend Melanie? So levelheaded in the face of crisis? Though Elizabeth was on laundry duty this morning, the last thing anyone would need, she did as Melanie had said.

The Moore family sat around the dinner table. From the outside looking in, one might never know this was a family torn apart by war, a family missing two of its members as they gathered this evening. But Henry Moore knew differently. Their presence was indeed missed by each member. And their empty chairs served as reminders of their absence. Still, those present reveled in the closeness they shared. And they put on brave faces for the others in their company. It was in the final stretches of the meal when, as the women watched, he produced a letter from his pocket.

"Who's it from, Father?" Susan asked, wide-eyed.

Martha's eyes met her husband's.

"It's from Jacob," he said as he pulled his eyes from her gaze.

"Please, do read it, Father!" Susan all but jumped up and down in her chair.

"You know how we do things," he admonished her. "We'll read it in the parlor once everyone is done with dinner."

"Let's go then," Susan begged, pushing her plate away from herself.

"I'm finished." Martha laid her napkin on the table.

"Me, too." Susan followed suit, setting her napkin next to her plate. She looked at her father with wide, expectant eyes. Was she willing him to say he was finished so they might retire to the parlor?

He waited a handful of seconds, eyeing Susan and Martha's expressions. "All right, then," he said at long last, laying his own napkin down. "To the parlor."

Henry led them to the small family room where they huddled around the fireplace. He took a seat to the left of the massive structure, Susan plopped on the floor near his feet, and Martha sat nearby on the sofa, picking at her cross-stitch.

Taking the letter back out of his pocket, he then opened it and began to read.

"Dear Mother, Father, and Susan, I hope this letter finds you well. I miss you all. We settled in our camp and I'm trying to get the hang of things. I'm learning all kinds of stuff. There are definitely things Benjamin failed to mention in his letters, but I understand. He just didn't think it was interesting. Like how we get up every day before dawn. That's boring stuff. But it's important, I guess, since we do it every day.

"We spend most of our time doing things to keep us from getting fat and lazy. But no one here cooks as well as you, Mother, so I don't think anyone is going to get fat. Don't worry, though, I'm eating well enough. I have met some people here and am making friends. I rode the train down here with one of our camp doctors named John. He gave me some good advice about life. My tent mate's name is Phillip. He's a couple of years older than me. We get along just fine, but he doesn't talk much.

"I'd better head out to lunch before it's all gone. I'll write again soon. Love, Jacob. P.S. I am eager to hear about Benjamin."

"That was nice that he became acquainted with one of the doctors," Martha said, working her cross-stitch, moving furiously with her fingers.

Henry supposed she'd rather not allow her mind to wander to those places every parent's mind must when receiving a letter from the front. *Would it be the last?*

"I wonder what he eats there," Susan said, looking up at her father.

"It's not as good as what you get to eat." Henry patted her on the head.

"But is it yucky food or just a bad cook?" Susan's brow furrowed.

"I think they get rations for the most part," Henry sighed, looking back over the letter.

"Rations?" Susan tested the word.

Henry nodded. "An allotted amount of food. Crackers, pork, and coffee, stuff like that."

"Coffee?" She blanched at that. "Jacob doesn't drink coffee!"

"Chances are he will when he comes back."

Susan looked at her father, eyebrow quirked.

"Susan, there may be other things that will have changed about Jacob and even Benjamin when they come home." His voice softened. He'd rather not say more.

"Like what?"

She was so innocent to the goings on of war. Too innocent.

"Oh, I don't know." Henry forced himself to continue the conversation with Susan. "It's just something I want you to know." He prayed that would be enough for her.

Susan shrugged it off. "Okay, Father. Will you read the letter again?"

"Of course. 'Dear Mother, Father, and Susan...'"

Jacob scrambled for cover as shots rang over his head. The battle had been raging for what seemed like forever. Cannons exploding and men screaming in pain filled his ears. It was nothing like he had ever imagined. This was the worst kind of horror he could have pictured. He wished he could recall some of his training, but it was all a blank, replaced by images of bloodied soldiers. One by one, his comrades fell. Blue uniforms stained with red littered the ground. In the distance, someone shouted commands, but he couldn't make out anything clearly amidst the muskets firing.

As he moved through the field, he kept low. Bullets whizzed past his head left and right. It was surreal. He was a target in this open field, and his eyes searched the haze created by weapons' fire to find a safe haven. His drive to survive pushed through dizziness and confusion until that was his only thought. Survive. Moving almost by instinct, he made his way stumbling through the field of bodies. By luck, he came upon a ditch protected by a berm and ducked into the safety it offered.

Other soldiers lay in the ditch, fighting from this position. They crawled up onto the berm on their bellies and fired into the enemy line. Leaning against the cool earth that made up the wall of the ditch, he gasped, trying to catch his breath. His fear and anxiety washed over him. He was alive! And that was all that mattered.

Having survived the first wave and made it to a safe position, the temptation to remain here throughout the rest of the battle was strong. But those men on the berm needed him. They counted on him to help defend their position or else they would all be lost.

After he got a hold of himself and steeled his senses, he climbed up onto the berm, staying on his stomach lest he create too much of a target. The man to his left nodded as he took position and began firing at the Confederate army. He did his best to aim at targets, as hard as they were to see. On occasion, he saw a glint of steel in the distance or the profile of a soldier running. And he tried to hit them. It was difficult to discern success.

Glancing across the enemy's line, Jacob spotted a dip on the far left flank. The Confederates had shifted to the right in response to the Union's first wave offensive. As the minutes of realizing he was alive passed, his confidence began to return. He remembered snippets of the briefing from his unit's commander and the mention of flanking the Confederates on that side. It seemed their offensive had started to work, but something must have gone wrong.

Jacob cursed himself for not listening more closely and assuming his platoon's sergeant would be here to keep things in order. Narrowing his eyes as he watched the movements of the soldiers, he remembered the plan of attack.

"The left unit. Hey! Where is the left unit? Aren't they supposed to be moving in on the second wave?" he shouted to the others crouched with him behind the berm.

They looked at each other, apparently more confused than he.

"I think they got pinned down back there," one soldier responded, his thumb pointed behind them.

It was Old Man. Jacob searched his memory, but couldn't recall the man's name. "What's your name again?"

"Daniel." His voice broke for just a second.

"The Confederates responded to the first wave and are moving to the right. It's up to us to move in to that dip over there and flank them from the left." Jacob pointed to the weak spot in the enemy's line.

Daniel nodded. Was he ready to take orders from anybody?

Jacob had a renewed sense of purpose. Maybe his ability to run fast would pay off.

"We'll split in half. Daniel, me, and you." He tapped the soldier to his right. "We'll make a fast run for that spot while you all continue to cover us from here. When we get there and start shooting, the rest of you will follow. That may hold back the Confederates just enough for the rest of our unit to catch up and take 'em!"

The rest of his new war brothers nodded in quick agreement.

"I'm Steven," the soldier he had tapped said, his voice shaking.

Jacob shook hands with him.

He and his small crew loaded their Springfield muskets and gathered up to the left edge of the berm. With a quick visual signal to the others, they broke out in a fast run.

Jacob's legs flew. It was as if he rode the wind. But he soon noticed how far their target truly was. Could they make it? *I've made it this far; we are going to get there!*

Loud artillery fire boomed. It was deafening as it hit a spot they had just passed. The shock knocked him to the ground. Daniel and Steven were startled. They looked to Jacob. Were their courage and morale hinging on his? He dragged himself to his feet and continued, as fast as he could. His comrades were close behind. As they ran across the fury of the battlefield, they wove around fallen soldiers. It was a bit much for Jacob, but he held it together and kept moving.

How far is that dip in the line? How long does it take to get there? It seemed like an eternity. But a moment later, he saw it. Jacob wanted to shout for joy. In a matter of seconds, he would be there. He had pulled out well ahead of the others. Would they arrive safely?

As he turned, a blast sounded and pain stung him. Falling to the ground, his eyes feverishly sought out his injury and the source of the blast. Here he was, sprinting like it was a race, forgetting that they were fighting for their lives.

Steven and Daniel caught up to him with wide eyes.

Finally laying eyes on the spot where he had been grazed by a ball, he looked past a torn piece of uniform near his shoulder. Feeling along his skin, he let out a sigh. It hadn't penetrated anything, just missed him. While it would be a noticeable mark, it hadn't entered his shoulder.

Jacob picked up his musket and started running again, at last diving into the dip in the line.

Steven and Daniel jumped in right behind him. They raised their weapons, looking for targets.

One enemy soldier looked in their direction. Was that the man who almost hit him?

Before Jacob could react, Daniel fired, and the man fell.

Another Confederate moved up from behind the fallen soldier, and Steven took him out.

Jacob was shocked into action, eyeing his men as they hastily reloaded. Picking up his Springfield, he trained his sights on another Confederate rushing in. His fingers twitched. What was he doing? He had to act! Yet he could not escape his hesitation.

Everything had been surreal. Marching, inspections, field stripping, rations. Almost like a dream. But now it was real. This was what war was about: killing another man. In the instant it took him to trace his thoughts, he understood one thing: if he waited, he or one of his war buddies would be dead, so he pulled the trigger.

He started to reload his weapon when he felt the shakes and he couldn't keep it down anymore, vomiting on the ground.

"First kill?" There was no judgment or mocking in Daniel's voice. Only gentleness.

"Yeah," Jacob said, wiping his face with his sleeve. His legs were weak.

"I did the same."

With that, Jacob had crossed a threshold he never knew existed. His father had told him he looked like a real man in his uniform. Now those words echoed true.

Jacob didn't get lost in thought though. This plan would be a complete failure unless they provided enough cover for the rest of his unit to take this position.

They had dropped three soldiers. Were there more nearby? He doubted it. Most of the Confederate unit was much further down the line and didn't know they were about to be flanked. Jacob turned to tell Steven and Daniel to finish loading their Springfields when he noticed they were already doing so. Time to give the signal for the rest of his unit to join them and hold this position.

Jacob stood, more exposed than he liked, to wave his hat at the men behind the berm. They were not quite visible, but he watched as they grouped together on the left side. His signal had been received. Reaching over and grabbing his weapon, he put his hat back on.

The sound of more artillery firing in the distance shook him. Was it closer or further away? As he slid into the dip, seeking better cover, the crack of a rifle was followed by hot, piercing pain in his left leg. Looking down, blood covered his leg. His gaze shifted, taking in his surroundings. The man he had hit earlier wasn't dead, but had gotten in a final shot with his loaded weapon.

Jacob let out a loud cry while Steven attacked the man with his bayonet.

Then things started to swirl. Jacob's vision blurred. As if everything was in a daze.

Daniel came to his side, applying pressure to his leg. As he started to fade out, he kept looking back, wondering if the rest of his unit had caught up to them.

And then, nothing.

The battle raged on. All Elizabeth could do was sit and listen to the cannons and gunfire in the distance, grimacing at every sound. There was no laundry to do, no sewing that was called for, nothing to be done. Just sit and wait for news. It was the longest wait of her life.

Looking at the water, she couldn't help but imagine the laundry they would have to do the next day. She envisioned the blood discoloring the water, as they would work to clean the dark blue uniforms. Shaking her head to clear such morbid thoughts, she tried to think of something more pleasant. Nothing came to mind. What was there to think of at a time like this? Nothing but war and bloodshed. Not for the soldiers, and not for her.

Though she had long since been released from duty, she was unable to leave her post. The camp seemed abandoned with the troops gone, the hospital staffed, and the other women...where? Where were the other women? Waiting and praying in their tents? Elizabeth sank to her knees by the water tub and sobbed, praying for the men in their unit that faced their mortality even then.

"Father, Keep Your gracious hand on these brave men. I would ask that You keep them safe from harm, but I know that it is Your will, not mine, that we should seek. Comfort those who are wounded. Give the doctors wisdom and skill. Be with John."

"Elizabeth!" Melanie interrupted her thoughts. "Elizabeth!"

Elizabeth rose and rushed toward her friend. "What is it? Is there news?"

Melanie, nearly out of breath, caught Elizabeth's hands. She nodded. "The fighting is over, but there are many wounded. They need help in the hospital. I told them I would bring you." Melanie turned and walked in the direction of the hospital.

Elizabeth froze. She wanted to help, but how could she avoid John in the hospital? He would see her for certain, and her time here would be over. Her head fell. What self-serving thinking! There were men wounded and in need of care, and she was worried about something so selfish! Embarrassed by her reaction to Melanie's request for help, she turned away.

"Come on." Melanie jerked on her hand. "What are you waiting for?"

Determined to do what she could to help the men in need, she turned back toward her friend. "I am sorry I hesitated. I am ready."

"I know it won't be easy," Melanie said softly, "But we will do what we must."

Melanie must think her squeamish. Elizabeth chose not to contradict her and nodded.

Tugging at her once more, Melanie led her to the hospital tent.

Nothing could have prepared Elizabeth for what awaited her at the hospital. The battle had been gruesome. Every space available had a solider, the tent filled with men in all states of horror. She did not have time to take it all in before a nurse approached.

"Take the men water, sit with them, and tell them the doctors are making it around. Do you know how to clean a wound?"

Elizabeth continued to stare at the sight, not able to make eye contact with the nurse. But she nodded. She was only somewhat aware that Melanie shook her head.

"Good," the nurse said to Elizabeth. "Do only superficial cleaning. You'll find supplies over there." She pointed to a shelf at one end of the tent. "And you," she turned to Melanie. "Come watch me for a couple of patients and you'll learn."

As she looked over the many men in agony, being recognized by John became a smaller and smaller concern. Elizabeth made her way to the shelf and grabbed the supplies she would need.

She stopped at the man closest to the shelf unit. He was young, much younger than John. His sandy-blonde hair fell over deep brown eyes that looked up to her as if to find some reassurance that all would be well. There was fear there as well. Fear remaining like an echo from the emotion of the battle, and fear that nothing would ever be the same. Fear of what might happen to him. Would she ever forget that look in his eyes?

"Hello, soldier." She put on her best smile for him. "I'm Elizabeth. What's your name?"

The man shook badly, with a terrible leg wound. He was in shock. In all likelihood he would lose the leg.

"A-Adam."

She offered him some water. He drank it, thanking her. She began to clean the wound, but didn't see much point in it. The leg was in need of a deeper cleaning. Still, she did as the nurse had instructed her and basically put a strip of cloth on the gunshot wound.

"I-is it b-b-bad?" Adam asked, seeking her eyes.

She shook her head. "You'll be fine," she told a half-truth. "The doctor will see you in a while."

Man after man, wound after wound, all Elizabeth could do was offer water and assurances that the doctors would see them. She knew at a glance that some of these men were not going to make it. And that broke her heart. But she put on a brave smile for them and spent more time by their bedside, talking with them, singing to them, praying with them. A few of them passed on while she was with them, but she refused to cry.

She returned to the shelf for more supplies. Stretching her back, she wondered how long she had been here. The ache in her muscles led her to believe it had been quite some time. A few hours maybe? Glancing around the hospital, she spotted Melanie, sitting with a young man, talking as she cleaned his leg wound. Elizabeth smiled. Perhaps Melanie had found her calling. The doctors made their rounds as well. Dr. Smith was there and Dr. Young. But where was John?

Her gaze flicked from side to side, searching. No John. She felt a little sick and her heart skipped a few beats.

Catching up to a nurse walking nearby, she grabbed at the woman's sleeve. "I'm looking for Dr. Taylor. Dr. John Taylor," she said, knowing her voice betrayed her worry.

"A doctor will be around to see each patient in turn," the nurse said, jerking her arm away.

"No." Elizabeth grabbed the woman's shoulders, desperate. "I'm looking for Dr. Taylor."

The nurse stopped to think. "He went to the front lines to patch the wounded there and prepare them for transport. I haven't seen him since."

Elizabeth's eyes widened. Her heart dropped into her stomach. The warmth drained from her face and she felt light-headed.

"Miss, are you okay?" The nurse's face contorted into a concerned expression.

Elizabeth couldn't speak, she couldn't breathe. She backed away from the nurse and whirled around, running out of the hospital. Where to, she did not know. At first she turned this way and that, unsure about what she was going to do. The world began to blur in front of her.

Stopping, she worked to catch her breath. She needed a plan. The front lines. If that's where John was, that's where she needed to go. But how? The laundry!

It was easy enough to get her hands on a small uniform, carry it back to her tent, and slip into it, binding her breasts. Shoving her hair into a cap, she rubbed dirt and mud on her face to mar her feminine features. And taking advantage of the mayhem from the recent battle, she made her way across the camp unnoticed and ran toward the battlefield.

The field was littered with bodies and limbs. Elizabeth had thought the hospital was bad, but this proved a million times worse. There were no words to describe the grisly state of the men there. She felt the urge to vomit, but held her stomach. Taking several deep breaths, she reminded herself that she was here for a reason; she had to find John. He might need her.

Walking the battlefield, she looked for signs of her beloved. With the front line a little ways in the distance and to the left of her position, she could search here for a while before risking being discovered. What was he doing out here in the first place? Why would he come? Hadn't he promised to stay a safe distance from the fighting? But she knew he would go where he was needed. *Stubborn, selfish fool!*

When the bodies thickened and the number of gray uniforms matched the blue ones, she knew she neared what had at one time been the front lines. She glanced to her left and saw that she was almost in line with the current front line, but far enough away to be clear of the fighting. At this point, she was forced to move bodies to check for John. Having to touch the bloodied corpses ended up to be too much and she did vomit. But, her determination took over and she moved onward.

She came upon a Union soldier stabbed with a bayonet, the blade protruding from his back. That was something she definitely didn't want to touch. And she noticed the man underneath him was a Confederate soldier, so she turned to move on. But a hand shot up. The Confederate soldier was alive!

"Help me," came the weak voice of the man trapped underneath the dead Union soldier.

Something in her told her to run, but another part bid her to stay. Gray uniform or blue, this man needed help. How could she, in good conscience, leave him to die knowing she could have saved his life?

With much effort, she pushed the dead soldier off him and saw that the Confederate soldier had a wound in his upper arm. It began to bleed. The weight and body of the Union soldier must have put enough pressure on it to stop the bleeding. What could she use as a tourniquet? Reaching for the Union soldier's sleeve, she tore off enough to fashion one.

"Thank you," he said, his voice still weak.

That's when she looked into his eyes. It was hard to imagine that this man, whose blue eyes she found herself gazing into, had played a part in the destruction around her, had killed men, perhaps this Union soldier she had just moved. But it was true.

Voices in the distance drew her attention. She jerked her head up, starting to stand as she scanned the area around her. Confederate soldiers! Headed her way! What was she going to do?

"Stop! Thief!" One yelled out, having spotted her. He raised his gun.

She threw up her hands and moved a step back.

He fired.

A hot, searing pain in her left shoulder whipped her around and threw her to the ground. Her head smacked something solid as she landed.

And then all was black.

Abigail sat in front of her vanity, putting the finishing touches on her appearance: a pair of earrings Elizabeth had gifted her at last year's birthday celebration. They were simple, beautiful pearl earrings. Elizabeth wasn't much for elaborate ornamentation, but Abigail treasured them. All the more today. They made her feel as if Elizabeth was with her.

Gazing at her reflection in the mirror, not a hair was awry and her gown had been pressed for show. Yet these things were out of place with face that looked back at her. Her features were downcast, true, but it was her eyes. They were soulless. As if the life had been drained from her.

She was as ready as she'd ever be. What other preparation could be done? But something was still missing. This feeling had haunted her since Elizabeth's flight. What was this emptiness? Was this what it felt like to lose one's child?

Thomas came from behind her and kissed the side of her face.

"You are beautiful, darling. Even if you must wear these ridiculous hats."

Smiling in the mirror at him brought life to her features, but not to her eyes. Still, she gave him an amused look. Thomas never understood women's fashions, the hat least of all. He couldn't comprehend why she needed such a collection.

Thomas stood once again and fingered his tie. The knot was askew. Had he attempted to work it himself?

"I don't know why you won't let someone help you with that." Abigail sighed as she turned. "Here." She batted his hands away. "Let me."

"I don't have someone help with it, because I prefer when you do it." He winked.

She afforded him another smile. What a charmer she had married! Even after all these years, he could make her smile. "I appreciate you coming to this event," she said, her voice serious. "It's very important to me."

"It's important to me, too." He put his hands on her arms as she finished, letting her hands fall. "Elizabeth is, after all, my daughter, too."

"Of course." She let her eyes linger on his. Could he see in her eyes what she had? She hoped not.

"Besides," he said with a sly smile. "You and Charlotte have been working night and day to make sure this is the grandest party of the season. I want to see it for myself."

"I just hope everything goes as planned," she moaned, her brows coming together. *What if it didn't? What if the Hall...?*

"I have every confidence it will." Thomas pressed another kiss to the side of her face. "We'd best get you there before it all falls apart," he said with a twinkle in his eye.

She gave him another smile and allowed him to lead her down the hall. Soon enough they were helped into their coverings and ushered out the door to the waiting carriage.

The ride to the Event Hall was quite unremarkable. Abigail busied herself going over her mental checklist, but Thomas kept talking to her. What was he saying? Something about the weather? She needed to focus. He continued with his questions, his eyes beckoning her to respond.

"What?" Her reply was sharper than she'd intended.

His eyes widened.

"Sorry," she whispered. "I'm...distracted at the moment."

He nodded. "I understand."

Thomas spoke not another word the remainder of their ride.

But she still couldn't focus her thoughts. She felt guilty for delivering the verbal punch.

They arrived at the Hall in short order. And Abigail would crawl out of her skin if it took one minute longer. How was the decorating going? Were they following the plan?

Stilling her movements, she allowed Thomas to get out first, though everything in her seemed to stretch forth.

Thomas reached a hand in for her.

She took it and he helped her down. Then she took off. Had he offered his arm in escort? Most likely. Could she wait for him to escort her into the event space? It was not physically possible. Abigail moved as quick as polite society would allow until she was inside.

Hands laid hold of her wrap. She slid it off with only a nod in the direction of the hands. The space captivated her. Banners were hung, flowers were on display, food tables were being prepped. Almost everything was done. And Charlotte stood in the midst of the hustle and bustle, directing it all.

Abigail shook her head. Of course Charlotte was here. How could she have given it a second thought?

"Charlotte," Abigail greeted her friend, crossing to her. "I should have been here to help you."

"Abigail!" Charlotte paused to embrace her friend and co-host. "Nonsense, I promise I just arrived myself."

"It seems as if everything is running smoothly." Abigail let her gaze wander over the Hall, admiring the realization of all their planning. The Hall looked better than they'd imagined. Tonight would be a success. She had to believe that.

"Appears so. I haven't checked the registration table yet. Would you mind?"

Abigail nodded. "Consider it done."

The next half hour became a flurry of activity as the final touches were put on the space and the two women worked side by side to make sure even the tiniest detail was managed. By the time the guests arrived, everything was set and running like clockwork.

And so the following half hour became a different kind of din.

People checked in, milled about, conversed, enjoyed the décor, and partook of the refreshments.

The time came for the guests to be properly welcomed. This particular task fell to Abigail. As she prepared to step in front of the crowd, shaking hands touched her necklace. Why was she trembling so? These were her friends and people from her community. And this event was for Elizabeth. She clasped her hands together to still them, but the quivering came from inside of her.

An arm snaked around her waist. She jumped back from the contact. *Who?* But the arm held her fast. And the presence seemed familiar to her. Turning, she met the eyes of her husband, her rock.

Thomas leaned toward the side of her head and whispered into her hair, "You'll do fine."

Abigail took a deep breath and smoothed her hands over her dress.

"Trust me," he said, pressing a kiss to the side of her face.

She nodded, squeezing his arm. The shakiness had subsided somewhat. Adjusting her hat, she then stepped up to the podium. But the crowd seemed too engaged in their own conversations. No one noticed she had stepped up to address them. Searching out Charlotte, she became desperate. Her friend was nowhere.

Clink, clink, clink. The sound drew her attention to where she had just been standing. Thomas used a spoon to bang against his glass, trying to get everyone's attention. As members in the audience noticed her at the podium, they chimed in with their glasses. Soon, all voices paused.

Once all eyes were on Abigail, she began, hoping she sounded more confident than she felt. "Welcome, esteemed guests and friends. As you know, this is a fundraiser for our brave soldiers who, as we speak, are fighting for our country. We hope you have come feeling patriotic and ready to give for the sake of those men who are sacrificing that our nation be made whole again. As many of you already know, our men need many things, so we accept all manner of gifts. Foodstuffs and monetary support are the most crucial at this time, but anything you can give will help.

"Tonight, we would like to put a face on this issue. I want to introduce my dear friend and co-chair for this evening's event, a woman who has given tirelessly to this cause herself and stands as a model of patriotism: Mrs. Charlotte Taylor."

Abigail prayed Charlotte would have appeared by the time she turned. Applause sounded and she turned her head in time to see Charlotte moving toward her to take her place. And Abigail clapped for her friend, never more relieved as she stepped to the side, allowing room for Charlotte to take center stage.

As Charlotte began her speech, Abigail moved off to find some water. All of a sudden, she was parched.

"Thank you, Mrs. Thompson, for that wonderful introduction and for your efforts in making this event possible. And thank you all for being here. Some of you may know that my son, Dr. John Taylor, is on the front lines fighting for this nation. Let me tell you a little bit about my son. John..."

Thomas came up behind Abigail and put his hand on the small of her back. "You were great," he whispered in her ear.

"Thanks," she said, not taking her eyes off Charlotte. But she wasn't truly listening to her either. Would that she were allowed to tell Elizabeth's story!

It was not a well-kept secret that Elizabeth was no longer at home, and some even knew she had fled to help out with the war effort. But Abigail would never be able to step up to a podium and talk about it. What Elizabeth had done was respectable, even admirable, but definitely beneath her station. Women of their station did not go prancing off to war. They did just what Charlotte and Abigail were doing.

If only Elizabeth were here, she could make a compelling speaker! But she wasn't. She was miles away in some war camp doing God knows what. No, Abigail had not come to peace with Elizabeth's decision. Would she ever?

Applause erupted around her. Abigail set her drink down and joined in.

"Enjoy yourselves, and please, don't hesitate to see any of the women in the Booster Club if you have questions about donations."

Charlotte stepped down from the podium and the din of the crowd rose again. But Abigail's thoughts were numb. She stared straight ahead. There was movement in front of her, but she looked through that and beyond somehow.

"How was that?" Charlotte appeared in front of her. *Where had she come from?*

Abigail focused on her friend's face.

Charlotte's eyes begged for reassurance, eyebrows raised.

Abigail wished she had been listening better.

"It was great," Thomas interjected. "John would be proud."

"Yes," Abigail said, nodding. "Of course he would."

Smiling, Charlotte seemed relieved. "Thank you."

"I think we're bound to get donations after all of this," Abigail said, sweeping her arms over the Event Hall.

"For certain," Charlotte agreed, looking around.

The three stood in silence. For a handful of moments, it was amiable. And then it became awkward.

Charlotte took Abigail's hand. It felt warm. Was that because Abigail's hand was cold? "If you'll excuse me, I need to find Franklin."

"Of course," Thomas said. "I think the last place I saw him was by the refreshment table."

"I have no doubt." Charlotte sighed.

Abigail squeezed her friend's hand before she walked away.

"Forgive me," Thomas said, his words coming out slow and careful. "But you seem as if you are miles from here."

Abigail looked back at her husband. "I am."

"Thinking of Elizabeth?" He reached up and touched her hair, his fingers grazing her locks.

Abigail nodded, fighting tears. Why did it sting so? These thoughts?

Thomas waited for her to speak.

"She should be here," Abigail started; tears welled, threatening to spill over. She stopped speaking, trying to gain control of herself.

Thomas pulled her to the side, to a corner where they would be less conspicuous. He kept his hands on her arms. It brought her some measure of comfort.

"She had no business running off! There is so much more good she could be doing here!" Abigail cried.

Thomas's eyes seemed deeper somehow in that moment. And his voice was soft, not much more than a whisper. "Can you not see that she did it for love?"

Abigail let out an exasperated gasp. She was in no mood to entertain such schoolgirl notions.

"We need not understand, my dear. We can only try to accept it."

"And what if I can't?" She looked up at him.

Thomas had no words to offer in response.

CHAPTER FOUR
PRISONER

When Jacob returned to consciousness, the first thing that came to him was the pain in his leg. A quick glance around and he knew he was no longer on the battlefield. Was he back at camp? Wounded soldiers surrounded him. The hospital? Rising up on his elbows, he jerked his head around, searching for Daniel and Steven. They were nowhere to be found. Were they all right? Or dead? Had their tactic worked?

In short order, he was heaving and sweating from the small effort of holding himself up and from the pain as well. A woman five or so years his senior stopped at his bedside. Long red hair was pinned out of her face and her green eyes seemed to dance as she smiled down at him. She was lovely.

"Hey, there, soldier," she said, sitting down next to him. "Care for some water?"

He nodded, gazing at the ladle she held out. Leaning toward it, he drank when the girl tipped it, dripping the liquid into his mouth. It didn't even matter that it wasn't cold. Jacob was grateful for the refreshment.

"My name's Melanie. What's yours?" She set her bucket and ladle down.

"Jacob." Even to him his voice sounded weak, haggard.

"Well, Jacob, I'm going to take a look at your wound and clean it up a bit." She said this as if it was something that happened every day. "You're not going to like me in a few minutes." Then there was that smile again as she met his eyes.

As much as he wanted to keep staring into those green orbs, his eyes traced her movements over his leg. He braced himself as she removed the dressings from his wound, crude as they were. It wasn't pleasant, just as she had promised. But even more unpleasant was the next part when she went about cleansing the area with water and another liquid of some sort that stung. The moment the cleaning agent hit his leg, pain shot through his limb anew. Arching his back, he came off the table several inches.

Melanie placed a hand on his shoulder. It distracted him only somewhat from what she did to his leg. Whenever she looked at his wound, she grimaced. But every time she looked into his eyes, she smiled. Was she putting on a brave face? How bad was his wound?

"Did we do it? Did we win?" he managed to choke out, his mind turning back toward the battle.

"I don't know any of the details of the battle. I'm sorry." Her voice was soft and soothing. He wouldn't mind having her do worse to his wound as long as she kept talking.

"What of my friends?" His voice became urgent. "Daniel? Steven? Did they bring me in? Are they here?"

Her eyes met his again. There was a sadness there. His breath caught.

"I'm afraid I don't know anything about them either."

He let out his breath. There was hope.

"Even if they were injured and in the hospital somewhere, I wouldn't know unless I'd treated them. I'm sorry, Jacob, but you'll have to be patient." Her hand again fell on his shoulder.

Jacob wasn't satisfied with her answers, but it wasn't her fault.

Glancing around the hospital, he took in the scene anew. The amount of wounded was unimaginable. Every available bed and floor space was taken.

"The doctors are making their way around as they can," she offered. "Perhaps they know more."

Another wave of pain shot through him and he gritted his teeth against it, trying not to cry out in front of her. He only somewhat succeeded.

Her brows furrowed.

"Can I have something for the pain?"

"I'll ask one of the nurses." She turned her head.

"You're not a nurse?" He jerked up in the bed. What was she doing tending to his wound?

Turning toward him once again, she said, "I'm just someone who's helping out."

Her response had done nothing to assuage his concern. "But you cleaned my wound."

"I have had a little training," she said, a small smile gracing her lips. "And now, I'm going to amaze you with my other skills." She winked at him. "I'll redress your wound."

He afforded her a smile, easing back onto the pillow. She was rather enjoyable to be around.

As she worked to redress the wound, she continued her attempts at conversation. "So, soldier, tell me about your girl back home."

"I, um, don't have a girl back home." He focused on the top of the tent, trying to distract himself from what she was doing.

"Come now, Jacob. Sandy blonde hair, hazel eyes, striking smile, and you expect me to believe you haven't got at least one girl back home."

He shrugged and nodded. "Guess I was always too busy with this or that to settle on one special girl."

"You keep them all guessing, is that it?" She winked at him again.

"No," he said, his face warming. "At least, not intentionally." He studied her face then.

"I bet you have a line of girls that would jump at the chance to be on your arm."

Was that true? It didn't seem at all likely, but maybe there were. She couldn't mean that brunette, Clara. They were just friends. Not even good friends at that. Clara always seemed friendly, but he never thought she liked him that way. Couldn't be. Or maybe she was just shy? He shook his head. There were always girls hanging around him at school. But none of those girls ever seemed interesting enough to hold his attention for long. And none of them had a smile like Melanie's.

A man came from behind Melanie as she started to secure the bandages.

"No need to tie that off, I'll be looking at it."

"Of course, doctor." She let the ends of the bandage fall, slipping through her fingers.

The doctor met Jacob's eyes. "Hello, soldier. I'm Dr. Smith. I just had to come and see the young man who helped advance the union line."

"You mean it worked?" Jacob tried to lift himself up on his elbows.

"It sure did, soldier. The Union troops are holding strong having advanced the line to where you sneaked into that opening. There's a lot of talk about you around camp. You're a pretty fast runner, eh?"

"Yes, sir." Jacob felt his chest puff up.

"Let's see what we can do to fix up this leg." The doctor began unwrapping the bandages Melanie had just spent several minutes putting in place.

As he maneuvered Jacob's leg, the pain came back full force. "Can I have something for the pain, doctor?"

"Of course," the older man said, patting his shoulder. "Of course."

The doctor turned to Melanie. "Go find my nurse. Tell her to bring the camp hero something for pain."

"Aye, aye!" Melanie said, smiling again at Jacob before walking off.

The doctor unwrapped the bandage and studied the leg wound. Jacob watched Dr. Smith's expression change as his smile fell ever so slightly before he caught himself. He then covered the wound again and patted Jacob's opposite knee.

"You're going to be just fine," he promised.

Melanie returned with the nurse, who gave Jacob a shot of something. Immediately, the pain started to ease.

The doctor spoke in hushed tones to the nurse. Melanie must have overheard because she piped up. As did his hold on reality.

The doctor turned his back to Jacob who worked hard to follow what happened. It was difficult. Dr. Smith glanced over his shoulder at Jacob and then pulled the two women a little further away. Then he started to speak. But Jacob's world swirled and the voices seemed distorted.

He saw Melanie quite clearly, however. Why was she so adamant? Did the doctor make her mad? She was even prettier when she was upset.

The pull to unconsciousness became too great and Jacob slipped further and further toward it. He wanted to stay awake and ask Melanie what had bothered her so, but the drugs won and he was soon surrounded by darkness.

Sound. The first thing on the edge of Elizabeth's consciousness; though the source of the sound was difficult to make out. With much effort, her eyes blinked open. Light. The world was hazy, but it was definitely daytime. She blinked. With each blink, the world came into sharper focus. It became apparent that she was in a tent. On a cot of some sort. And there was pain. From where?

It required several minutes of concentration for her to identify that the pain radiated from her head. Reaching up, her fingers touched the soft gauze of a bandage. But moving her left arm had been a mistake. Pain shot through her shoulder. She let out a yelp. Then clamped her mouth shut, biting her lip to prevent any further utterances.

Where was she? What had happened to her?

The tent was large with many low cots as the one she lay on. And there were shelves stocked with all manner of things. But she was the sole occupant at the moment. Motion off to her right drew her attention. A woman rushed into the tent, coming directly for her. So her movements and vocalizations had alerted at least one person to her presence.

Elizabeth searched for some place to run, some place to hide. But she doubted she could do either in her current state. She would just have to stand her ground and hope for the best. Her gaze returned to the woman advancing on her.

The woman had a stern face, the kind of face that had witnessed too much and had little compassion left to offer.

"Try not to move so quickly," the woman's sharp voice came as she halted just short of Elizabeth's figure. "Doctor," the woman called, looking somewhere off to her left. "Doctor, she's awake."

The tent flap opened again and another blurry figure appeared. A man this time. Few long strides were needed to bring him to Elizabeth's side. His face held more kindness than the woman's, though it betrayed more years.

"How do you feel?" he asked, pulling at the shoulder of her nightdress only enough to bare her wound.

Elizabeth stared at the two strangers. Could she trust them? She didn't even know where she was. Everything seemed hazy. No real details came to her about where she had been, what led to her injuries, nothing. But these people were, by all appearances, the ones who had patched her up. Perhaps it was worth the risk.

"I'm in some pain. My head, my shoulder."

"Just as I expected," the doctor said. "But you can hear. You can talk. Can you see all right? How many fingers am I holding up?"

At first his fingers were hazy, but the world became clearer by the second.

"Four."

"Good." He took a deep breath. "Do you remember how you ended up here?"

She shifted her gaze between the two. Was this some sort of game? Didn't they know? Her head ached just thinking about it. So she closed her eyes briefly, opening them to gauge the doctor's reaction. "No."

If that surprised the doctor, he didn't show it. "You came to us with a gunshot wound and a concussion. That's probably why you don't remember the injury. We were quite surprised to find out you were a woman."

"What?" Why would that surprise them?

"Because you posed as a soldier." He spoke matter-of-factly.

"I was what?" He spoke nonsense. Pose as a soldier?

The doctor's impassive expression melted to one of concern.

"What do you remember?"

Elizabeth again fought through a growing headache to search out some detail, some answer, some clue about herself.

"Nothing," she said, her voice rising.

"When you say nothing..." the doctor started then stopped. "Can you tell me your name?"

She hunted for that piece of information, which should be so simple. But there was nothing. A big blank. It wouldn't come to her.

"No." Try as she might to fight them, tears threatened to fall.

"Can you tell me anything about yourself? Where you're from? How old you are?"

"No!" came her immediate answer. What was she going to do? Without any knowledge of who she was? Was she even safe here? Moving to sit up, pain shot through her again.

"Calm down," the doctor soothed, his hands on her arms, gently pressing, encouraging her to lie back. "It will be all right."

"What is the last thing you do remember?"

Elizabeth searched the darkness of her mind. "Waking here."

The doctor and nurse exchanged a look. Elizabeth twitched, unable to remain still.

"What's wrong with me? What's going to happen to me?" Shifting in the cot, she tried to sit up again.

The doctor and nurse both laid hands on her to stop her from doing so.

"Calm yourself," the doctor said, a bit more firmly. "You are safe. We'll find all the answers you need. You have amnesia. You've lost your memory."

"Amnesia?" Elizabeth lay back, forcing herself to breathe.

"Yes. In many cases, patients are able to remember everything eventually. So, don't worry. I assure you, everything will be just fine."

Elizabeth wanted to believe him. But how was she to remain calm? She had lost who she was! Were there people looking for her? The same people who had harmed her?

"Right now, I think it's important you get some rest," the doctor said, glancing over at the nurse.

Elizabeth nodded after a few moments, leaning back into the pillow. She let her eyes close to appease the doctor and nurse. Sensing the doctor and nurse moving away, she strained to hear them. They spoke not too far away, but try as she might, she could not make out what they said. So, she instead concentrated on finding a memory beyond two minutes ago. But, it was useless. It was all a blank.

Matthew slammed his hand on the table harder than he intended. His palm stung, and the vibrations coursed through his entire body, including his injured arm, tucked into a sling.

"Would you listen to the doctor? It's amnesia!" he argued.

"I don't care," the colonel said. "We cannot risk a Union spy in our midst."

Mathew pushed out a breath through clenched teeth and shoved himself away from the table. They had already gone around and around about this. And now they were practically in each others' faces.

"Look, Mr. Tucker," Lieutenant Colonel Simmons piped up from the sidelines, "I know she probably saved your life, but we don't have the luxury of giving prisoners such considerations. We have to think about a whole camp of men. What of the cost to those men if she were to carry off information about our location to her Union Commander, Lieutenant?"

They were right. Matthew also risked insubordination charges speaking to his commanding officers the way he was, but he couldn't stop himself. "And just how do you suppose she's going to do that if she can't even remember her own name?"

The colonel's eyes met Matthew's. Steely gray eyes narrowed. Matthew had run up against his commanding officer's limits.

"Sir," Matthew added as he took a step back.

The tension in the colonel's shoulders eased.

"Doctor, what kind of guarantee can you give me that the prisoner is not faking her amnesia?" the colonel asked.

Matthew had almost forgotten that the doctor was there.

"She's not faking the concussion. However, I cannot guarantee that she's not faking the amnesia, no matter how improbable I find it."

"There. It's possible she's making this whole thing up in order to receive better treatment."

The colonel and Matthew glared at one another. Who would speak first?

"What if I vouch for her, sir?" Dr. Wilson spoke up.

The colonel paused. Matthew knew it wasn't easy for him to go against the doctor's word. Perhaps the colonel would see reason and remember that this helpless woman was in this mess because of one of his trigger-happy soldiers. If they had bothered to capture her properly, they would have a prisoner, not a patient. And this whole discussion would be moot.

"She will be restricted to the hospital..." the colonel began.

Matthew opened his mouth to protest.

"...until such time as we can determine for certain that she is not a threat." The colonel stood to his full height. This was his final offer.

A fair compromise. No one would be completely happy with the decision, but wasn't that the basis of all good compromises?

"Thank you, gentlemen, you're all dismissed," the colonel said, sitting and shuffling some papers on his desk. It was clear he was done with this matter.

Matthew and Dr. Wilson moved out of the tent. The doctor stepped toward the hospital, moving with a purpose. It meant Matthew had to pick up his step if he wanted to speak with him.

"Doctor," he called.

Dr. Wilson turned and allowed Matthew a moment to catch up.

"Thank you," he said, meeting the doctor's eyes. "For the support in there."

"Not a problem," Dr. Wilson replied. "I only spoke the truth."

Matthew smiled at him. "When, ah, when can I see her?"

"Now, if you'd like. I can't say how receptive she'll be. But you're welcome to come and see her."

"Thanks, doc."

They walked in silence the remainder of the way to the hospital tent. Matthew attempted to shake off the heated discussion as fresh memories of the battle, and of her, flooded his mind. The moment she had appeared over him out on that battlefield, he had been sure she was an angel sent from heaven. As she had come into focus, he then thought she was a Union soldier ready to finish him off. But then, against all odds, she had helped him, saved him. Only to be shot down in the midst of her attempted rescue. Guilt for her predicament washed over him. Perhaps that's why he fought so hard for her to be treated well.

The oversized hospital tent loomed in front of him. What would it be like to see her again? His glimpses of her whilst in the hospital just after being brought back to camp had been limited. He wasn't sure he could say he would know her on sight in the least. Except, those eyes.

Matthew followed Dr. Wilson into the tent. The good doctor wasted no time in moving through the tent toward their destination. For his part, Matthew tried to glance around the man. It wasn't until they slowed to a stop and the doctor stepped to the side that he was able to see her.

She sat on the thin cot, eating rations, eyes widened as she watched him. Her gaze darted between him and the doctor. The skin of her face had been cleaned. It was fair, creamy even. And though her head was bandaged, the curly blonde hair that cascaded down past her shoulders appeared freshly cleaned as well. Quite lovely. He blinked a few times and resisted the urge to shake his head to clear it.

"How are you feeling?" The doctor lifted her chart to check the latest entry.

"Much better now that I have some food in me." Her eyes followed Matthew's subtle movements.

"This is someone who wanted to come and visit, if that's all right," Dr. Wilson explained.

"Do I know you?" It was a question, but also a statement. There was recognition in her eyes. Did she have some vague memory of him?

"You saved me," he said, moving closer to her cot. "Out on the battlefield."

Her head tilted to the side as if she tried to recollect the incident, but any hint of recognition that had been in her eyes was gone.

He looked to the ground, to the side table, anywhere but at her. "I wanted to come by and thank you. But I can see that you're busy. I'll get out of..." He turned to leave, but she interrupted him.

"And you. Are you the one who brought me here?"

He stopped. Then turned slowly and met her gaze before nodding.

"So, I should be thanking you, too. For saving me."

"You're most welcome." He returned to his place by her cot. Her blue eyes captured him; they were the same hue as his. Truly she was beautiful, even in a hospital bed, all bandaged up. She was an angel, fallen to earth.

Dr. Wilson cleared his throat. "I'll leave you two to talk," he said before moving across the tent.

After several seconds, Matthew pulled a chair over to sit next to Elizabeth.

She continued to glare at him as if she still tried to place him.

"Do you know where I come from?" she asked, hopeful.

"Sorry, no," he shook his head.

"What about my name?"

He shook his head again.

"So, I saved you and that's it?"

He nodded. It sounded weak and he knew it. Matthew wanted to offer her something. "Perhaps until you remember your name, we could come up with something to call you," he suggested.

She raised an eyebrow. After a somewhat lengthy pause, she said, "What should my name be?"

He was taken aback. Surely she didn't mean for him to name her, did she? But as his eyes continued to gaze at hers, she watched him expectantly. Swallowing hard, he chose his words carefully when he opened his mouth to speak again.

"I've always figured that if I had a girl, I'd name her after my grandmother—Annabelle." Her brows came together. Was he on the wrong track? "Forget it. I'm just too nostalgic for my own good." He looked down at his hands, his face heating.

"Annabelle," she tried the name. Thin brows lifted from their creased state. "I think I like that. I like it a lot. Annabelle."

"Annabelle it is, then," Matthew's eyes met hers, smiling.

Dr. Wilson appeared again. How much had he heard? "Ah, we've come up with a temporary name, have we?"

"Yes." Elizabeth looked up at him. "Annabelle."

Dr. Wilson picked up her chart and made a notation. "All right. 'Annabelle' it is."

Matthew returned his gaze to Elizabeth's face, but she was already watching him. Something coursed through him in that moment.

"I think it's time for Miss Annabelle to get some rest," Dr. Wilson said gently, eyeing Matthew.

"Of course, doctor," he said, rising. He leaned over to Elizabeth once again. "I'm glad you are better."

"Thank you."

Matthew turned to leave.

"Wait," she called out.

He spun toward her.

"Will you come visit me again?"

"If that's all right with you. I would like that very much." There was that warmth in his chest again.

She nodded. "I would like that, too."

Was he a schoolboy again? It seemed so as he smiled back at her. Then he took his leave.

Miles away, John awoke in a Confederate jail. The same walls and bars greeted him that he had fallen asleep staring at the previous night. He lay on the makeshift bed, or what they passed off as a bed. Would the floor be as comfortable? Perhaps. Less likely he'd be bitten by bedbugs.

The cell closed in around him, the space uninviting. Then again, that was the whole point. What did they intend to do with him? Who did they think he was?

His body ached from the rough treatment that had been visited upon him since his capture. He had first been held in a small Confederate camp. They had tried to get information out of him there. But he had nothing to give them. Nothing they wanted.

Then he was moved here. Not more than a couple of miles south-east. Though blindfolded, he had been able to feel the sun, burning on the right side of his face as he lay in the back of a wagon.

Motion nearby drew his attention toward the cell door. He turned his head in that direction and regretted the movement as pain shot through his head. *Small movements. Remember, smaller movements.*

A soldier worked the lock. "Stay back."

His warning was wholly unnecessary. John had no intention of fighting his way free. Yet. So he did as he was told.

The man brought in a plate of food and set it on the only other piece of furniture in the space—a small stand. Eyeing John, the soldier backed out of the cell, secured the door, and moved down the hall in the direction he had come.

"Excuse me," John said, moving to stand next to the bars. "Can you tell me why I'm here?"

The man didn't answer. He didn't even look at John. Just walked off.

"Anybody?" John called out.

There was no answer.

Grimacing, John eased back down onto the cot. He glanced at the meal provided him. Rations, no doubt. Some pork, beans, and bread. None of it looked appetizing, but he might as well keep up his strength. So he ate every last bit. Who knew when he'd get another meal? Nothing was promised him here.

That was why he also attempted to sleep as he could, but to no avail. There was no rest to be found. His body was too alert. Too on edge.

Not for the first time, his mind went back to that fateful moment on the battlefield. On the front lines, patching soldiers and sorting through those who had hope and those who did not, he had been in the thick of it. Deep down, he had known he shouldn't be out there, but some of the soldiers were bleeding out on the field unnecessar-ily. A simple tourniquet could save lives. The left unit had been pinned down and he patched soldiers there. Then they were surrounded.

A few men died protecting him. He saw their faces even now. And when the shooting stopped, he was the only one the Confederates deemed worth taking. For what purpose, he didn't know. Did they think he was someone of value? True, he was an officer. But that was a rank given him because of his medical standing, not his military position. Surely they must know that.

Lost in his memories, it took a moment for him to realize he had company. How had he missed the *clip-clop* of boots? It seemed so loud now. The Confederate soldier was back.

"Care to tell me why I'm here?" he tried.

The man didn't respond. He simply demanded, "Hold out your wrists."

John stood, making slow movements, and did as told. The man reached through the bars and cuffed John's wrists. Only then did the soldier open the cell. Was he such a high-risk prisoner?

The soldier indicated that John should step out of the cell and follow him. He then led John through the small jail and into another room. Perhaps the sheriff's office at one time? It had since been converted into an interrogation room of sorts with only a table and chairs. Hands on John's shoulders pressed on him until he was seated in one of the chairs.

John did not resist.

The man posted himself behind John, by the door.

Who are we waiting on? John kept his facial features even. If he had information they wanted, he had no intention of giving it up. He would have to work to keep his face an expressionless mask. No one had trained him for this.

Soon after, more footsteps sounded in the hall. Someone bigger than this soldier. John was tempted to turn his head as the larger man drew near, but he forced his attention forward. The man's labored breathing helped John track the man as surely as the floorboard creaks. As he passed by John, his back became the first view

John caught. He was big, appearing all the more massive in the small space. When he turned, John peered at the markings on his uniform. Though he hadn't taken time to learn much about Confederate uniform insignias, he was certain this man was an officer of mid-level ranking.

"Hello, Captain Taylor, is it?" the man said as he made his way around the table to sit in the chair opposite John. He carried a file with him. Tiny in his large hands.

"Dr. Taylor," John corrected him.

"Your uniform indicates that you are a Captain."

"I am, but it is a rank bestowed as the assistant surgeon of the regiment."

"As you wish, Dr. Taylor." The man seemed to dismiss his response. He opened the file and leaned over, holding John's gaze. "I'm Colonel Wallace. I understand you've been cooperative."

"I see no reason to cause problems."

"Good," the man said, smiling. "Then we're going to get along."

John remained silent.

"Let's start with something simple." He pulled a map out of the file and set it in front of John. It appeared to be a map of the area. Battle lines had already been marked up and John could identify where he had been captured. "Can you point out to me where your camp is located?"

"I can't." John replied without giving the map much more than a glance.

"You can't? Come now, doctor." The colonel leaned back in his seat. "I thought we had an understanding."

"I'm not good with maps," he lied.

"Let me help you, then." He traced the battle line with his finger. "Here's where the fighting took place when you were captured." His finger stopped at one point in the line, drawing an invisible 'x'. "Here's where you were captured. Now, where is your camp from there?"

John leaned forward then and pretended to look intently at the map. "I can't be sure."

The colonel's eyes flicked to John's face and his mouth formed a thin line. "Did you walk far to get to the front line? Was it close? Did you go east? West? Downhill? Uphill?"

"I think I must have hit my head when your soldiers roughed me up. I can't seem to remember." John cocked his head to the side and narrowed his gaze.

The truth was that the Union camp had, in all likelihood, been moved. The Colonel had to know this as well. But John did not plan on giving even an inch.

Colonel Wallace laid his large hands flat on the table on either side of the map, straightening to his full, seated height.

John remained silent for a moment as if he were thinking, then shook his head. "I can't recall."

Wallace's eyes narrowed, his face reddened, and he drew in a breath through clenched teeth, but he kept his cool. His voice remained even and calm. "Take him back to his cell. Nothing but stale bread and water until he's ready to talk."

The soldier grabbed John's arm and lifted him.

"Wait! I do remember something." John's words rushed out of him.

The Colonel held up his hand to stop the soldier.

John leaned over the map. He shouldn't, but he couldn't help himself. Pointing to a place on the map a couple of miles into Confederate territory due southeast of the front line, he said, "That's a place I've always wanted to visit." He smiled. "I bet it's a nice little town."

The Colonel looked at the map and frowned.

John had pointed to the town where the jail was located.

Lieutenant Colonel Simmons sat at his makeshift desk, rubbing the bridge of his nose while he waited on his next meeting. It was not going to be pleasant. Private Thomas 'Tommy' Dickson had been a wild card from the start. And now he had to have another talk with the man. There didn't seem to be anything he could say that he hadn't already said. Even in wartime, there were certain rules, things that made sense and things that didn't. And shooting an unarmed man...well, woman, when she could have been taken prisoner and used to gather intelligence just didn't make sense.

Simmons' aid lifted the tent flap and stuck his head in to let the lieutenant colonel know Private Dickson had arrived.

"Send him in." Simmons sighed, sitting up and preparing himself for what he knew would become a confrontation.

Dickson stepped into the colonel's tent and saluted. Even for a soldier at attention, his posture and movements were stiff.

"At ease," Simmons said.

Dickson relaxed his stance ever so slightly.

"I trust you know what this meeting is regarding, Private," Simmons said, leaning forward.

"Sir, no, sir." Dickson didn't even bother to glance in his direction, but kept his eyes trained forward, fixed on some spot on the back of the tent behind Simmons.

"Private, you shot an unarmed Union soldier out of battle when there are standing orders to take any and all opportunities to capture such soldiers for interrogation."

"I believed the so-called soldier to be thieving the bodies, sir." Dickson's voice was firm, resolute.

"My orders still stand." Simmons raised his voice a level.

"Sir, yes, sir," he fairly spit out.

Simmons got to his feet and approached Dickson. "This isn't the first time we've had this conversation. I'm starting to think you are trigger happy, Private."

"Sir, no, sir. It was just a Union soldier." Even as Simmons approached him, Dickson refused to look at him, still staring at that one spot.

"Just a Union soldier? Are you even listening to me? That is the point! She may have had information we could have used. Now we'll never know. Now we are stuck harboring an enemy because not only did you decide to go against a direct order, you had the bad aim to wound her and the bad luck that she was struck with amnesia."

"Sir, yes, sir." There was that same stubbornness Simmons had seen before. All proper in here, but a loose cannon out there.

"I have no choice but to sentence you to digging latrines for the whole camp for the next month," the lieutenant colonel said before walking back toward his desk.

"Sir?" came Dickson's surprised response and the first hint of emotion Simmons had gotten out of him. And it was the wrong time to show such emotion.

Simmons spun around. "What?" Simmons's words were strong, challenging.

"Sir, yes, sir," Dickson said through gritted teeth as his eyes narrowed, back to staring at that blasted spot on the tent wall.

"Dismissed, Private." Simmons said with a wave of his hand as he sat at his desk and turned his attention to the next item on his list.

Simmons didn't bother to watch as Dickson left.

A stillness fell over the camp. All was peaceful as the soldiers lay resting. All, that is, except for the hospital. The two remaining physicians had worked well into the night performing the necessary operations to keep their patients alive. And Melanie was grateful for their hard work. Even now, she waited for this one particular surgery to be completed. Dr. Smith concentrated on fixing Jacob's leg as best he could.

Should she feel selfish that this surgery took so long? How long would an amputation have lasted? That was no matter. They were going to save his leg. Together.

When Dr. Smith told the nurse to mark Jacob for amputation, Melanie had pled for his leg, asking if there were any way they could save it. The doctor remained doubtful that anything could, but he said routine deep cleaning might fight off gangrene if they had the resources and staff to do that. Of course, if they would only teach her, she would volunteer to add that to her duties.

She just couldn't imagine a man so young, with so much promise, having to go through life without one of his legs. Especially the man who had just been declared the 'camp hero' for the day.

Dr. Smith must have been moved by her sacrifice for he said they would all work to try and save his leg. He must have made an enormous exception for Jacob.

Looking over the hospital, Melanie saw several amputees. Some from battle, some from surgery. All would have to learn a new way to live. Melanie's heart went out to each of them. But at least they were alive. Why couldn't she have said the same thing about Jacob?

Something about him had spoken to her heart. He was special. Was it just because he was so young? As she looked around this tent, she saw several other boys his age. Was it because of his heroism? There would be another hero tomorrow. Could she save them all? Or was it because she had seen enough devastation for one day and she had to have some hope?

Dr. Smith stepped out of surgery, scrubbing blood off of his hands. Jacob's blood.

"Dr. Smith!" She rushed over to him. Questions filled her, but she bit her lip, holding back the torrent. He would tell her what he could as he could.

Smith raised his head to look at her. Was he as tired as he looked? Or perhaps more so?

"I repaired the damage, but I am still doubtful we can fend off gangrene. It's going to take a lot of diligent work on your part and even then..." He left the sentence hanging.

"I know." Reaching for his hand, she squeezed it. Her gratitude poured out of her. "Dr. Smith, thank you. I wish I had the words to say more, but I..."

He bobbed his head. "It's time for me to get some shut eye. Tell the nurses that if they need anything to talk to Dr. Young."

"Yes, doctor," Melanie said, releasing his hand. As she watched the doctor move to the other side of the tent and out beyond, she clapped her hands together. Setting about to do as Dr. Smith had requested, she moved through the hospital tent.

By the time she had made rounds to all of the nurses, Jacob had been moved to his bed to recover. Melanie took hesitant steps toward him. Moments later, she was by his side. He appeared even younger when he slept.

Surely he must have lied about his age to end up here. He can't be 18. What must it have been like for his mother and father when he told them? Her own mother and father could not have cared less when she told them of her plans to contribute to the war effort by joining the women's camp. They had stopped caring what she did long ago. And while she wanted to believe they were concerned about her, she would just be kidding herself.

Melanie sat with Jacob for several minutes more. But he did not move save the rise and fall of his chest. Not wanting to disturb his rest, she decided to leave. Another long look at the boy who would be a soldier, and she rose to her feet.

She then made her way back to her tent. It would be daylight in a few hours. Slipping into the tent without making a sound for sake of her tent mates' rest, she plopped down on her mat with no other nighttime preparations and drifted into a sleep filled with disturbing dreams of war.

Matthew moved through the camp. The tents and soldiers milling around him were but a blur. Would anything halt him from his daily rendezvous? It had been this way since she came. Each afternoon he made his way to the hospital. Dr. Wilson still followed the progress of Matthew's arm but that was not the reason he so faithfully trekked to the hospital day after day. He had become quite drawn to her.

Though Annabelle had not regained her memory, she had become more comfortable around him. Some days they would converse easily, other days he would do most of the talking. It all depended on her mood. But she always seemed eager for his visits. Whether she was anxious to see him or just to break up the monotony of the day, Matthew did not know. Whatever the reason, he was thankful for the time spent with her.

He came to find that he looked forward to these moments with her. And it was much more than simply the enjoyment of her company or some sense of responsibility for her. There was something happening within him. Was he coming to truly care for her?

As much as Matthew hoped she would regain her memory, it concerned him, too. What would it mean for her? For him?

He arrived at the opening to the large tent and stepped through, his eyes searching her out. Of course, she sat in her cot as she always did. Only today she was enraptured in a book. This gave him a few extra moments to watch her. She bit at her lip, her eyes intent on the page even as she turned to the next one. And as he watched, her breath caught. A smile tugged at the corners of his mouth. If only he could watch her like this for hours. But even if she did not notice him, for certain the hospital staff would.

So he pulled himself out of the moment and stepped toward her. He could not help the silly smile that now filled his features.

"Annabelle?" he said softly as he approached her.

She jerked in response, dropping the book. It landed in her lap.

He, too, was taken aback by her sudden movements, but regained his composure soon enough. "Are you well? I didn't mean to startle you."

Her face had paled, but she nodded. "I am, sir. I just...it was..." She struggled for words.

Closing the distance between them and sitting beside her cot, he caught her flailing hands in his larger one. "It's all right. I understand." He attempted to stifle a laugh, but failed.

She quirked an eyebrow at him.

"I saw that you were quite caught in your book. I should have come back later."

"Oh." Her face colored.

"No need to be embarrassed. I am likewise afflicted. I've always enjoyed reading."

Her shoulders relaxed. Had he put her at ease? But she stared down at her hands, still caught in his grasp.

They had never held hands before. He withdrew his touch, wondering if he should apologize for his boldness.

An awkward silence fell between them and he opened his mouth to speak, but she filled the space before he could.

"What are some of your favorites?" She played with the corner of her sheet.

"I like the writings of Edgar Allen Poe." He watched her fidgeting. A nervous habit?

She grimaced. "That's some dark stuff."

"I like the mystery and suspense," he said, shifting his weight so that he could lean closer.

"Hmm." Her face relaxed, but it was still clear she didn't agree.

"Have you read much Poe?" he challenged, wanting to keep her talking.

"Some. *The Raven, The Tell Tale Heart*...not my style. I'm a typical girl when it comes to poetry. I'd prefer Shakespeare's Sonnets." A smile spread across her features.

He gazed into her eyes and recited, "Shall I compare thee to a summer's day? Thou art more lovely and more temperate."

"You know them then?" Her eyes widened and her voice rose.

"Of course," he said. "Every young man who plans to woo a young lady should."

Though he did not think it possible, her smile broadened.

It was nice to have something in common. In common? How did she know...? "Wait! Do you realize we've been talking about things you remember? You remember reading Poe, you remembered those lines from Shakespeare."

"You're right." Her face brightened. It wasn't exactly crucial to her identity, but it was something.

Seeing her face light up brought a warmth to his heart. "Can you remember anything else?"

She became quiet as she concentrated, then her face fell.

"Maybe it only comes when you're not thinking about it." He reached out for her hand, but thought better of it and drew back.

She shrugged. "Maybe."

"Either way, I think it's great progress, Annabelle."

Smiling again, she nodded.

She seemed happy to have remembered something from her past. And that pleased him. But it concerned him, too. What would Colonel Jones think of her memory returning? Even if it were these insignificant snatches? This would be something he kept to himself. Unless, of course, she posed a real threat to the camp. That, however, seemed rather unlikely.

As she healed, Elizabeth was permitted to walk a short distance from the hospital with Matthew for fresh air. Dr. Wilson deemed it a necessary part of her recovery. Of the people they passed, many nodded at them in polite greeting. A few looked at her suspiciously, which she didn't understand. When she asked Matthew about it, his face darkened and he dismissed her question.

Some of the women tossed knowing glances their way, smiling at Matthew, and his face would color. These glances Elizabeth understood, and her face warmed too. But one man in the camp looked familiar to her. And she was quite certain he scowled at her.

"Who is that man?" she asked as he walked away.

"Don't mind Tommy. He rubs everyone the wrong way." Had Matthew seen the face the man made at her?

Elizabeth tried to brush off the uneasy feelings she had from the encounter, but it wasn't that easy. It was difficult when her memory was untrustworthy and someone acted as if she had wronged them.

"Did I...did I do something to that man?"

"Of course not, Annabelle. He's just one of those fellas that's always got a chip on his shoulder."

Elizabeth wasn't sure she believed him, but she let the issue go.

With Matthew's help, it wasn't long before she had made several acquaintances among the men and women in the camp, enough to keep her mind off Tommy. Their walks became more routine, and they saw many of the same people on their strolls. When she was able to greet them by name, it helped her feel some sense of belonging when they responded in kind.

Their daily walks soon took them farther away from the hospital until they walked to the nearby stream each day. Then a new routine emerged. They would stop at the stream, eat their lunch rations, and read some sonnets. It was a beautiful spot they settled on. A large oak tree perched on a gently sloped hill above the small stream served to support their backs. This oak tree also became their canopy during their midday lunches and readings.

Elizabeth watched on as he read Sonnet 52. Closing her eyes, she enjoyed the way his voice raised and fell to the meter. She had grown quite fond of their time together and rather attached to Matthew. Was that so wrong? He was handsome with his sandy-blonde hair and blue eyes. While she had been thankful his injury kept him from being sent into battle, it did not escape her notice that his wounds were healing. He hadn't been wearing his sling the last couple of days.

Matthew's voice broke in laughter. Opening her eyes, she joined him, laughing more at the sight of him than at whatever had tickled him. He boldly reached over to push a stubborn curl behind her ear, allowing his hand to cup her face for just a moment before letting it fall. But she caught it and held it, wanting to prolong their connection.

He looked at her, a question in his eyes.

She wanted more.

Lifting her hand to his lips, he then pressed a kiss to her palm.

Elizabeth breathed deeply, staring into his eyes. "I so enjoy our time together, Matthew."

"As do I." He kept her hand in his, but let it fall into his lap.

"I hope it won't have to end."

"Why would it?" There was confusion in his eyes.

"If you should have to go…" Her voice broke and she looked toward the stream. "Go to battle."

"We don't have to think about that right now." He tugged on the hand he held captive.

She turned to look at him again, fighting the emotions welling in her. "I think about it often." Her heart ached.

He was silent.

"I don't want to lose you," she said plainly, though she realized this was too much to put on him.

"You won't."

"How can you promise that?" she balked.

"Because I can't think about it any other way."

She gazed into his eyes for a few moments more. Then she shifted to move closer to him, hesitantly maneuvering to lean against his chest and wrap her arms around his midsection. He enveloped her in his arms, pressing a kiss into her hair.

The Moore house was full of noise and laughter when Henry Moore stepped through his front door and into the entry. This surprised him, but pleasantly so. Happy sounds coming from the reaches of his home was a first since Jacob had left for war. It lifted his spirits. And the aroma that filled the home testified that the women of the house had been baking. Such delicious smells enticed him to move farther in.

Henry's wife was a renowned cook in the area and no one appreciated that about her more than he. So, he became all too excited to find his wife, their daughter, and their maidservant rolling out dough for biscuits. And a plate of cookies sat nearby. Unattended. He reached for one.

Martha's threat bellowed from across the room. "Not on your life, Henry Moore. Those are specially designated."

Henry didn't have to put on a distraught face; he was truly saddened at the thought that he would not be partaking of the delectable treats. "Not even one, dear wife?"

Martha's face was stern. "Not even one."

He pretended to sulk, but part of his disappointment was real. Those cookies looked and smelled amazing. They were, after all, her famous chocolate chip walnut cookies.

Their maidservant opened the oven and pulled out another batch. The aroma filled his nostrils again and his mouth watered.

"What is all this for?" he waved his hands over the collection of goodies, swallowing as he salivated. "A bake sale?"

Martha, Susan, and the maidservant exchanged looks.

"Now that's an idea," Martha started to say.

"A bake sale to raise money for the troops," the maidservant said at the same time.

Perhaps this was not their intent. But he had obviously sparked an idea for more baking that would not satisfy the churning in his stomach.

"No," he said, louder than he intended. "No more baking unless I can partake. And one of you had better tell me what all this is for." He stepped between his wife and daughter.

"We're making packages for Benjamin and Jacob, Father," Susan said in a matter-of-fact manner. "Remember how Jacob said he missed Mama's cooking?"

"Why, I sure do," Henry said, laying a hand on his daughter's shoulder. "I think it's a wonderful idea."

"Mama says we'll write the letters after dinner and mail the packages tomorrow." Susan's eyes lit up as she spoke.

"Then that's what we shall do." Henry squeezed his daughter's shoulder before placing a kiss on the top of her head. Turning toward his wife, he pressed a kiss to the side of her face. "I fear, however, that I am two unnecessary hands in this rather busy kitchen. And I don't want to get in your way." He made his way back across the kitchen to the doorway. Nodding once more, he took his leave of them.

Seconds later, however, he poked his head back in. "Are you sure I can't have just one cookie?"

"No, you can't," Martha said, laughing, and tossed a handful of flour in his direction. "Now, get out of here."

Henry feigned fearfulness and scooted away from the door. He heard Susan's giggle in response.

It wasn't long before he was several paces away from the kitchen and moving toward the stairs. Climbing them with care, he made his way to his cozy office. It had been a long day. The banter with his wife and daughter had lightened his mood, but it could not alleviate the weight that he carried.

A heaviness from supporting a family and a community that was losing its younger men settled on him. Trying to shield his family from the politics and economics of a country at war was proving to be a task in and of itself. And then his boys.

His boys' participation in the war was inevitable. He supposed he should be proud they enlisted before they were pressured to. In this way, they had made him proud. But he worried about them every moment of every day. It was different than it was for Martha. Henry had to be strong.

Sitting at his desk, he unloaded his satchel and organized his paperwork. Then he went through the mail that came in that day. Nothing from either Benjamin or Jacob. Susan would be disappointed. He opened his top drawer and pulled out all the letters they had received over the last few months. Smoothing over the ruffled pages, he reread the most recent ones, trying somehow, to keep the boys close to home.

The first letter was the one in which Benjamin told them about the dog that had wandered into camp. That was the last thing a group of soldiers needed to worry about, but still they had adopted the starving animal as the camp pet. Benjamin went on and on about the antics of that crazy dog.

Jacob's latest note came next. Indeed he was fixated on the food in camp. This letter told all about the cook who couldn't cook.

Each of the boys did share news from the front, but Henry knew that, for the sakes of their mother and sister, they did not share the grim extent to which they had experienced war. Their lack of detail was likely because they just didn't want to dwell on it. Home was a safe place, a place where these atrocities didn't happen. And they wanted to keep it safe from such things. So they didn't share them. Not for the first time, Henry wondered about his boys transforming into men. What were they seeing? What were they experiencing? How was it changing them? Would they be recognizable to him when or if they came home?

After he put the letters away, he leaned back, thinking on his family. And the weariness of being strong for his wife and daughter and everyone else overcame him again. Pinching the bridge of his nose to help ease the tension of his frustration, he reflected on his boys and how he wished he could be there for them in some real, tangible way. A cross he bore every day. This feeling that he should be there with them, beside them. Yet at the same time, he knew his place was at home, being strong. Even so, he often wished that just for one moment, he could set this weight to the side.

A quiet, almost timid knock on the door drew him out of his musings.

He put his glasses back on and sat to his full height. "Come in."

The door creaked open and his little Susan entered his office. Sliding through the door ever so slowly, she looked as if she feared something would jump out and grab her. Her movements were unsure. The children were not permitted in his office, as this was his private sanctuary and workspace. After several seconds of standing just inside the door, Susan raised her eyes to meet her father's gaze.

Henry held out his arms, welcoming her into the room. Would that ease the trepidation she felt?

She did move closer to him, but with slow steps. As she approached him, she pulled a handkerchief out from behind her back and held it out to him.

His eyes moved from the handkerchief to her eyes. What game was this?

"Susan, what is...?"

She put a finger on her lips and pushed the handkerchief closer toward him.

He took it after a moment. Only then did he feel the weight of something else within the folds of the cloth. Unwrapping the edges of the delicate linen, he was surprised to find a cookie nestled in the center. Smiling at his daughter, he mirrored her gesture and put a finger to his lips. Without hesitation, he split the cookie in half and handed her one piece.

She offered him a big smile with her eyes bright as she bit into her part of the cookie.

He chomped into his portion as well. Then he gathered her into his arms, grateful to have his sweet little girl still under his roof.

CHAPTER FIVE
DANGER

John's sleep proved fitful. The thin, uncomfortable mattress of the cot was not the problem. His stomach was empty and had been for a while. It had been several days since he had eaten. And his jailers took turns clanging the bars to rouse him. How long had it been since he'd had a restful night? He did not know.

Ignoring the churning in his stomach, he closed his eyes and drifted off into another bout of restless sleep. It didn't last long, however. Jerked to consciousness by a man's voice in his ear and rough hands on his shoulders, he cried out.

"On your feet!"

John did his best to pull himself together as the man succeeded in getting him upright. His feet were unsteady though, and John stumbled before regaining his balance. There wasn't much time for that either before the Confederate soldier shoved him out of the cell. Unable to maintain his footing, he fell to his knees. Another soldier, who must have been outside of the cell, grabbed at John's uniform and dragged him toward the interrogation room. Try as he might, John could not get his feet to obey him.

In seconds, he was in the now familiar office and the soldier helped him into the chair. It almost toppled over. The man grunted and stepped out of the room.

Now that John sat still, he allowed his tired eyes to focus. Daylight streamed in from the window. What time was it? He had long since given up keeping track of the days. And, as was typical for these sessions since they had started denying John food, Colonel Wallace sat at the desk eating a well-portioned dinner of beef and potatoes.

John's stomach grumbled and churned painfully. What he wouldn't give for one morsel off that plate! But that one morsel would cost him. And he had nothing to give.

A Confederate scout had already discovered the former location of the camp he had been in. So, the one piece of information he did have became useless to them.

He was glad, after all, that he didn't have information to trade. For he wasn't sure he would be able to hold out under such duress.

Instead of sitting and watching the oversized colonel eat what would be equivalent to three days worth of rations, John brought up a mental picture of Elizabeth. She had become the one guiding light that would get him through this. The only way he had survived thus far was to think of her and push through, knowing he had to get home to her. He could not give up. There she was, in his mind's eye, in his favorite blue dress. She stood in the doorway of his house, blonde curls around her shoulders. Smiling at him, she stretched out her arms to welcome him home. If only he could run to her, take her in his arms, and...

"Well now, Dr. Taylor. Let's hope we have a better session today than we did yesterday."

Colonel Wallace's gruff voice cut into his thoughts and caused the vision of Elizabeth to dissipate.

"I do hope I can share my meal with you," the colonel shoved another bite into his mouth. "After all, I have an over-abundance." A smile crossed his face. From all appearances, Wallace behaved as if they were the best of friends sitting down to a weekly dinner. One thing was for certain; this man was good at what he did.

John stared at him, heaving a weak sigh. "I don't know anything."

"What is in your stock of ammunition?" Wallace started, as if John hadn't said anything.

"I am a doctor, not a tactical officer," John insisted. He tried to put all the force he could into his statement, but even he knew it came across weak. His body was so tired.

"Where are your weapons supplied from?" The colonel blotted his mouth with a napkin.

"I don't know anything." John pled. "Why won't you believe me?"

"Who does your unit commander take his orders from?" Wallace neither rushed nor raised his voice. His tone remained neutral, but he continued to throw out questions with force.

"I only know who I report to: Dr. William Smith." John hung his head.

Colonel Wallace took one last, long look at John. And John knew. The colonel didn't like the answers he was getting. He also knew, because his jailers made sure he knew, that the colonel would like nothing more than to torture him to death.

Finally, the colonel knocked on his desk. Three loud raps. The soldier who had dragged John into the interrogation room stepped back into the office.

"Yes, sir?" The soldier's gruff voice sounded in the silence.

"He doesn't know anything. Send him back to the front lines. Perhaps they'll find a way to make use of him as a physician."

The Confederate guard nodded and took hold of John's uniform again, all but jerking him to feet.

As they were almost out of the door, the colonel called out, almost as an afterthought, "And give him some rations."

John felt as if he could cry he was so happy to know he would have food soon. Half-dragged, half-walking back to his cell, he landed hard on the floor. But he didn't care. All he could think about was the food he would partake of soon.

The Confederate guard returned soon after with the same rations he had received the first day: pork, beans, and bread. This time, however, John was sure that it was the most delectable meal he had ever eaten. He had to force himself to eat slowly lest he upset his stomach.

What would happen next, he did not know. But he was getting out of here. And as long as he didn't have to trade information he didn't have for food, cooperating by using his skills as a physician, even to save Confederate troops, would not be something he had a problem with.

Hazy shapes took form. That was the first thing Elizabeth noticed as she opened her eyes. What had disrupted her sleep? Shapes became clearer and she recognized the form moving next to her as Suellen. She placed a bowl next to Elizabeth's cot.

Elizabeth drew a hand across her face. How long had she been sleep? *Oh no!* She drew herself up on her elbow. Had she missed dinner again? Sighing, she released her weight back into the pillow. It wasn't the end of the world, but she enjoyed being around everyone and having the opportunity to spend more time with Matthew.

As she turned, Suellen's eyes caught hers. "I'm sorry. Did I wake you? Seems I can't ever drop off your dinner without waking you."

Elizabeth smiled at her, shifting in the cot to move to a sitting position. "It's all right. I'm a light sleeper." Reaching for the bowl, Elizabeth spotted a note next to her spoon.

"Somebody dropped that off for you," Suellen started, then leaned closer to Elizabeth and continued. "Actually, it's from Matthew. He wants to meet you at your 'special place'!" Suellen seemed unfazed by the fact that she had invaded Elizabeth's privacy and read the note.

"Oh?" was all Elizabeth said.

"Yeah. He was real upset at dinner that you weren't there. But he didn't let on, not one bit, that he had planned a secret meet-up."

Elizabeth rubbed her head. It was a little soon after such a deep sleep for all this chatter. She still worked to pull herself out of her dream. That man had filled her dreams again. The one with the dark hair and dark eyes. He visited her every dream. Who was he? Someone from her past? Shaking her head, she tried to pull herself back to the present. Looking up, she found herself staring into Suellen's expectant gaze.

"Thank you, Suellen." She reached for a piece of bread.

"You'd better hurry up, now. He said he wants to meet you just after dark." Suellen folded her hands by her face. "So romantic!"

Elizabeth yawned and nodded, picking up the note and opening it for herself. As she read its contents, Suellen slipped out of the hospital. It did not matter. Suellen had told her everything in the note. So Elizabeth set to eating her dinner. She was quite hungry after her deep sleep.

After polishing off her stew, Elizabeth smoothed over her dress and wrapped herself with a shawl. Then she headed out of the hospital and toward the stream. What could Matthew be thinking? Did he truly just miss her? Or did he want to conjure up a romantic setting for their first kiss? She smiled at that. Unsure what his intentions were, she decided she trusted him enough to come when he requested.

The stream's banks were empty when she arrived. So much for rushing here to meet Matthew. He was nowhere in sight. Maybe he got held up somewhere along the way. She sat down and waited where she had been earlier that day when Matthew had kissed her hand.

Several minutes passed before she heard something. Standing

and cocking her head in the direction of the sound, she discerned it to be rustling in the bushes nearby.

"Matthew? Is that you?" she became worried. Something wasn't right about this. Was it some wild animal?

More shuffling, but nothing came for her. She gathered her shawl around herself.

I shouldn't be out in the night like this. It was a mistake to come looking for Matthew. He clearly had not sent her the message. Turning back toward the camp, she moved in that direction.

A movement in her periphery came into shape. The bushes. Something jumped out of the bushes and tackled her to the ground. Her gut reaction was to struggle against whatever had attacked her. It wasn't long before she distinguished that she fought not against an animal, but a man. Soon enough, he had her hopelessly pinned. She looked up into his hate-filled eyes. It was Tommy.

"I got in a heap of trouble because of you, Union tramp," he said, grabbing her roughly and slamming her against the ground.

Pain pierced her from the back of her head and spots filled her vision.

"And you prance about the camp as if you own it." There was a lilt to his voice when he said 'prance,' but his voice took on a menacing quality soon after.

"Please, stop. You're hurting me," she screamed.

"Are you scared?" he sneered.

"Yes," she said, nearly breathless.

"Good, 'cause I'm gonna finish what I started." He pulled out a knife from his belt and held it against her throat."

"Please," she pleaded, shutting her eyes tight as tears welled.

He laughed in her face.

"Is this what you call sport?" A man's voice interrupted from above. "Attacking a defenseless women in the dead of night?"

Elizabeth craned her neck. Matthew!

"Leave us be, Matthew. You know she has this coming to her."

"C'mon, Tommy. You know your fight is with me. Let her go and we'll do this man-to-man." Matthew's voice was strong and firm. How was that possible? Elizabeth shook all over.

Matthew drew his knife and moved into a threatening posture, indicating that if Tommy shed her blood, his would be next.

Tommy got to his feet, pulling her up with him.

The movement made her dizzy and she felt as if she might vomit. The blade of the knife was still cold on the skin of her neck.

"And what of her?" Tommy said, not even trying to disguise his anger.

"I'm the only thing standing in your way," Matthew said, his voice even.

Tommy sneered at him and tossed Elizabeth to the side.

As she hit the ground, her world went dark.

Zigzagging through the camp, Melanie made her way to the hospital. She dodged a myriad of soldiers on her route, smiling as she passed them, but otherwise paying them no mind. It was time for her daily appointment with Jacob. Actually, with Jacob's leg.

But today she had a surprise for him. Glancing down at the package in her arms, she imagined how his face would light up when she presented it to him. He wouldn't expect it in the least. Mail didn't come to the hospital until later in the day. But she heard his name at mail call during breakfast and collected the precious bundle so he wouldn't have to wait.

As she entered the hospital tent, ducking to avoid catching her hair on the raised tent flap, she spotted him. He was propped up in his bed. Even from this distance, she saw the piece of paper in his lap, pencil in his hand, his mouth twisted and eyebrows furrowed.

Putting on her brightest smile, she stepped over to his cot. "What are you working on there? A drawing?"

Just the mention of it made her think of Elizabeth and her heart fell in her chest. No one had seen her since that first battle. What could have happened to her? Had she gone off to the front lines for some crazy reason? If that was the case, she must have been killed or captured. Either way, they were not likely to ever see her again.

"No, it's a letter," Jacob's response broke through her thoughts.

Melanie's eyes shifted to once again meet his. Did he read her momentary lapse? She could not see it in his expression if he did. He seemed focused on his paper.

Moving around his cot, she glanced over his shoulder. 'Dear Mother, Father, and Susan,' was scrawled across the paper. "Not far along, are we?"

Jacob groaned and, tossing the pencil down, rubbed his hands over his face. "I just don't know how to tell them about the battle or about my injury. You know, I don't want to worry them." All of this was muffled as it was spoken from behind his hands. Shaking his head, he released his face, plopping his hands down on his legs and looked up at her.

"Hmmm," was all Melanie could offer. That was a problem. But she didn't have any words of wisdom. Her own relationship with her parents had been strained at best.

There were people who were meant to raise children and people who weren't. That's what she had concluded anyway. And her parents definitely fit into the second category. They never seemed to be the right fit for the role. Maybe that's why she was the only child they had. Even then, they found a way to let her know she was an accident. Unintended. She knew what they meant. Becoming parents was never part of their plans. Her birth was a mistake.

"Melanie?" She was startled out of her thoughts by the feel of Jacob's fingers on her arm.

"I'm sorry, what?" She attempted to gather her wits about her.

"I said, 'What have you got there?'"

Looking down at him, she saw that his eyes now held concern for her.

He opened his mouth, perhaps to ask her what had disturbed her so, but she cut him off.

"It's for you," she plastered a smile on her face. "Isn't it wonderful? Someone sent you a package." She maneuvered around the small space next to his cot—moving the pencil and paper to the side, setting the small crate on the cot with him. "I picked it up at the mail call for you. You don't mind, do you?"

"Mind? Why should I?" Moving his hands over the lid, he worked to open it.

Melanie reached over to help, and with some effort, they got the top off.

Now that their only obstacle was out of the way, Melanie peered with him into the crate. Melanie gasped at the treasures that lay within. Someone had filled this care package with biscuits, cookies, hard candies, sweet bread, and letters bearing names that Melanie didn't recognize. Were they Jacob's family members?

He reached into his precious cargo with hands that trembled slightly and touched the envelopes. Then his hands drew back.

Stealing a glance at him, Melanie saw him wiping at his eyes.

"Your parents must miss you a lot." She laid a hand on his shoulder. In many ways, she was glad for him, but she could not deny the ache in the middle of her chest at the thought of his sweet parents whose thoughts were with him as they were apart.

Jacob managed a nod, but remained silent.

Melanie swallowed past a lump in her throat that she didn't expect. "Would you like me to read these letters to you, or do you want to wait and read them yourself?"

Jacob's eyes were on hers again. This time she knew that he saw. How, she did not know. But he did. She turned away so he wouldn't see more than she wanted him to.

"I would like if you would read them to me." His voice was soft.

Melanie sniffed. Why was this affecting her so? *Focus.* There was a job to do here. "Before or after your cleaning treatment?"

"One before, um, Susan's. The others after." He lifted the letters out of the box and placed the lid back over the prized contents.

"All right." Melanie offered him a smile she didn't feel.

He glanced at the writing on the envelopes and handed her one that bore the writing of a young hand. She pulled out the paper covered in more of the child-like script and began to read.

Susan shared childish thoughts—wishes that he was well, stories about things going on in the neighborhood with people that Jacob must know. A sweet letter. This young girl cared about her brother and his well-being. Something Melanie would never know. Pushing that thought to the side, she finished the letter. When she looked over at Jacob, he smiled ear to ear.

"That brightened your mood," she observed, placing the letter back into Jacob's possession with great care.

"Yeah. She's a lot of trouble, but she's a good sister."

"Seems like it." Melanie stood and walked to a nearby shelf to gather the things she would need to clean his leg.

"Do you have brothers or sisters?" Jacob called over to her.

Melanie's hand froze over the fresh bandages. She recovered quickly. "No."

"No siblings?" came Jacob's surprised voice. As if it were a novel idea that one could be an only child.

"Nope. Just me." Melanie sighed and brushed a stray hair out of her face. She would not let these emotions drag her down. So that famous smile went back up before she turned toward him again. "But I was never lonely. I had my friends and always plenty of dolls and whatnot." *Yes, I always had plenty of things.* She sat and began opening the bandages already on his leg.

"Girls and their dolls." He rolled his eyes.

"Boys and their guns." She rolled her eyes.

He laughed. "If you don't like boys and guns, you're in the wrong place." His laugh became a wince as she began cleaning.

A valid point. "There are plenty of boys that don't have guns," she retorted, attempting to take his mind off the discomfort brought on by the cleaning.

"Who? Dr. Smith and Dr. Young? They're hardly what I'd call 'in your age category'."

She frowned at him. "You know what? I admit defeat. I can't deny that there are plenty of rather handsome men here that do like their big guns."

"Muskets." He corrected her.

"Pardon?"

"Muskets. We don't call them 'guns.' They're 'muskets'."

"Ah. Muskets." She nodded, eyes back on her work.

"And who might you be referring to?" He ribbed her. "These 'handsome men'?"

She gave him a sly smile. "That man, Daniel, who visits you often for one. He's quite handsome."

"Oh?" Jacob's voice became a little quieter.

"And I've got my eye on that bugle player, too." She leaned in and whispered as if she were sharing a great secret.

"I see." His tone was flat now, as if he didn't like what she was saying. Or maybe it was the pain. Soon enough he was gritting his teeth as she got deeper into the process. This part was hard for Melanie, but necessary. And almost as soon as it began, it was over and she worked to reapply his bandages.

"What about you?" Melanie shot a glance his way. He needed to think about something other than his leg. "You ever going to tell me about those girls back home?"

His cheeks colored.

"Ah, see! There are girls chasing you. I knew it!" She chuckled.

"I don't know if 'chasing me' is the way I would put it." His eyes were on her face; she could feel it. But she remained focused on her work.

She sighed. "The good ones never can see the forest for the trees."

"What?" His question came out a bit sharp.

"Oh, nothing," Melanie said, shaking her head. "Just something my mother used to say." And she again fought to keep from being swept into memories she'd rather keep locked away.

At last, she finished tying off his bandage.

"There. All set. Now shall we get to those other two letters?" she injected all the cheerfulness into her voice she could manage.

Jacob nodded, leaning back on his pillows. He seemed much more relaxed, but she knew better. The cleaning always took something out of him. Reaching over into the box, he picked up another letter and passed it to her.

This one, it turned out, was from his mother. She reiterated how proud she was and what a fine man he had become. Martha, as Melanie came to know her, also wrote about how missed Jacob was and how eager they were for him to return. Melanie feigned a sneeze when her emotions got the better of her. What was with her today? His mother gave him a piece of advice—look out for yourself, be safe, and the like.

As Melanie handed the letter back, she noticed more color in Jacob's cheeks. Why was he embarrassed? Surely he must be glad his mother cared so much for his well-being. Perhaps he didn't like for Melanie to read about his mother fawning over him so. It was sweet.

The final note was from his father. It seemed Henry had been elected to pass along what the family garnered from Jacob's brother, Benjamin's, last letter. He was alive and well. His regiment advanced and had apparently taken on a homeless dog as a mascot of sorts. Henry shared in earnest about how things were at home, about Martha's good days and bad days and her renewed purpose these last weeks thinking of ways to reach out to her boys, such as these care packages. The letter closed reminding Jacob that he, too, was proud and wished him safety and good health.

Melanie folded the last letter and returned it to the box. Warring emotions about her own family tumbled about inside her. She stared at the letter still in her hands. And her words spilled out, "You have such a sweet family, Jacob."

There was no response. Looking over to where he lay against his pillows, she realized he had drifted off to sleep. Placing the letters back in the crate and securing the lid on top, she then slid it under his bed lest anyone else be curious enough to take a peek.

Then she shifted his pillows and pulled his blanket over him. With that, she took her leave of the hospital. If she could, she would take her leave of the whole camp. But what good would that do? She had already run this far to escape the raging regret in the pit of her stomach. How much farther could she go?

Matthew barely flinched as he watched Annabelle crumple. His life, and hers, depended on his concentration.

Tommy leapt towards Matthew, swinging his knife.

Matthew jumped to the side, half expecting this crazy man's attack. He spun around keeping his eye on what Tommy might try next.

"Tommy, you're crazy. Why are you doing this?" Matthew raised his hands in the air.

Tommy didn't answer. Instead, he lunged towards Matthew, extending his arm, trying to reach him with his blade. Again, Matthew dodged to the side, and seeing Tommy overextended, hit him with his free hand. This caused Tommy to stumble forward and hit the ground.

Matthew realized he had a chance to end this fight. With Tommy face down on the ground and a little disoriented, Matthew could have pounced on his back. But something in him froze.

He and his brother had grown up hunting in the woods with their Pa. There were many times they had shot deer and wild boars, and skinned rabbits caught in traps using the same bowie knife he now held in his hand. But this was different.

This wasn't hunting wild game; it was the possibility of killing another man. Of course Matthew had fired his musket at enemy soldiers on the battlefield, but a hot-blooded knife fight was totally different.

His hesitation cost him dearly. Because he struggled to make a decision, Tommy scrambled to his feet and then dove onto Matthew, rolling them both to the ground. Matthew knew he had made a stupid decision.

Crashing to the ground, they both dropped their knives as they braced themselves hitting the ground. Due to Tommy's initiative, he ended up on top, and started punching Matthew's face. All Matthew could do was throw up his hands to guard himself. Things didn't look good.

Tommy paused and looked around. He reached over toward his knife. In that brief pause, Matthew saw where Tommy was leaning, and heaved as hard as he could, pushing Tommy with his legs. It was difficult, because Tommy weighed a lot more than Matthew had realized. Matthew was pinned, but somehow, through a combination of adrenaline and will power, he managed to push Tommy off balance enough and roll away from him.

Tommy, with his knife in his clutches, twisted around, madder than a rattled hornet's nest.

"You're gonna' die, Union lover!" Tommy shouted as he climbed to his feet.

Matthew searched for his knife, and spotting it, scrambled for it. He picked it up just in time to see that Tommy was about to lunge at him again. This seemed to be Tommy's favorite move. Remembering how much it hurt when Tommy landed on top of him, Matthew somehow shifted his weight on the balls of his feet just enough that Tommy barely missed him.

Tommy landed on the ground again, harder than before. While he somehow kept a hold of his knife, he let out a loud *oohf* as he hit the ground. He landed on his side, with his knife arm on the ground.

Realizing this might be his last chance, Matthew dove on top of Tommy and swung his blade with all the power he could muster into Tommy's back. The tip of the blade poked through to the surface of

Tommy's chest. A big pool of dark red began to discolor Tommy's uniform on both sides.

Tommy's eyes shifted towards Matthew, and then froze with an eternal look of hate.

Matthew knew he would never forget this dead man's face for the rest of his life. He collapsed onto the ground.

After a couple of minutes, as his heartbeat slowed to near normal, he managed to pull himself together. Just then, one of the platoon second lieutenants happened upon them. He was wide-eyed, his mouth opening and closing without making a sound.

"Tell the unit commander that Tommy went crazy and tried to kill Annabelle. I tried to talk him down, but he wouldn't hear of it. He drew his knife and attacked. I had no choice."

The junior officer, still not able to form a coherent sentence, just shook his head in acknowledgment, and ran off, seeking his commanding officer to report the incident.

Yeah, that's about all second lieutenants are good for, Matthew could hear his Pa saying. He briefly chuckled at that thought. Yes, he would have to share that with his Pa. And he'd also have to tell him what had happened here with Tommy. Pa was someone who would understand. That left Matthew with a small feeling of peace.

But that would come later. There were more important things to focus on now. Matthew crawled to where Annabelle still lay unconscious.

"Annabelle." He moved the back of his hand across the side of her face. "Annabelle."

She shifted and groaned.

He gathered her into his arms. "You're safe!"

Her eyes blinked open. As she took in the sight of him, she moved her arms to embrace him. "Matthew!"

He pressed his lips to her hair, her forehead, her face, and, eventually, found her lips in a desperate kiss.

She responded eagerly, ready for him to deepen the kiss.

They pulled apart in need for air. He held her still, stroking her face, her hair.

"How did you know?" Her voice was quiet, broken.

"Suellen mentioned something about a late night rendezvous and I put it all together. I was so worried."

She let out a whimper.

"Don't ever scare me like that again, you hear me?"

"I don't intend to, Matthew. I don't intend to."

"I don't know what I would do if something happened to you, Annabelle. I love you."

His lips met hers again. This time in a gentler, sweeter kiss.

Days had passed since Abigail was willing to set foot outside the front door of her home. There had been no word from Elizabeth and it darkened her spirits to the point she just couldn't be out in society. She spent her days fraught with worry. Each day, she found it harder to force herself out of bed and allow herself to be prepared. And each day, she was more convinced that she would never see her beloved daughter again. Her heart sank impossibly lower into a bottomless pit. Why had they not received word?

Elizabeth's letter had assured them she would write often, yet they had not one letter from her at camp. Had something happened? All the fundraising in the world would do nothing to help her daughter if she had been killed. *No,* Abigail shook her head, *I can't think like that. Why must I jump to the worst possible conclusion?*

As she sat in the chair in her bedroom, she allowed the torrent of worry to wash over her. It gripped her heart, clamping down on it like a vise. Reaching for her tea, she took a long sip, letting the warmth bring her what small comfort it could. Not only had she not been able to leave the house these last several days, the truth was that she had barely left her room these last two days. Would she become all the more reclusive the longer they went without news? The days dragged on and there was no respite to be found.

Just then she heard movement downstairs. It was faint, but there it was, the unmistakable sound of the front door. Who would come for a visit, uninvited, with her in such a state? Charlotte?

Setting down her teacup, she forced herself out of the chair and into the hall. Craning her neck as she neared the stairway, she searched out a better view of the main entrance. She intercepted her husband as he came up the stairs. Frozen to the spot, her hand raised to cover her heart, which had stopped beating.

"Thomas, what has happened?" It was more than a little unusual to see him at home in the middle of the afternoon.

The corners of his mouth became a smile and he closed the few steps between them to embrace her. "A letter has come," he said into her hair.

Fresh tears fell on her face as her arms moved to hold her husband to herself. At last, a sign of life!

"My darling, you're shaking!" Thomas said, holding her more tightly.

Not caring, she pulled away and grasped at her husband's hand, drawing him toward the bedroom. She didn't stop until they were in the bedroom's sitting area. On the edge of the seat she had just earlier vacated, she looked up at Thomas. His eyes fell on hers, brows furrowed. Waving her hands as if to dismiss any further comment, she then placed a hand on the seat next to her.

"Please, sit. We have waited so long."

He watched her for a moment longer before taking the seat and then tearing open the envelope. There was a slight tremor in his hands as well. Several pieces of paper were within. Two letters and several sketches. The letters were written by two different hands. One Elizabeth's, the other was that of a stranger.

Abigail looked at her husband as if he could offer some explanation. His eyes were on the papers in his hands, brows gathered together.

Then he did the oddest thing. Thomas flipped over the envelope and glanced at the front. Why would he do such a thing?

"What's the matter?" Something was going on in that brain of his.

"It's the dates. Elizabeth's letter is dated weeks ago. But the postmark is but a week and a half old."

Abigail licked her lips, but her mouth felt dry. What could this mean? The intensity of her worry threatened to overtake her. But she managed to swallow against the dryness. "Read Elizabeth's letter first, please." Her voice came out strangled.

Thomas nodded, shuffling the papers.

"'Dearest Mother, Father, and Andrew,

"I trust you are all well as this letter reaches you. I have been at camp for many days now and it has been a learning experience for me. I've learned how to cook, how to do laundry, and how to sew and mend. The women have been quite patient with me, but I think I'm picking it up well. Although, I don't think the soldiers care much for my cooking.

"My accommodations are not as nice as those I enjoy at home, but they are sufficient. I share a tent with three other young women. Two of them, Sarah and Lily, are nurses. We don't see them much. They are up and out before we arise and retire early. The nursing staff are some of the hardest working people I have ever known. My other tent mate, Melanie, is one of the chattiest people I know. But she is a good friend to me.

"I've seen John on a few occasions, but I am trying to make sure he doesn't know I'm here. That has been truly difficult for me. But just knowing he's here and that he's safe is enough.

"I've included some of my drawings of the camp. I don't have a lot of free time to draw, but I take advantage of what time I do have. The soldiers are rather willing subjects for portraits too. They all seem to appreciate my work.

"Just as I mention I don't have much free time, my time to write this letter is coming to a close. I'm on kitchen duty tonight, which means I'm helping with the cooking again. Perhaps practice makes perfect. I'll write again soon.

"Love always, Elizabeth"

There, nothing seemed amiss. Abigail took a deep breath. But something nagged at the edge of her mind and a weight hung in the pit of her stomach. If only they could stop there. How she wished there wasn't another letter that bore more news, which might destroy any hope she now felt. She knew, however, that they could not stop there. There was more to this story.

Abigail turned to look at her husband. He seemed frozen, still staring at Elizabeth's letter. Was he struggling with the same thoughts? She gathered all the bravery she could muster and laid a hand on his arm, giving it a gentle squeeze.

Turning his face toward hers, he offered her a weak smile as he laid his opposite hand on hers. Then he sucked in a deep breath, moved Elizabeth's letter to the back of the stack and plunged into the stranger's letter.

"'Dear Sir and Madam,

"My name is Melanie. I was a tent mate of your daughter, Elizabeth. I only found this letter recently. I regret to inform you that your daughter is missing. She was last seen in the hospital assisting with the care of the wounded. A nurse reports that she was looking for Dr. John Taylor, who had gone to the front lines to patch the wounded there. It is suspected that she went there as well where she was either captured or met with an untimely end...'"

Abigail cried out. She lost all strength and fell forward, grasping for something sturdy.

Thomas grabbed for her hands with his arm closest to her but continued, "...No remains have been recovered. Your daughter was a bright spot in our camp and worked diligently in all that she did to see that everyone else's needs were taken care of. We will never give up hope that she shall be returned. Regards, Melanie"

"Oh, Elizabeth!" Abigail cried, hot tears pouring out of her eyes.

It was as if her heart had been stabbed and was pouring out. There was pain, sharp pain, emanating from the core of her being.

Thomas shifted from his seat to kneel in front of Abigail. Then his arms surrounded her, supporting her and enclosing her. Even as firmly as he held her, she felt as if she were going to shatter into a million pieces, never to be made whole again.

"What are we going to do?" was all she could manage between sobs.

Silence stretched out for several long moments that seemed drawn into eternity. Why wouldn't he say something? She needed him to say something!

At long last, he did speak, his words coming slowly. "We have to be strong. And do just as this young woman suggests—hold out hope that Elizabeth will be returned."

"But what if she's dead?" she shot back, unable to stop herself.

"Shh," he soothed. "Don't talk like that. Not yet. I'm not about to give up on Elizabeth." His voice was stronger then, filled with determination.

How could he be so sure? Was there truly room for hope? Even if there wasn't, was hope all they had?

The day was fresh and new, even if the memories of the night before remained. Matthew and Annabelle walked toward their favorite spot by the stream. As Matthew reached for her small hand, grasping it in his, he looked over in her direction. She offered him a quick glance and a playful smile, keeping pace with him. There was a pause in the small talk. Something simple and sweet passed between them.

As Matthew returned her smile, Annabelle's gaze drifted off and the corners of her mouth fell. Something wasn't right. What was she looking at? Following her gaze with his, he saw that her eyes were trained on the place where, hours earlier, he had been locked in a struggle for his life. The grass was matted from where his and

Tommy's bodies had been as they fought. He became lost in those memories, too. Not the risk to his own life. But how he had come so close to losing her. If he had been just a few minutes later... His hand tightened on hers.

Looking back toward Annabelle, he noted that her face paled. It also came to his attention that they had stopped moving. They stood, frozen to that spot.

"Annabelle," he said, stepping between her and the site of last night's fight to the death. He maneuvered his head until he caught her eyes. "We can find somewhere else to go."

She remained quiet for a moment, staring into his eyes. Her bright blue orbs clouded. "No," she said, her voice soft. "Just give me a minute."

Her grip on his hand tightened until his fingers were nearly numb.

She stayed quiet and unmoving for so long. Perhaps it would be better if they found another place. "Annabelle, truly we can..."

"No." There was a flash in her eyes.

He took a step back and gave her the emotional space she needed to deal with the memories of what had transpired in this place by the stream so close to their sacred spot. As she continued to grip his hand with more strength than he thought possible, he had to resist the urge to pull it away. So he bit his lip and allowed her to squeeze his hand as tightly as she needed.

It seemed as if eternity passed before she loosened her grip on his hand and refocused on his face. She nodded. He released her hand to wrap his arm around her and pull her to himself. The most natural thing to do. Annabelle leaned into him. Kissing the top of her head, he then breathed in the scent of her hair, wishing he could hold her like this forever. Then he could keep her safe.

Eventually, he turned their bodies in the direction of the hillside that had served as the setting for many of their more tender moments. Would he ever be able to remember those moments without this place being tainted by the memory of Tommy's murderous attack? He wanted to kick himself for bringing her here without considering the cost, but it was done. And she seemed determined that the attack would not overshadow her love of this place either.

They arrived at the large oak on top of the hillside and Annabelle plopped down on the ground, leaning against the trunk of the old tree. Her gaze drifted to the stream and her eyes closed. She made such a solemn picture. One that he wished he could capture. But he had neither paper, nor her skill for it. So he would just watch her.

It wasn't long before her eyes opened and she caught him staring at her.

"What is it?" she said, stifling a laugh.

"Nothing." He shook his head, his cheeks warming. "Just admiring the portrait you would make."

It was her turn to shake her head, but she granted him one of her finest smiles. "It would be all the better if you joined me." She patted the ground next to her.

He maneuvered his body to the ground. Some of his muscles ached as he did so. Once seated, she wrapped her arms around his and leaned on his shoulder. And they gazed out over the stream. Matthew enjoyed her closeness and the serenity of their place. But the remnant emotions from the previous night's events still haunted him.

After some moments had passed in silence, he gathered all the bravery he could muster and broke the solitude.

"I have my marching orders," he said softly.

Her body stilled. Was she breathing? He tilted his head to look down at her. There was movement, ever so slight, from the rise and fall of her chest.

Reaching over, he gripped her hand again.

"Will you say something?" He needed to hear from her. It took all he had not to gather her in his arms. But it was best to give her space to take in the news.

"I don't know what to say," came her response, almost too quiet to discern.

He didn't know how to respond either. She was right. What was there to say? This was not the way he wanted this conversation to go. But what had he hoped for?

She cleared her throat and continued. "That is...I want to say so many things—I don't want you to go. I don't know why you have to fight. I don't understand..."

He pulled back. "You don't know why we fight?"

She looked up at him. Her blue eyes so wide, so innocent. Yet the depths of them betrayed that there was more to her than he could see on the surface. If only he had time to explore those depths. Wouldn't he be happily lost in them forever?

"No," she said, her voice much firmer. She sat straighter, looking forward and pulling her arms into her lap. "Maybe it's my memory. Maybe I never understood this war to begin with."

She let her gaze wander back toward him. But after meeting his eyes briefly, she looked away again.

"I'm not making any sense," she grumbled, shifting her attention to her skirt, playing with the fabric.

Matthew chewed on his lip, pulling his knees up to prop his crossed arms on them. Long had he been concerned about this very thing. She was, after all, from the Union side of the war. That was a piece of information Dr. Wilson continued to keep from her. Should he tell her now? How would that affect her? Affect them? He dipped his head. This decision was too big for him. Was it his to make?

He let his legs drop into a cross-legged position and leaned forward so he could look at her. "We fight for our way of life, for the right to live as we see fit. The Union would impress upon us their ideas about how we should run our lives. Now they refuse to let us live apart from them. So, we fight for our freedom."

Annabelle met his eyes. It was as if she wanted to understand, but held back. Something held her back. What was it? They sat for several moments in this stalemate. Matthew made the first move to break it. Leaning toward her, he reached for her hand. He lifted her small hand to his lips and pressed a kiss to her palm.

"Let us not discuss such heavy matters," he said, his voice barely above a whisper. "I just want to sit with you and enjoy the setting sun before I go off to battle." His eyes wandered over the lines of her face, the waves of her hair. An ache grew in his chest. Whenever he was around her, many sensations streamed from the center of his being. Yes, he was captivated by her.

Nodding, she leaned into him. The feel of her body, soft against his made him light-headed, almost drunk. He wrapped an arm around her and pulled her closer still, relishing in the rush of emotion.

Together they watched the sun set. Matthew marveled anew at how the sky changed colors. But never before had he been more aware of how alive he was, with his Annabelle next to him. After some time, he took her hand in his, laying it in the palm of one hand and using the other to caress her fingers.

"What are you thinking about?" the question spilled out of him.

A deep sigh escaped her. "About you. About the war. About how much I don't want you to go."

Turning his face, he pressed a kiss to the top of her head. "I may not have you to save me this time, but I'll be fine." Was it just him or were his words slurred? She was intoxicating.

"How can you know that?" she countered, bending her fingers to grasp his hand.

"Because—" He used his now free hand to tip her chin so she was looking at him. "This time I have something to come back to."

The last of his lunch rations were gone. But Daniel continued to stare at his plate. The course metal of the tin was cool in his hands. Crumbs of hard tack remained, but he left them alone. His fixation on the empty plate was not due to lingering hunger, but because he dreaded his next errand.

It had not been his intention to skip his regular visits to Jacob these last several days. The truth was that he, if he were willing to admit it to himself, had been avoiding Melanie. Just the thought of her caused a jolt of electricity to fire through his being. There was something about her. Something that made him think. And think about her he had been. Nonstop.

And this was not acceptable. It was an outright betrayal to his friend. Daniel was no mind reader, but it didn't take one to see that Jacob had feelings for Melanie. There were glances. Smiles. Looks. And Daniel did not want to get in the middle of that. His regard for Jacob was too high. Still, could he help the way his heart flipped when he caught sight of her in the meal line?

Today. He determined that today he would visit his friend no matter what. That wasn't to say he couldn't try to avoid Melanie at the same time. So he would go directly after mealtime. In all likelihood, she would be working with the other women on chores around the camp. Perhaps that's where she was now.

It had not escaped his notice that she was not in the lunch line today. Was he looking for her? His thoughts accused him. *Certainly not!* he assured himself. This was just an observation. Perhaps she was busy with laundry duty or mending.

Rising to his feet, he walked over to put his plate by the wash bin. A young lady worked on cleaning them.

"Thank you." She offered him a smile, which he returned, nodding. Her name escaped him, but he knew her. One of the younger wives. And God had smiled down upon her. That husband of hers survived the first battle in one piece.

A short walk to the makeshift hospital did not distract Daniel's thoughts from where they always were these days—Melanie. Where was she after all? What could possibly keep her from a meal? She needed to keep up her strength. They all did. One never knew when... well, when life would take a drastic turn.

The oversized tent was in front of him. He scanned the area around him as if fearing she'd appear from around the back of one of the nearby tents. *This is crazy.* She was not lying in wait somewhere like some sharpshooter.

Gathering his wits about him, he took a deep breath and straightened his uniform. Then stepped into the tent. And froze in his tracks.

There she was. By Jacob's bed. Leaning over his cot, she held his hand. The scene stole his breath. Melanie was the most tender of angels come down to grace this place full of pain and suffering.

But he could not escape the vise that clamped around his heart at seeing her tenderness bestowed upon Jacob. His friend. Jacob was his friend. He shouldn't be having these thoughts. He needed to go.

As he turned to leave, however, his eyes focused in on Melanie's. Something stopped him. Her green eyes betrayed a pain that tugged at him. He couldn't tear himself away. Rather it drew him in. Moments later, he stood over the two of them.

As his shadow fell over Jacob's figure, Melanie's face turned up to meet his gaze. She leaned back from Jacob and wiped at her eyes. How had he not noticed she cried?

"Am I disturbing you?" How had it not occurred to him that he might be interrupting a moment? "I should go," he said, turning to leave.

"No," she called out.

He halted.

"Please," she said, her voice thin. "Stay. I know Jacob would like you being here."

Daniel shifted his body back toward his friend. And though he was there because of Jacob, he couldn't tear his eyes away from Melanie.

"Are you..." his voice caught. He cleared his throat. "Are you well?"

Her tears continued to break through. A protective instinct flared in him. The urge to pull her into his embrace was almost irresistible. Almost. He still remembered Jacob, after all.

She fell silent. Her gaze rested on Jacob, tears falling. After some moments, it seemed to overtake her and she shook her head. Raising a hand to her mouth, her body trembled.

He could hold back no longer. Stepping around the cot, he stopped just short of her. Instead of gathering her in his arms, he crouched in front of her. Only then did he see a red tinge to her eyes. She had been crying for some time.

"Tell me." His eyes, his heart, were fixed on her. He was hooked.

Several seconds passed as she worked to calm herself. Then she met his eyes and spoke. "Jacob is feverish. He has been the last two times I came to change his bandages. And there's this stuff coming out of his wound..." She shook her head and waved a hand as if to erase her words.

Without thinking, he caught her hand. "It's all right. What does the doctor say?"

She struggled to hold back another fit of tears. "I've been too afraid to tell him. I know it's my fault." The words poured out of her.

"No," he said a little more harshly than he intended.

She jerked back a little.

"I won't hear you say that, Melanie," he softened his tone. "No one has worked harder to keep Jacob well and in good spirits than you have. Don't say such things."

"But it hasn't been enough." Another tear escaped down her face.

His heart twisted. He took both of her hands in his. "You're not a miracle worker. And Jacob knows that."

She turned so that her eyes again rested on Jacob. And there was silence again. After allowing some moments for her to take in his words of comfort, it was time for words of reason.

"Melanie," Daniel said, his voice not much more than a whisper. He squeezed her hands gently, trying to draw her attention back toward himself.

She continued to stare at Jacob.

"Melanie," he tried again. He had words to say that she wouldn't want to hear. "There may be an infection spreading. I need to get the doctor."

There was a nod, almost imperceptible, but there all the same.

He stood, allowing her hands to slide from his, regretting the break in contact. But Jacob needed him, needed him to be strong and walk away from Melanie, needed him to speak up for his well-being. Still, Daniel could not resist placing a hand on Melanie's shoulder as he passed her on his way to fetch Dr. Smith.

The doctor wasn't difficult to find. He was across the hospital speaking with a nurse. As soon as their conversation came to a close, Daniel intercepted him before the doctor had a chance to move on.

"Dr. Smith," he started, interjecting himself in the man's path.

"Yes, soldier?" There was an edge to his voice. The doctor was a kind man, but he had many patients that needed to be attended to and that left little time to suffer distractions.

Daniel was taken aback, but determined, he trudged forward. "I'm here on behalf of Jacob Moore. I've just come from his bedside and his nursemaid, Melanie, has noticed some strange things about his wound."

The doctor's face darkened. He nodded to Daniel and moved past Daniel in the direction of Jacob's cot. What could Daniel do but follow?

Melanie must have been watching for their approach as she was on her feet as they neared. She stepped out of Dr. Smith's way once he came around the cot.

"Talk to me, Melanie," the doctor said, looking at her with serious eyes. "Tell me everything." He then worked to remove the bandages on Jacob's leg.

"He's been feverish these last couple of days. I thought it might be something he caught in the hospital. Then I noticed more and more oozing when I cleaned the wound. And there's been some swelling. But I haven't seen any green."

By then, the doctor finished unwrapping the leg and was examining the wound. "Not all types of gangrene are green," he informed her shortly.

"Jacob told me that it no longer hurt when I would clean it," she argued.

Her lower lip trembled and she was wringing her hands. Was she about to fall apart again?

The doctor's face fell. He looked at Melanie and the hardness in his exterior softened. "I'm so sorry."

The words were simple and delivered with as much gentleness as any man could muster, but Daniel knew that they hit Melanie as painfully as would an arrow.

"But, he was better," Melanie said, desperate.

Daniel moved closer to her.

"Gangrene can make the patient numb," the doctor tried to explain.

Melanie was beside herself. "Can't you just give him medicine or something?"

The doctor shook his head.

Tears flowed down Melanie's face and she shook.

Daniel put an arm around her. He couldn't help the warmth that pervaded his body.

"Dr. Smith, you can't! You can't take his leg!" Melanie cried openly now.

"I have to," came his simple reply. He raised his hand, turning toward a group of nurses nearby. Once he caught the attention of one, he shifted his attention back to Melanie.

"Young lady, you did everything you could. There just wasn't enough blood flow to the area and the tissue began to die. There's nothing any of us could have done. My most capable nurse couldn't have prevented this were she in your place. But if I don't take his leg, the gangrene will continue to spread and infect more healthy tissue. He could die."

Melanie shook her head. She covered her face with her hands, and turning toward Daniel, buried her face in his chest.

He put his arms around her, supporting her while she cried. And it was strange, all of the emotions within him. His heart leapt at Melanie's closeness, every nerve seemed alive. Yet he was broken for her pain. And for his friend. Then there was the guilt. He shouldn't be holding Melanie like this. But he couldn't pull away.

Movement out of his periphery caught his attention. Dr. Smith pulled off his glasses and wiped the sweat from his forehead. Was he loath to do what he must?

A nurse brushed past Daniel, leaning over Jacob.

The doctor's sad eyes caught Daniel's. He motioned for Daniel to take Melanie elsewhere.

Daniel expected a fight, but it took little effort to lead her from the tent.

CHAPTER SIX

REUNITED

The men marched out in the morning before dawn. Elizabeth had been awake. She listened to the unit commander yelling orders as they went. Marching feet threatened to lull her back to sleep. But it was not to be. For she knew where those feet carried them. And that Matthew was among them. Overcome with nausea, she shifted onto her back, staring at the top of the hospital tent. A wave of emotion threatened to overtake her as her thoughts drifted where she'd rather them not—the likelihood of Matthew's return.

Elizabeth couldn't deny she had come to care for the man deeply. The turning of her heart as thoughts of his possible fate filled her mind was evidence enough. Straining to hear the men as they passed farther out of the camp, an emptiness drew the warmth from her body. She pulled her thin blanket up to her chin. It was no use. So she sat and reached for her thick shawl. Wrapping it around herself, she gathered her arms close to her body.

Now that her wrap fought off the cold that seemed to come from within her, she longed to lie back down and escape into sleep. Maybe then this day wouldn't happen. That too, would not serve her. She had to face it as surely as those soldiers. Rising to her feet, she gathered her clothes and prepared for the day.

Once she was dressed and fed for the morning, Elizabeth went about her chores—seeing to the patients in the hospital. They were few and her task was completed in short order. Then the time was hers to spend as she pleased. Today, that was torture. Minutes passed into hours as she, and the other women, awaited news from the front.

Elizabeth had ample time to consider her worry after Matthew. She sat in the hospital tent, wringing her hands. Could she bear it if he didn't return? Did he know how she felt? She hoped he did. For she had never told him. Why had she held back? The truth was that she had been a coward, afraid to be vulnerable.

A tear escaped. Raising a hand to brush it away, she chose hope. And she set in her heart that if he did return, she would tell him. She had learned a great lesson this day. War left no time to be afraid of anything, least of all your own feelings.

Sounds on the edges of the camp alerted her to the presence of soldiers. Elizabeth was on her feet in a heartbeat. She rushed out and into the thick of an influx of wounded men. Yes, the battle was well under way.

Her eyes searched the faces of the wounded for Matthew. And her heart twisted in her chest as if someone wrung it with their hands. But she pushed past it and continued to search for him. She saw something in the faces of these men—their pain. How could she be so selfish? These men were suffering and needed help.

She rushed for the closest man. He walked on his own feet, but held his arm, grimacing. A hand-made tourniquet squeezed his upper arm, soaked in blood. *Must be a gunshot wound. Probably not critical.* Smiling at him, she placed an arm on his opposite shoulder.

"Head for the hospital. You'll be seen by a doctor there. Don't take that tourniquet off."

The man nodded and moved on.

She stepped toward the next man. He lay on a stretcher. And she was not prepared for the gruesome sight that awaited her. This man had been hit by something much bigger. His midsection was ripped open and... Raising a hand to her mouth to keep from being sick, she worked to gather her wits about her. Then she reached for the arm of the lead man carrying the stretcher.

"This way," she commanded, leading them into the hospital.

Grabbing for bandages and cleaning supplies, she made her way back to where the man now lay on a hospital cot. She applied pressure to the open wound and felt her hands sink into his abdomen. A fresh wave of nausea rose and threatened to overtake her, but she swallowed it back. Looking up at the men that remained there, she started barking commands.

"You." She pointed to the dark-haired soldier. "Put your hands here."

The man's eyes were wide, but he obeyed, taking her place pressing on the wound.

"And you." She spoke to the red-haired man. "Get the doctor. Tell him I have a critical case."

The man nodded, relief clear on his face, and raced off into the hospital.

Elizabeth continued her work. She attempted to clean the wound as much as she could. There was so much blood. An artery must have been injured, ripped, or nicked at the very least, she realized with dismay. The man's chances of survival just plummeted, if he had any.

She felt more than heard someone behind her. But she couldn't be bothered to turn away from her patient. It wasn't until the doctor came alongside her that she realized it was him.

Dr. Wilson relieved the soldier who was now white as a sheet. The man stepped back into the recesses of the tent as the doctor examined the man's injuries.

A hand fell on her shoulder. "Annabelle," he said, his voice firm, but still gentle somehow.

Brushing her hair out of her face, smearing blood on her forehead, she continued her work to staunch the wound.

"Annabelle," the doctor repeated, pulling on her arm.

She halted but did not shift her gaze from the body of the man she worked to save.

"Annabelle, you've preformed as well as any nurse in this hospital. But this man is...he's not going to make it."

Tears blurred her vision. She moved her face against her shoulder to wipe them away. This was no time to fall apart.

"He's not in any pain," the doctor said.

She knew he only attempted to comfort her.

"He will just slip away."

She nodded.

"I need your help with other patients," he said, his grip on her arm loosening. "You are as fine as any of my nurses."

Looking at him at last, she nodded again.

He afforded her a small smile. "Good, come this way."

Dr. Wilson led her farther into the hospital. And Elizabeth continued to help with the wounded, cleaning injuries, bandaging, determining if amputation was likely, preparing patients for the doctor. In a few hours, she heaved from the effort, and patches of her dress were well soaked with sweat. But they had made good progress. The wounded had stopped coming in, and they neared the end of the line.

And then Dr. Wilson appeared behind her again. "Why don't you step outside?" He laid a hand on her shoulder. "You've done enough here."

Part of her wanted to argue, to stay until the last patient had been seen. But a bigger part of her knew how weak she was. So she nodded and moved away from the patient who would lose his arm, but would live to see another day.

Stepping outside, she took in several breaths of fresh air. The air inside the tent had become tainted by the smells of the battle and the wounded. These breaths filled her nostrils with the smell of grass, of the breeze, of a world beyond the pain and suffering. It was wonderful.

She stumbled farther into the camp, seeking out a wash station. All around her were reunions between soldiers and their wives. But the last several hours left her numb to the joy they shared. Finding the washbowl, she attempted to wash her hands clean of the red that stained them. It required some tough scrubbing, and scrub she would. Scouring her hands, she attempted to remove the memories of this day.

Directly to her right a soldier and his young wife embraced, not caring if they put on a display. She couldn't help but watch them. There was such relief, such elation, such love between them.

Would there be such between she and Matthew? Matthew! Her heart came to life again. Had he made it back? She hadn't seen him in the hospital, and glancing around, she didn't see him among the soldiers within the range of her sight. Did that mean he was…?

Now moving through the camp, she sought him. Had he not returned? Her heart sank in her chest and tears long fought won the battle.

Hands grabbed her from behind. Spun around, she found herself pressed to a gray uniform, locked in a firm embrace. Breathing in, she knew it was Matthew. The liquid spilling out of her eyes became tears of joy as she clung to him and cried.

"I thought you were gone!" she said, unable to keep herself from saying what filled her heart.

"I know, but I'm here. I'm here." He stroked her hair.

She pulled back to look into his dirty, blood-streaked face. "I love you, Matthew. I love you so much!"

"I love you." He pulled her to himself for a deep kiss.

She remained there, locked in his arms for long minutes before he pulled back again.

"I can't imagine a life without you, Annabelle," he said, breathless. "Would you marry me?"

"Marry?" The words struck her. Her stomach flip-flopped. It was not a pleasant feeling.

"Yes." He seemed oblivious to her reaction. Rather he was all happiness and eagerness. "The colonel can do it. What do you say? Be my war bride?"

War bride. What was it about those words? Someone else had spoken them to her. She stood in the comfort of Matthew's arms, but could not find an answer for him. She was lost in pieces of memories that seemed hazy.

"Elizabeth!"

Someone screamed from her left side. She turned toward the sound. Whether it was the voice or the name that seemed familiar to her, she did not know.

"Elizabeth!"

The man from her dreams glared at her from across the yard. He was in a Union uniform, being escorted through the camp by two Confederate guards. But he pulled hard against them.

Matthew jerked her back into his embrace. Did she need to be protected from this crazed man?

"Get your hands off of her. Elizabeth!" the man screamed.

And then he was gone, dragged into a tent across the camp.

Somehow both his voice and that name meant something to her. And though she found herself leaning into Matthew in this moment of uncertainty, she was determined to find out what it was.

Later that evening, dinner service was in full swing. In celebration of the survival of so many, the women had cooked a fine stew. Elizabeth's nose took in the delicious smells. The day had brought many things. Peace was not one of them.

Her mind had been plagued by the appearance of this other man. Who was he? What was he to her? What could this mean? Despite

Dr. Wilson's insistence that she rest, Elizabeth volunteered to distribute the stew as Sally and Suellen filled the bowls.

One thing she had needed since that man entered the camp, since Matthew's proposal, was space. And serving proved the perfect opportunity to do so rather than sit next to Matthew, who was no doubt eager for an answer.

"Someone needs to take a bowl to that prisoner," Sally spoke up. She looked between Suellen and Elizabeth. Clearly, she did not consider herself an option.

"I will," Elizabeth said, perhaps a bit too soon.

The other women turned curious gazes on her.

"After all," she attempted to cover, hoping they didn't notice her cheeks color. "I'm the only one who doesn't have a husband waiting on me at dinner."

"Ah, but you have a beau," Sally teased. She poked at Elizabeth. "Don't you think Matthew will miss ya?"

"I don't mean to disappoint him." Her tone was quiet, shy almost as she moved her hands over her skirt, nervous. "I just thought..."

"She's only teasing you, honey," Suellen assured her, putting a hand on Elizabeth's arm. "We appreciate you volunteering. There'll be a guard there if he tries anything. Don't you hesitate to scream now, ya hear?"

Elizabeth felt some of the color drain from her face. "Yes, ma'am."

Sally handed her two bowls of soup, each with a spoon. "But we do want to be right kind to him." She lowered her voice as if she shared a great secret. "We hope he'll help our doctors patch up our fellas. That's what he's here for. Best for everyone if he does it willingly."

Elizabeth nodded. "I'll see what I can do," she said, smiling.

"I don't think there's anything that pretty face o' yours can't do." Suellen returned her smile. "Now, get. Before that soup gets cold."

Elizabeth made her way through the camp with easy steps, careful not to spill any of the precious stew. She nodded at the men she passed, thankful for each one and their return from battle. It wasn't long before she stood in front of the prisoner's tent.

"Good evening," she said to the guard. "I brought supper." She raised the bowls.

The man, shadowed in the night, took the still-steaming bowl. He sniffed it before shoving a spoonful into his mouth.

"I have some for the prisoner as well."

The guard jerked his head toward the tent.

She sucked in a breath before she entered, steeling herself against her nerves. As she stepped inside the dimly lit tent, her breath caught in her throat. The man whose face haunted her dreams was bound and tied to a post on one side of the small area. His face appeared red, swollen, and bruised from where he had obviously been beaten. Was it because he resisted his captors trying to get to her? Against her better judgment, her heart went out to him. It was curious to her that it should.

He looked up at the intrusion. The second his eyes met hers, something electric shot through her.

"Elizabeth," he said, trying to move toward her. His bonds kept him place. "Elizabeth, you're here! I don't know how, but you are!"

With a great deal of caution, she moved to crouch before him. Unable to stop herself, she reached out a shaking hand to touch the face she had seen so many times in her dreams. His eyes never left hers.

The man reached up his bound hands to brush the hair off her forehead. A breath escaped him. "What have they done to you?"

Her hand went to her forehead. The scar from her fall.

"That was from an accident," she recited. "I fell and had a concussion and...amnesia."

"Amnesia?" his brows furrowed.

She nodded. "I have no memory of who I am. But I know you... somehow."

He brushed the back of his fingertips against her cheek. "I'm not surprised." Then he clasped her chin between his bound hands and brought her lips to his for a gentle kiss.

Elizabeth allowed her lips to linger for only a few seconds before pulling back. *What would Matthew think of me allowing such a thing to happen?*

Jerking away from the man, she stared at him. She should slap him for his advances, but she could not raise a hand against him. Nor could she scream for the guard and allow more harm to be visited upon him for his indiscretion. After all, she did not know what he was to her. For all she knew, he could be her...

She shook her head and stirred the stew. Then she offered him a spoonful. He opened his mouth, taking in the bite with obvious gratitude on his face. What had they been feeding him? The meal continued in silence, she spooning the meat, vegetables, and broth into his mouth. Once the bowl emptied, she gave him a slight smile and stood, turning to leave.

"I was so wrong, Lizzie," he said, halting her where she stood. Her hand already pressed against the tent flap, but she turned to look at him, curious.

"I should have married you when I had the chance. Taken what time we had."

She took a deep breath. So that was it; they were to be wed. *A fiancé.* The thought overwhelmed her. How could she have had such an intimate relationship and forgotten the pieces of it? Should she doubt his claim? But her heart, beating hard in her chest at the nearness of him, testified to the veracity of his claim.

Elizabeth studied him. How had this all come about? The two of them in this war, yet torn apart? How had he let that happen? She opened her mouth, but found she could not speak. He appeared too lost to her. Too caught up in his own emotions to assuage hers.

She turned to leave again, but Sally and Suellen's words about his cooperation came back to her, and she thought better of it. Stepping toward him once more, she crouched down again.

"If you truly care for me as you say you do, you won't make me watch them brutalize you. You will do as they ask." The back of her eyes pricked as she saw once again the effects of the soldiers' treatment of him.

"But I..."

"If you care about me," she repeated.

His deep brown eyes, so familiar to her, searched hers. And after several seconds, he nodded.

She stood, turning to leave again.

"Wait," he called after her. "If I do. If I cooperate, will you continue to bring me dinner each night?"

So he attempted to strike a deal. Her first instinct was to refuse him. How dare he play games with her? She whirled around to do just that, but something gave her pause. The thought of watching him being beaten, or worse, for refusing to comply with their orders, became more than she could handle. Besides, this was not exactly a deal with the devil. It wasn't as if he was asking her for much. And so, steadying herself so as to appear unfazed by his challenge, she said, "I will."

He nodded and the pact was made.

Elizabeth at last took her leave of him.

Well into her evening routine, Elizabeth brushed her hair. And thought about the name the prisoner had called her. Elizabeth. What else was it that he had called her? Lizzie. That was it. Lizzie. Lizzie. Little Lizzie...and she became still as a vision began to form...

"Hold still, little Lizzie!" a portly woman with greying chestnut brown hair said as she attempted to tie a bow in Elizabeth's hair. The woman had a kind face, though it twisted in concentration from trying to still Elizabeth as she squirmed for freedom.

"Now, don't you dare go running around outside or your mother will have a fit!" the woman warned, her voice serious.

"Why do I have to wear this stupid dress?" Elizabeth quipped, tugging at the fancy skirt.

"There are important people coming to dinner, Lizzie," her nursemaid explained for perhaps the hundredth time. "A doctor. You should like that. Your father hopes he will join his practice. He has a son close to your age."

"A boy?" Elizabeth pulled back again.

"Yes, a boy." The nursemaid's eyes widened for emphasis. She seemed amused.

"Hmmm," Elizabeth murmured. Nothing exciting about meeting another boy. All the boys at school chased her and pulled her hair. She didn't care much for boys.

"Now, stand still," the nursemaid commanded. "Let me look you over." She smiled despite herself. "You are a little angel."

Elizabeth grimaced and tugged at the big bow on the front of her dress.

"Now stop that, Lizzie!" The nursemaid smoothed over the dress where Elizabeth had just fumbled with it. "Ladies do not tug at their clothes. Now, you have a few minutes before they get here. You may go play quietly with your dolls inside while I see to your brother."

"All right." Elizabeth was glad to be dismissed to play, even if she had to stay inside. She had great difficulty keeping her clothes neat and nice, but she was determined to do it for her father. And imagine, another doctor come to dinner! How she would enjoy hearing the two doctors discuss their cases. It couldn't come fast enough. So she would just have to bide her time checking on her dolls, seeing what ailed them in Elizabeth's Hospital that day.

Minutes later, the nursemaid came into her room to check on her. No sooner had she entered the room when she stopped short, catching sight of Elizabeth.

"Good heavens, Lizzie! Your hair!"

"Sorry, Nanny," Elizabeth apologized. She truly was sorry. After all, she had tried so hard to stay nice. "There was an emergency and I had to crawl under my..."

"It's all right," the nursemaid cut her off, bidding Elizabeth to her.

"Just come here, child, so I can try to fix it." Her eyes found the clock; her voice betrayed her anxiety.

Elizabeth stood and walked to her nursemaid, head down. Nanny patted her on the shoulder as she directed her to the vanity. The woman had never worked so quickly, Elizabeth was sure of it. But, just as she tied off the second braid, they heard the doorbell ring.

"They're here," Elizabeth said, jumping up from the stool and bounding away toward the door.

"Remember your manners," Nanny called after her. "Ladies do not bounce so."

"Yes, ma'am," Elizabeth called, not looking back.

Elizabeth's brother met her in the hall and they walked down the stairs, followed by their nursemaid. As they descended the stairs, she saw that their guests were already in the foyer being greeted by their mother and father. The steps creaked beneath them, alerting the people below to their presence. All eyes were on them. Elizabeth felt a little uneasy.

"These are our children — Elizabeth, our first, and Andrew." Her father introduced them.

"Nice to meet you," both of the adults said in tune.

"This is our son, John," the lady whose name she did not know said, putting her hands on the shoulders of the young boy with them who stood a head taller than Elizabeth. He had deep brown hair and equally deep brown eyes.

"Hello," was his simple greeting. He then turned his attention back to the grown-ups.

Just then, the butler came out into the foyer and informed Father that dinner was ready. So they all filed into the dining room. Elizabeth studied the boy throughout the meal, but he remained quiet and aloof, more inter-ested in the adults than she or her brother. In fact, after dinner, when they were welcomed to play, he preferred to adjourn to the parlor with the adults.

She decided that if he thought himself too good for Elizabeth and her brother that was just fine with her. Besides, she didn't need a boy cramping her style.

Elizabeth was jarred out of the memory. She gripped the hairbrush so tightly that her knuckles had turned white. Releasing her aching joints, she threw it down. *Elizabeth*. That was her name. Not Annabelle. Elizabeth. Who should she tell? Matthew? Would everyone know then that she was connected somehow to this Union soldier and lock her up, too? It was too great a risk, she decided. So she would keep it to herself for now.

'Waking from a dream into a nightmare' is how Jacob would forever describe this day. As darkness opened into full consciousness, pain slammed into his awareness. A lot of pain. He cried out, the pain was so great. Realization flooded his mind. Something was radically different about his body.

Jerking the covers back, he saw the stump that was once his leg. His head spun, as did the world around him. He couldn't seem to focus on anything. Screaming for the nurse, he fought to breathe. This must be some kind of nightmare. So he didn't care who heard him or whom he might disturb. It wasn't long before a nurse was by his side.

Her hands were on his arms. "Calm yourself, soldier." She attempted to lay him back on his pillows.

He resisted her, his nightshirt becoming damp with sweat. "My leg! My leg!" was all he could say.

The woman called for another nurse to grab something. Whatever she said was indistinguishable to him. He fought more and more to just breathe. And there was a pain in his chest. Was he going to have a heart attack? He tried to jerk away from the nurse's hands while she attempted yet again to hold him down. Out of nowhere, another set of hands appeared, this time with a cloth over his nose and mouth.

"Just breathe," the nurse yelled above his screams. "You are safe."

"My leg!" he continued to wail as whatever the sweet smell on the cloth was calmed him.

The hands that worked to hold him eased their grip.

"I know this is difficult," the first nurse said, maneuvering so that her face was mere inches from his.

He no longer had any fight in him. No, he felt numb, sedate, and his limbs became heavy.

"Your leg became gangrenous. It would have killed you," she went on to explain.

Jacob, even in the midst of his nightmare, knew that he'd had this one before. But he never remembered the calming drugs or the kindness of the nurses. In his earlier nightmares, there had been sneers and saws. He had been able to feel a lot more sensations too. His heart began to beat hard and fast. And his breathing quickened.

The nurse held the cloth to his face again and he breathed in the sweet scented medicine again. Then he was dragged toward the darkness of sleep again. *Wait!* If he was being pulled into sleep, that must mean this wasn't a nightmare, that his leg was truly gone. He had only a few seconds of realization before the darkness overcame him again.

The sun shone on Charlotte Taylor as she walked down the street. It was but a few blocks from her door to the home of her dear friend. Despite the brightness of the sun shining down on the earth, her heart was sad. She had made this trip on many occasions, most with her whole family in tow. That thought tugged at her heart.

Her son. He was so far away, perhaps never to return home. *Now, Charlotte, you mustn't think like that!* She allowed her attention to be drawn to the homes that she passed. They were so neatly placed on the block. Lining up with perfect symmetry, they fit together. If only life could be so neat and orderly.

As she arrived at the house she had come to know so well, she took a deep breath before mounting the few stairs that would take her to the front door. She rang the bell. It wasn't long before a maid-servant answered the door.

"Good day to you, Mrs. Taylor. Let me take that wrap for you." The maidservant moved out of her way so she could step inside. Then the maid's hands were on her wrap, lifting its weight from her shoulders.

The maidservant then led Charlotte down the hall to the parlor. The house seemed particularly quiet today, Charlotte noted as they moved through the home that was as familiar to her as her own. Soon enough, they were at the door to the family parlor and the maid waved her in.

"I'll let Mrs. Thompson know that you are here."

Charlotte nodded, moving into the space and taking a seat on the settee within. Her eyes wandered over the space. Kept up well, every-thing was in its place. But there were no disturbed books. No sewing projects out. It seemed as if no one had inhabited this parlor in quite some time. Odd, Abigail often enjoyed hours in here. What could it mean?

Though she expected to wait mere minutes before she was face to face with her dear friend, the minutes ticked by until nearly a half hour had passed. Charlotte had all but decided to call for the maid when she heard the sound of someone in the hall. Was the maid coming to dismiss her? But when the door opened, it was Abigail come to greet her.

A small smile was plastered onto her face. Charlotte knew her well enough to know that this could not be as genuine as the sadness in her eyes. Abigail appeared as if she had dressed in a hurry. Had she just dressed when Charlotte came to call?

Closer inspection of her friend's features yielded more clues. Unmistakable dark circles under her friend's eyes were quite telling. Whether they were from crying or lack of sleep, Charlotte did not know. But her overall appearance was enough to stir great concern within Charlotte. She made no effort to disguise it.

Charlotte was on her feet in a moment, taking steps toward her friend. "Are you quite well?"

Moving into the parlor and waving off her friend, Abigail took a seat on her favorite chair catty corner to the settee. "Yes, I'm well. Why do you ask?"

Why did she insist on hiding? On behaving as if this were any other social visit on any other day? Charlotte watched her, confused by her behavior. It was a far cry from the behavior of friends who had no secrets and shared everything. Was Abigail so proud that she wouldn't talk about whatever bothered her? Was Charlotte so fearful that she wouldn't push? No, she cared too much about her friend.

"Abigail, you look as if you've been through a lot these last days," she said, moving to a seat closer to her friend, leaning toward her.

Charlotte was pleased her friend didn't draw away from her touch. But she didn't open up either. She sat, her mouth a thin line, holding firm to her hard exterior. One look in Abigail's eyes, glistening over with unshed tears, told her there may be a crack in that brave exterior.

"Tell me, friend. You know you can trust me." Charlotte reached out to touch Abigail's hands that lay in her lap, twisting a handkerchief.

As soon as their hands made contact, Abigail burst into tears and the words began to pour out of her. "I have kept to my room. Since we received word about Elizabeth, I can't seem to function. It's all I can do to get out of bed each day."

Charlotte attempted to move closer to her friend, placing a hand on Abigail's shoulder. She and her own husband had received word not too long ago about John, that he had been captured and was believed to be a prisoner in a Confederate camp.

"There, there," Charlotte soothed. "It's perfectly understandable."

"But look at you!" Abigail blotted at her tears with her handkerchief. "Your son is a prisoner of war, and you're out and about calling on friends."

Charlotte rubbed Abigail's arm in hopes of reassuring her. "No, not calling on friends. Calling on one friend. A dear friend. One who can empathize with what I'm going through." She felt tears welling in her own eyes.

Abigail nodded and let her gaze fall back down on her handkerchief in her lap. That did seem to bring her some comfort.

"No one expects you to be able to hold it together. Especially with the news you received. Least of all me."

Abigail's eyes shifted toward her friend. She startled at seeing the tears in Charlotte's eyes.

But Charlotte offered her a smile.

"Thank you," Abigail said, her voice quiet. "You are a dear friend to me."

Charlotte nodded, wiping at a tear that had escaped. "A dear friend who just wants to help any way I can. Just tell me how."

"Sit with me for a while?" Her eyes were hopeful.

Charlotte nodded. "That, I can do."

When Elizabeth awoke, it was to a hospital full of wounded and dying soldiers. The battle was over, but in here, another battle waged on. She went through her morning routine and began her day as any nurse would—making rounds.

Bringing the soldiers their rations, she checked wound dressings and redressed any as needed. Elizabeth also alerted the doctors to any cases that seemed worse than the day before. And she took the time to sit with anyone who dealt poorly with the reality of his wound or treatment.

On the battlefield, many men lost their legs and arms to amputations. The risk of gangrene was too great and the medicine to prevent it too scarce. Some of the men would rather die than lose limbs, but the doctors were not in the habit of handing out that choice. So, when the reality of it set in, they often needed someone to talk to or a hand to hold. This was a service Elizabeth could provide.

By the time one round finished, it was noon. Elizabeth prepared to pass around lunch rations, but Dr. Wilson dismissed her. He told her there were others who could do this work, and that he wanted her to rest. With the weight of the last few days on her, she did not argue.

As she stopped her work, she noticed that the captive doctor, John, was in the hospital as he had promised, doing his part to help the wounded men. A guard with a gun stood inside the hospital tent keeping a watchful eye on him. This made Elizabeth uneasy, but it had to be she supposed. John was their prisoner, but they did need the extra doctor.

The prisoner seemed to feel her eyes on him because he turned and met her gaze. When he smiled at her, a part of her warmed at the sympathy in his eyes for her. Had he been watching her all morning? From the look in his eyes, she wagered he had. She returned his smile, but turned away when she thought better of it. And again she wondered what Matthew would think of her.

They hadn't seen each other since he had proposed yesterday. She didn't want him to think she didn't care anymore. The thought crossed her mind to find him, but a weariness took over and she went to her cot. As she lay down and sleep overcame her, she was visited in her dreams by another memory coming to the surface...

"Teacher's pet! Teacher's pet!" The boys, Elizabeth's schoolmates, taunted her as she left the school building. She had received the highest mark on a test in their grade level. And the teacher had made much ado about it as many of the students had done poorly on the test.

Hugging her books to her chest, she pretended it didn't bother her, but these boys had a way of getting her goat. Why did they have to single her out so?

A couple of the boys ran ahead of her and stopped short. She almost bumped into them.

"We found a pet for the teacher's pet," one of the boys said, holding up a mouse by its tail.

Elizabeth jumped back as the small rodent dangled, squealing to be freed.

"Stop it, Freddie!" she said, "Let it go."

"Maybe we should let it go in your hair," another boy said, laughing as he came up alongside Elizabeth and tugged at her blonde locks.

Elizabeth gasped and backed away from the semicircle of boys, not realizing she backed into an alley.

The boys chased her farther in the narrow crossway.

Elizabeth turned and ran, trying to fight tears, making it difficult to see. One second she was running, the next her foot swept from under her and she tripped and fell. Pain throbbed through her leg as she hit the ground hard. Her books were around her and her dress was dirtied, but she didn't care. All she cared about was her ankle. She had hurt it badly.

"Now, what are you going to do, teacher's pet?" Freddie said, stopping in front of her, dangling the mouse in her face.

The other boys were around him in an instant. There was no escape.

Then someone broke through the boys and stood between her and the others. "I think you've done enough and you should leave her alone."

It was John!

"What are you gonna do? Snitch?" the boy that spoke sounded less certain.

There were three of them, but John stood a good head taller than any of them.

"Maybe I'll knock you into next Sunday," John threatened, raising his fists.

"C'mon, guys," one of the boys said. "She's already down in the dirt anyway."

The boys turned and slowly retreated.

Only then did John shift his focus toward Elizabeth.

"Thank you," she said, with tear-streaked face.

"No problem. I can't stand those hooligans. Are you all right?" There was a genuine concern in his eyes she had never known from him. He had always been so aloof.

"No, it's my ankle. I hurt it when I fell."

"Let me see," he crouched in front of her, massaging her foot, moving it this way and that.

"Ow!" she exclaimed when his ministrations hurt.

"I don't think it's broken, just sprained. Here..." he took his jacket off and tore his shirt sleeve at the shoulder.

"What are you doing? You can't walk around with no sleeve." Her eyes were wide.

He put his jacket back on, and winked. "See, no one will ever know."

"Except your mom." Her voice was harsher than she liked, but she had never been coached on how to act when she had just been saved from certain death by someone who had never seemed to care two snits about her.

"Trust me. She'll understand. Do you have any pencils?"

"Yes," she reached into her bag and pulled them out.

He put the two pencils on either side of her ankle and used his sleeve to wrap it. "There, you should be able to hobble on it to get to the clinic."

She nodded, unsure of what else to say.

John gathered his books and hers then he reached down to help her up. His hand felt warm, a pleasant sensation. But she pulled her hand back as soon as she was on her feet. He worked to steady her, positioning himself on her injured side and serving as a human crutch to get her to the clinic.

It was a short walk, but it took some time to get there with her hobbling along. And she wished away the time. His closeness proved bothersome to her. She was all too glad when they arrived and he settled her in a chair in the waiting room.

The receptionist must have spotted them and summoned her father, as it wasn't long before he rushed into the waiting room.

"Lizzie! Are you well?" His eyes darkened.

"Yes, Father, I fell." She fought fresh tears upon hearing her father's tender voice.

Dr. Thompson got down on one knee in front of her and examined her splinted ankle. "Who wrapped this?"

"I did, sir," John spoke up.

"You did a good job, young man." Dr. Thompson offered John a big smile. "As good as any nurse. And I must commend you on your creative use of supplies."

"Thank you, sir. I also checked for broken bones. I don't think there are any." John's voice was more confident.

Elizabeth's father unwrapped her ankle and began his own examination. "I concur. We'll just need to get you back to an exam room and redress it with proper bandages. Not that the sleeve wasn't a smart wrap in a pinch. How did you injure it, Elizabeth?"

"I tripped on my way home from school," she lied, praying John wouldn't give her away.

John tossed her a look.

"We'll have to be more careful, won't we?" His admonishment held but the tiniest hint of a scold.

"Yes, Father." Elizabeth just wished for this whole ordeal to be over with.

Father lifted her easily into his arms. Turning back to John, he said, "Would you like to come back and watch me wrap the ankle?"

John nodded, eyes wide.

The trio made their way back to the colder exam room where he would see to his patients. Father placed Elizabeth on the examination table, laying her out so he had easy access to her ankle. Turning to gather his supplies, he talked through the nuances of wrapping an ankle with John while he went through the process.

The two were down by Elizabeth's feet and her father's back was turned to her such that she wasn't in the best position to hear him. And as they manipulated her ankle to just the right angle, she busied herself trying not to cry out. She was relieved when it was done and her father helped her sit up again.

"Now, Elizabeth," her father said, turning toward her. "I want you to stay off of that foot as much as possible. Let me get you a crutch to

help you get around. John, would you be so kind as to see Elizabeth home?"

"Of course, sir." John's chest puffed out. He seemed ready to take on any task the doctor requested of him.

In short order, they stood in front of the clinic, crutch in place, and ready to start the long walk home. John moved to start walking and Elizabeth did what she could to keep pace with him.

"Thanks for making those boys leave me alone." Elizabeth broke the silence.

"You're welcome. They're just rabble-rousers, Elizabeth. Don't let them bother you."

She nodded. "You did a good job with my ankle today. How did you know how to do that?"

"I read a lot in my father's books and I listen to him. I want to be a doctor someday."

"I wish I could be a doctor, too." There was an edge of sadness to her voice.

"Maybe someday you can be." He looked over at her. She had never realized how nice his eyes were.

She looked away. "Women can't be doctors, John, that's silly."

"Maybe one day it won't be silly." His voice was serious.

Elizabeth became quiet and thoughtful. When John said it, it didn't sound impossible. If he believed it, maybe she should too. That would be nice.

"What else do you like to do?" She suddenly wanted to learn more about John.

"When I'm not reading medical books, I like to look at the stars." His voice became more timid then, almost as if he were afraid to share.

"Me, too!" Her response caused his eyes to light up. "My father got me a book about constellations. Maybe we can look at them sometime."

"That would be fun." There was that confidence she had come to associate with him. She liked that about him. He wasn't like other boys his age. No, he wasn't interested in pulling pigtails; he was interested in stars and doctor things.

They walked in silence for a little while.

"John?" She decided to break into the silence.

"Yeah?"

"Why weren't you this easy to talk to before?"

"I don't make friends easily. My mom says it's because I'm so focused on becoming a doctor. I'm always reading or listening to my dad or other doctors." His face colored a little as he spoke.

"Well, you don't have to worry about that now, because I'm your friend. And I like all that doctor stuff, too." She offered him a big smile even as she struggled with the crutch.

"You know what?" He returned her smile. "I think we're going to be great friends, Elizabeth."

Everything was still and calm when Jacob's eyes opened again. Looking around him, he caught sight of Melanie. She sat by his cot, in the middle of reading something. He didn't want to disturb her so he lay still, opening and closing his eyes to make sure he truly was awake. Then he moved his hands down to feel his legs. When his right hand grazed the end of this thigh he began to panic.

Small hands landed on his right arm. Melanie's. "Jacob," she said quite loudly. "Jacob, look at me!"

He turned his head toward her, his breathing already heavy and labored.

"You are well. Just breathe with me." She took deep breaths in and out, continuing to encourage him to breathe along with her. Soon, he was able to measure his breaths out with hers and he began to calm.

"My leg..." was all he could say once he had reached a sedate level.

"I know." She pushed errant strands of hair out of his eyes. "I'm sorry. We couldn't do enough. There was an infection we couldn't get to."

"But you said you were doing deep cleanings." He shot at her.

"I was, Jacob. But, there was a problem deeper in your leg that I couldn't get to."

"I don't understand." Why was he being so mean to her? He couldn't seem to control himself.

"I don't either. But that's what the doctor says." Her voice became so quiet, so timid, but he didn't care.

"He's lying. He wanted to take my leg from the start!"

"No, Jacob. He's not lying. No one was more heartbroken than he."

His eyes narrowed into slits. Now he knew she was lying.

"Please, believe me. Everyone did everything they could to save your leg."

He turned away from her, not wanting her to see him cry.

"Jacob, please don't shut me out. Not now." Her voice broke. Was she about to cry? This wasn't about her.

"Just go away. You've done enough."

"Jacob, I..." He heard in her voice that she cried, but he refused to see her tears.

"I said, 'Go away'." And he meant it. Filled with anger toward her. Toward the doctor. Toward every one of them who played a part in this.

So Melanie retracted her hands, and the last he heard of her was the gentle *whoosh* of her skirt as she left his bedside. And part of him regretted sending her away. But the bigger part of him blamed her for all of this. After all, she was supposed to be taking care of him, making sure this didn't happen. Now, here he was, an invalid. For the rest of his life. And it was all her fault.

When Elizabeth opened her eyes, she found herself staring at Matthew. He sat in the same place he had on numerous occasions upon visiting her little space in the hospital. How long had he been there? She tried to shake the sleepy haze from her mind, but everything seemed foggy still.

"Hello," he said, noticing her movements, his voice gentle and soft.

"Hello." She was still a bit asleep.

"How are you?" His brows met in the middle of his forehead.

"Tired." She shifted into a seated position.

"You must be to have slept through all of the evening rounds." His expression became one of amusement.

She jerked up. That wasn't possible. "No! I couldn't have! I have to..." Elizabeth moved to get out of bed and start doing something. What, she didn't know, but she had to do something.

He moved to sit on the edge of her cot, putting a hand on her shoulder to still her. "Slow down. The only thing you have to do is take care of yourself. You were obviously tired. You wear yourself out with your duties here in the hospital. It worries me."

She nodded, knowing he spoke truth. Only then did she notice the bowl in his other hand.

His eyes followed hers. "I brought you some dinner."

"Dinner?" Something wasn't right about that. There was something important about dinnertime.

"Yeah, it's dinnertime. I thought we could..." He started, reaching for the bowl he had set on a nearby table.

"Oh, no!" Her hand flew to her mouth. Now she was in trouble. She had missed an even more important appointment.

"Annabelle, what is it?" She could hear in his voice that his concern deepened.

"I'm supposed to take dinner to the prisoner."

He breathed a sigh of relief. "Someone else is taking care of it, I'm sure. Don't worry yourself so..."

"No, you don't understand. It has to be me. That was the deal." Her eyes met his and she knew they were wide now, all thoughts of sleep having dissipated.

"You made a deal with the prisoner?" Matthew's voice held an edge of anger.

"Yes, he said he would use his skill as a doctor to help the wounded soldiers if I would take him dinner every night."

Matthew scowled.

"It's not exactly a deal with the devil."

Matthew's face tightened. "I don't like it."

"I know," she said, softening her tone. "But I had to do it. And it's fine. Trust me. I just take him dinner and that's all. Besides, he's tied up and there's a guard there. What can go wrong?"

Matthew continued to glare at her with hard eyes, perhaps wagering how safe he thought it was. In the end, he responded by shaking his head and repeating, "I don't like it."

"I know." She hoped her words were sympathetic enough. As she slipped from the bed, Elizabeth grabbed for her shawl. "But I have to go."

"Can I wait here for you to come back?" A muscle in his jaw twitched.

How to get out of this one? She didn't want him waiting here, as she didn't know how long she'd be gone. The last thing she wanted was for him to sit here stewing.

"Can we make a date for tomorrow? To walk to our special place?" They hadn't been there for several days.

He fell silent for a handful of seconds. "Of course," he stood and walked over to her, leaning down to press a kiss to her lips.

This time, though his kiss warmed her, it didn't feel right. Something in her had changed. Was it these memories? She didn't know. Either way, she hoped he wouldn't sense anything different. So she closed her eyes and kissed him back.

When they broke apart, she offered him a smile. "See you tomorrow, then."

"Tomorrow." His features were still dark, and she knew he wasn't happy about her arrangement with the prisoner. But it was done and out of his control. So he could brood all he wanted; it wouldn't change a thing.

Elizabeth pulled away from him and rushed out of the tent. Making her way to the dinner line, she prayed she wasn't too late. But as she neared the service area, she saw that she was. It had closed for the evening. Refusing to give up, she hunted down Sally. The older woman still scrubbed plates in the nearby wash bin.

"What about the prisoner's dinner?" Elizabeth's words rushed out as she approached the woman. Sally's startled reaction made her regret how rude she'd come across, but she was on a mission.

"Suellen volunteered to take it tonight. Been there and back already." Sally turned her attention back to the pot she worked on.

Elizabeth's face fell. What was she going to do? She had to see the prisoner, to make sure he understood and would still do his part. But how was she going to get the guard to let her see him? An idea struck her, and she went back to the hospital to grab some bandages. Relieved to find that Matthew was not still there stewing, she gathered the supplies she needed and headed toward the prisoner's tent.

Sure enough, just as she predicted, she was stopped by the guard.

"I need the doctor to talk me through how to wrap my ankle," she said, hobbling on one foot.

The guard gave her a once over, settling his slitted eyes on her face. It was clear he didn't believe her.

"Would you prefer I wake Dr. Wilson from the first sound sleep he's gotten in three days?"

Without a word, the guard shrugged and lifted the tent flap for her to enter.

Tonight the man lay on a cot, hands bound to a post behind the head end of the cot. At least they let him sleep a little more comfortably. That's what cooperation gets you.

She knelt by the man, who was dozing, and touched his arm. His eyes opened.

"So you didn't forget our arrangement." His voice was not accusing, but kind. Almost relieved.

"No, I overslept." Why did her heart beat a little faster in his presence?

"I'm glad you came." He offered her a tired smile.

"Did you truly wrap my ankle with a couple of pencils and your sleeve?" Her eyes searched his. She was desperate for the truth.

He was quiet for a moment, then his face broke out in a broad smiled. "Yes, yes I did. You remember."

"Bits and pieces. Since you came to camp, I've been having flashbacks and dreams of memories. Or at least what I think are memories." Why did she feel so free to tell this man so much? She should be cautious.

"Ask me anything. I know everything about you, Lizzie." He reached his hand forward as if to touch her face, but he seemed to think better of it, allowing his hand to fall back down.

Elizabeth cleared her throat. "What are my parents' names?"

"Thomas and Abigail Thompson."

"Are they alive?" Her voice broke with emotion.

"Yes." His answer was firm and resolute.

She believed him. "Do they know where I am?" There was no stopping the tear that came down the side of her face.

He paused a second, then spoke with measured words. "I don't think they do, Lizzie."

"What about you? What are you to me?" She wanted to hear him say it. But more than that, she wanted to turn away from those deep brown eyes that stirred things in her.

"I would rather you remember it. It won't mean much to you if I tell you."

"What makes you so sure I will remember?"

"I just know," he said softly. His voice was so tender it tempted her to be drawn into those lips.

Elizabeth stared into his eyes for a moment longer. But she found herself pulling away, shaking her head to clear it moments later.

For Matthew's sake, she could not let this continue. At least not until she had a better handle on who she was. *What would that mean for Matthew?* She pushed that thought to the side. There would be time to worry about that later.

"I'd...better be going now." She stood, moving to leave.

John's gaze followed her face and his body leaned up as if he wanted to follow her. But he soon relaxed back onto the bed as she moved away from his cot and toward the exit of the tent.

Ping-ping.

It had started to rain, and leaving the prisoner's tent, Elizabeth heard the rain against the metal around the camp.

Ping-ping.

And she found herself in the throes of another memory.

Elizabeth's nanny had not long since left the room when she heard a familiar ping-ping *on her window. Slipping out of her bed, she made her way over to the window. Sure enough, there was John, outside and below her bedroom, throwing rocks at her window.*

She opened it. "John, Nanny just left the room. It's too early!"

"C'mon, Lizzie, it's the first night for Cassiopeia."

Elizabeth jerked her head around, looking at the door. "All right, John, but this might be the night we get caught."

She shut her window and got dressed in the outfit discarded not so long ago. Sneaking down the back stairs, she moved toward the door, quietly turned the knob, and ran out of the house.

"John Taylor, you are going to be the end of me," she whispered when she got to him. "My mother's going to find out for sure!"

"Not until we see Cassiopeia." He gave her one of his winning smiles.

"Let's go," she urged him, not wanting to be out one second longer than she had to.

They made their way to the park, to the clearing where they always went. Arriving breathless, they fell on the soft grasses there, laughing. They lay on their backs in the grass gazing up at the stars, pointing out the different constellations they saw, including the famed Cassiopeia.

Their conversation moved on to other things as it always did. Sharing secrets and gossip, they talked about their frustrations and problems, and raved about the good things that happened. After all, they were the best of friends.

"I'm glad we're friends, Lizzie."

"Me too, John. And we'll always be friends, won't we?"

"Always and forever."

"Always and forever," she repeated.

Henry Moore made his way down the street toward his home. Most days, he had a lightness to his step and a whistled tune for his walk to his family's abode. But today he was deep in thought. It had been some time since they had heard from either of their sons, and he didn't like it.

He kept up a brave face for his wife and daughter, encouraging them with words like 'life at camp is busy even if they aren't at battle' and 'Jacob's in the middle of recovering from his injury, give him time to adjust'. But he was worried.

Approaching the house that had been home to his family for many years, he took a moment to collect himself. It just wouldn't do for him to enter the house in a sullen mood. No, he needed to have that lightness to his step they were used to seeing. So, he checked himself and put on a smile he didn't feel.

Stopping to collect the mail, he leafed through, hoping for an envelope bearing Benjamin or Jacob's penmanship. There was nothing of the sort, however there was a letter that appeared it had come from a regiment, but the writing belonged to neither of his sons. This gave him reason to pause.

Until he resolved this matter in his own mind, he wasn't going to be able to put on any kind of front for the women inside. He should open it and read it now. A quick glance around at the busy sidewalk dissuaded him from that idea. It would be best if he could sneak up to his office unnoticed.

Opening the door ever so gently, he grimaced at every squeak it made. The sounds were magnified in his ears, but he knew they weren't truly that loud. No one passed through the foyer. Good. He closed the door with equal care, turning the knob so it wouldn't click. Once he had shut the door, he released the knob so it would latch.

The house seemed quiet enough. In all likelihood, Martha worked on dinner and Susan did her schoolwork. On any other day, he might come in the house and tromp up to his office without a care and not be disturbed, but on this day he wanted to take extra care to not be intercepted.

He paced the few steps that would get him to the stairway and took the stairs as soundlessly as possible. His office was the first door at the top of the steps, thus reducing his chances of alerting Susan to his presence if she was in her room down the hall.

It wasn't long before he found himself in the safety of the office. He let out the breath he had been holding. *I didn't even realize I was doing that.* Dropping his briefcase, he set the mail on the desk long enough to shrug off his jacket. Then he all but collapsed into his chair and sifted through the envelopes to find the one letter that had caused him such trepidation.

There it was. He stared at the writing, hoping, in futility, to gain some clue about the contents without having to read it. Yes, he feared this letter and what message it might hold. After a few moments, he turned the envelope over. Moving his fingers to open the flap, he found that his fingers trembled.

He closed his eyes and tried to calm himself, but it was no use. Opening his eyes again, he was determined to get to the letter and uncover its mystery. Delaying it would serve no purpose. So he ripped open the flap and pulled out the sheet of paper within.

Dear Mr. and Mrs. Moore,

My name is Owen. I regret to inform you that your son, Benjamin, was lost in battle yesterday. He was hit while defending the flank, saving lives. He was an honorable soldier that served his country well and did you proud. He never...

The letter continued, but the words blurred as Henry's eyes filled with tears. His head fell and his hand crumpled the letter as emotions overtook him. Benjamin, his son, was gone. Gone. His dear boy who had been so full of life. And there was nothing Henry could do to bring him back, nothing he could do to make any of this make sense. How was he ever going to tell his wife?

CHAPTER SEVEN
REMEMBERING

The day seemed brighter when Elizabeth opened her eyes. Sunlight streamed into the hospital tent, alerting her to the presence of the welcoming day. Yawning, she stretched as much as she could in the confining cot. It felt good to release the tightness from her muscles and feel the increase of blood flowing to her extremities.

Looking at the underside of the tent top, she thought over her plans for the day. She and Matthew were to spend time together, something she both looked forward to and dreaded at the same time. Would he expect an answer to his proposal? Elizabeth hadn't considered his marriage offer. Her mind had been too clouded from resurfaced memories and the dreams bombarding her since John's arrival.

Where was her heart? It was clear John had been special to her. A fiancé. By choice or by arrangement by their parents? Or was he lying to her about that altogether? She did care deeply for Matthew, even loved him. But dare she commit anything to him when she didn't know what lay in her heart for John?

Rising to a seated position on her cot, she gathered her racing thoughts and went through her short morning routine. And then she was off for her morning rounds. Most of her patients fared well. Even improved. A few still struggled to accept they would have to continue life without some body part. Elizabeth couldn't fault them. How would she handle if she woke up and someone told her she had lost her leg or her eye?

It was all too easy to get caught up with the patients. She spotted Matthew out of the corner of her eye. Hadn't she just started her rounds? Waving at him, she attempted to indicate that she was with her last patient.

He nodded and moved to her little corner of the hospital to wait. Finishing her conversation, she stood and turned in that direction. As she approached Matthew, she noted that he had already taken the liberty of gathering both of their lunch rations.

Standing, he offered his arm. She slid her hand into the crook there. He then led her toward the large tent's opening. Elizabeth caught a glimpse of John off to the right as they passed. There was a dark look in his eyes.

Elizabeth mulled over that and what it might mean as she and Matthew made small talk on their way to the stream. She did feel guilty that even now her focus was split. What could be done about it? John had become a part of her life...that is, John had always been a part of her life, but so was Matthew. It was all rather confusing.

Shaking her head to clear it so she could answer Matthew's questions, she drew a curious look from him. Still, it was difficult to concentrate on him the remainder of their walk.

They arrived at their favorite spot, and Elizabeth sat herself against the trunk of the oak. Placing her rations in her hands, Matthew sat next to her. Maybe a little too close. Why did she feel that way? This was her beau. He had every reason to think it proper to sit so close.

She concentrated on the bread in front of her while Matthew continued speaking of the most recent camp gossip. And Elizabeth made more of an effort to engage with him. It felt good to be in comfortable conversation with him again. As they finished the last bits of their lunch, he reached for her hand.

Lifting it, he kissed her fingertips and then leaned toward her to press a kiss to the side of her face.

Elizabeth closed her eyes and sighed.

"Annabelle, look at me," Matthew's voice was husky and deep.

She turned and looked into Matthew's blue eyes, so much like hers.

Elizabeth chose a light blue dress for her debutante party, one that matched her eyes. Gazing at her gown in the mirror as her maidservant curled her hair for the party, Elizabeth was struck with how well it suited her.

John planned to escort her, of course, but there had been this strangeness between them. Something had changed with him these last couple of weeks and Elizabeth was unsure what exactly it could be. He had become a little...distant.

Was it as her mother said? That he was too old to be her friend anymore? Nanny had always said that friendship can lead to the best marriage, but she and John were not interested in each other like that. Is that what had happened? Was he interested in something more? Elizabeth searched her feelings and found the caring consideration of one best friend for another. Nothing more.

"There, miss, you're all done," her maidservant said as she stepped back from her charge.

Elizabeth examined herself again in the mirror; she looked so much older with her hair up.

Her door swung open and Mother came into the room.

Staring at her mother's reflection in the mirror, Elizabeth marveled at the vision her own mother made. Would she ever measure up to the delicate creature that stood at her door? Would she ever have her mother's mild manners?

"You are perfect, darling."

"Thank you, Mother, I..." She was cut off by the sound of the doorbell ringing.

"Now, who could that be?" her mother mused, a smile gracing her features.

Elizabeth moved across the room to look out her window. John stood below, handsome in his shirt and tails. A servant opened the door to admit him. She stepped away from the window, heart pounding, and took a deep breath. Why was he early? Whatever the reason, there was no sense hiding in her room.

"It's John," she said simply to her mother before moving out of the room and down the stairs to meet him.

Her mother opened her mouth to protest, but was cut off by Elizabeth's rushed exit.

John must have heard her on the stairs, as he looked up to watch her descend.

"Elizabeth," he breathed. "You have never looked more beautiful."

Her face warmed at his intense gaze.

"You're early," she said, raising an eyebrow. A tease.

"Yes, I..." he spotted a passing servant. "Shall we go to the parlor?"

"Of course." She led him to the family's receiving room, hoping that some deep breaths could calm the racing of her heart. As she ushered him into the larger space, she closed the door behind him. They had been alone together many, many times. But never had she felt such trepidation as she did now with him looking at her as he was. She swallowed hard, but met his eyes.

He remained silent for several seconds. But he did find his voice soon enough. "There's something I've been wanting to tell you, and I didn't think the party was the right setting. You see...I..."

Fear filled Elizabeth. She didn't know what she would say if he finished that sentence. "There's something I've been wanting to tell you, too."

"Oh?" He seemed all too glad to let her go first.

"Yes. On this momentous occasion," she exaggerated the word the way her mother always did, smiling. "I've come to think back at how important you are in my life."

He quirked an eyebrow.

"And how important your friendship is to me, and how I hope we

always remain friends and that never changes." Though every nerve ending in her body was firing, she moved to embrace him.

And so she didn't see his face.

"Of course," he finally said, his voice dry and sullen. "Always and forever."

And then someone shook her, "Annabelle!"

She started to come around.

"Annabelle, are you all right? You blanked out." Matthew's voice anchored her to the moment.

"I, um, yes." She pressed a hand to her forehead. "I was trapped in a memory," she said before she could stop herself.

"You're remembering things?" Matthew's voice seemed excited and nervous at the same time.

"Only bits and pieces. Some things are vague, and some don't make much sense to me at all. I'm not truly sure of anything. That's why I haven't told anyone." She wasn't sure she wanted to tell him now. But it was out.

Matthew looked away, hurt. And he had every right to be. He wasn't just anyone. This was the man she professed to love.

"I'm sorry, Matthew." She reached out and cupped his face, turning his eyes to look at her. "I should have told you. But this has all been so confusing for me. I'm not sure of anything anymore."

"Not even sure of us?" The pain was naked on his face.

She wanted to lie, wanted to tell him that nothing had changed between them.

"I'm sure that I love you and that you love me, but..."

"No 'buts.' That's all that you need to know," he interrupted her, taking both of her hands in his. He used them to pull her closer to himself and pressed a kiss to her lips. "This is real."

She nodded, looking down. How could she explain it to him? He couldn't understand. So instead of trying, she leaned in to rest her head on his shoulder and let him hold her and keep all the worries of the world at bay.

Melanie scrubbed the blue cloth. It was her day on laundry duty and she took out her frustration on the dirty uniforms. She had replayed her last visit with Jacob in her mind a million times and could think of so many places where she should have said or done something differently. Yes, she had made a real mess of things. Now, he might never want to speak to her again, and she wouldn't blame him.

"Go easy. You have something against that uniform?" a voice off to her left said.

She looked up. It was Daniel. He stopped just short of the wash bin. Pulling her hands out of the water, she used her arm to wipe the sweat from her forehead. "No, just a little frustrated I suppose."

"Let me guess. Jacob?" He crossed his arms.

"Yeah." She reached for the next uniform.

"I just came from there. Believe me, I think he feels worse." Daniel's eyes were on her face.

She turned her attention back to her task. "But I'm the one who messed up." Melanie struck the uniform with soap and dunked it in the water.

"I'm not so sure he feels that way." His voice was gentle, more so than she would have expected from Jacob's best friend.

She lifted her hand to wipe away the tears that started to form.

"Your hands!" Daniel gasped, coming around the tub. He took her hands in his. "You have scrubbed them raw!" Reaching for clean bandages from the laundry pile, he urged her to follow him. "Come here." He led her to a couple of stools where they sat while he wrapped her red, swollen, bleeding hands.

"But, I have to finish," she protested.

"No, you don't. You need to give those hands a rest. I'll take over." His eyes were intent on her injured hands.

Did he just say he would finish the laundry?

Sure enough, after he finished wrapping her other hand, he pulled off his jacket, rolled up his sleeves, and walked over to the barrel. And started washing the next garment. After a moment, she realized her mouth was agape and she shut it before he looked over at her.

"What exactly happened between you two? If you don't mind my asking." He rubbed the uniform jacket over the washboard at a more reasonable pressure.

"He told me to leave him alone." Her reply was simple, but there was nothing simple about it in her mind.

"I'm sure he didn't mean that." Daniel looked up to meet her eyes.

"I'm quite sure he did," she shot back. Melanie hadn't meant to sound so harsh. It was her pain talking.

"Jacob is still dealing with the shock of having his leg amputated. He probably didn't want you to see him getting over-emotional."

Daniel's words seemed reasonable, but she wasn't ready to accept them. Not yet. The anger from Jacob seemed to fit her too well.

"I doubt that. I've seen him be emotional."

"Don't underestimate the façade a man wants to show the woman he cares about," Daniel said as he walked over to hang the freshly washed jacket.

"The woman he what?"

Daniel jerked his head around, confusion written all over his face.

Did he think she and Jacob were in some kind of relationship?

"Jacob cares for you a great deal, Melanie," he said, grabbing another uniform.

She nodded. It was true that Jacob cared for her as a friend. Surely there was nothing more to it than that. "I don't know why he would feel the need for a façade."

"Pride," Daniel said, shrugging.

"Men and their pride..." she shook her head, letting out a breath.

"Hey, it does a lot for us," he said defensively. "It makes us brave, makes it possible for us to declare our love to that special woman."

She gave him a long look, then smiled. "Do you have some declaring to do to someone?"

"Nope." He gave her a smirk.

"I bet you'd be hard to say no to." Her voice became soft.

His steel blue eyes met hers.

"I think you're about to scrub the color off of that shirt," she said, distracted.

He looked down at what he was doing. "Sorry!" he hung the shirt out to dry and put another in the wash. "Will you go visit him?"

"I will." She paused, not wanting to give in to her fear. "As long as you come with me."

He nodded. "It's a deal, then."

"I have dinner for the prisoner," Elizabeth said, handing the guard his rations.

"Looks like that foot of yours healed up right quick," he observed.

"What can I say? Dr. Taylor has a magic touch."

The guard scowled and took his rations to his post.

When she entered the tent, John was brooding. No longer tied up, he was merely confined to the tent. He must have earned some trust.

"I have your evening rations."

"No soup?" he said shortly.

"We cannot afford that luxury as often as the Union camps, sir," she flashed. "Rations sustain us through most meals here." She turned to leave.

"I didn't mean to insult you. I have appreciated the way I've been treated here...for the most part."

She remembered his beating and flinched. He was being kind.

"I'm just upset about seeing you going off with that man today. Who is he?" His voice was soft.

She half turned. "Someone who has become important to me."

"I see." He looked down at his rations, but she saw the hurt on his face.

His pain stabbed at her heart. Clearly, they were very close. She felt the urge to run into his arms and kiss the pain away. But she held back. Too much was still unknown to her.

"Please tell me," she started, hesitating.

"Anything." His eyebrow lifted, she knew he would answer most any question she asked him. But he had already refused to reveal things about their relationship. Would he now at her behest?

"What happened between us? I only have pieces." She hesitated. Should she trust him whereas she had refused Matthew? Staring into his eyes, her heart whispered that she should. "I have many of my memories back. I remember the debutante ball...and how I..." She paused. "What happened after I pushed you away?"

He smiled. "I pushed you back."

"What?" That confused her. What could he mean?

"Do you remember Diana?"

She rolled the name around in her mind. "Diana? No..."

John's expression was hard to read. His eyes were bright but his mouth became a thin line. "Think on that. I'm sure once you have it, you will have the rest."

An odd silence fell between them. Elizabeth found it difficult to pull away from his gaze, but she did so and took her leave of him.

Minutes later, she was in her bed, tossing and turning...Diana, Diana, Diana. There was a girl she vaguely remembered from her schooling days named Diana. She focused on the hazy memory of this girl, and a face came into focus. Diana had dark, almost black, hair, ivory skin, and deep brown eyes. Then, as a fitful sleep overcame her, Elizabeth remembered that Diana had always been her biggest rival in school for everything – grades, boys, parts in plays, everything. Why was Diana so important?

Then, as she drifted in sleep, it all became clear...

John invited Diana to the Christmas Dance. Diana! Imagine! He knew how Diana got under Elizabeth's skin. Of all the girls in Boston, why did he have to pick her? The girl was pretty. Does he care about Diana? *Elizabeth wondered. As deeply as he cared for her? Perhaps more so.* What will happen? Will he continue to see Diana and eventually marry her and have children? If so, *Elizabeth had thought, tearing up,* that will be just fine. *But she couldn't help the tears that started to gather and fall down her face. Why couldn't she stop this well of emotion? What was she going to do?*

The maidservant did what she could to prepare Elizabeth for the ball, but nothing could be done to disguise an afternoon of crying. Her eyes were quite puffy. Elizabeth leaned her head against the vanity and considered not going. She didn't want John to see her like this. Neither did she wish to stay home and not see how he and Diana were together. Nor was she sure that she wanted to see them together. Her stomach twisted in knots and she wasn't sure of anything. Mother made the decision that she should go for the sake of the host, Mr. Fields, who had so graciously invited them all to the ball. So, she was resigned to her fate.

The carriage ride to the Fields' home was uneventful. Elizabeth, for her part, kept her eyes drawn out the window as her parents chattered on about things of little importance to her.

"Elizabeth, you are rather quiet this evening. Is anything the matter?"

Elizabeth turned her attention to her father, letting the curtain on the window fall into place. "Not at all, Father," she fibbed. "Just enjoying the shine of the street lamps on the wet pavement." Well, it was a half-truth at least.

"Ah. Why isn't young Mr. Taylor accompanying us this evening?" He leaned toward his daughter.

Mother shot him a look that he caught a little too late.

"He is escorting Diana Balleu to the ball."

Elizabeth tried to hide her disappointment, but knew her parents would see through any façade she put up.

"Is that so?" her father's eyebrows went up.

The carriage ride continued in silence, her mother shooting Father dark looks, and Elizabeth with her stomach all knotted from the prospect of seeing John with Diana.

"We have arrived!" her father announced a little too happily as their carriage turned the last corner and the Fields' residence came into view. Moments later the carriage slowed.

Father exited the carriage first, then helped first Mother, then Elizabeth down, careful of the wet steps. They were then hastened into the house lest the drizzle of wintery mix threaten their gowns and hair. As they stepped into the foyer, their wraps were taken. Mr. and Mrs. Fields were just beyond the foyer to greet their guests.

"How good of you to come Dr. Thompson, Abigail, Elizabeth! What horrid weather for a ball!"

"Nonsense. As long as it is dry and warm in here, who cares what's going on outside?" Father asserted.

Elizabeth, for her part, found it very fitting that it should be so dreary this evening. For that's exactly how she felt—dreary.

"Please do come in and enjoy some refreshments," Mrs. Fields said as Elizabeth strained to see into the rooms beyond.

"I happen to know of some eligible young men who hope to see Miss Elizabeth this evening for a waltz," Mr. Fields commented, bringing a slight blush to Elizabeth's face.

She was all too happy when the pleasantries were over and they could move further into the house. Although she wasn't sure if she wished to find John or a place to avoid him. Unable to settle, she decided to get some punch. No sooner had she reached the concession table then she felt a tap on her shoulder.

She turned. It was John, but Diana was nowhere in sight.

A smile was on his face, but it fell when he noticed her puffy eyes. "Lizzie, are you well?"

She brushed his question off. "Where is your date?" she asked.

"Sitting down," he indicated where she sat, reserving a seat for him. "I'm coming after punch for the two of us, but I wanted to see you and put my name on your dance card first."

Elizabeth held it away from him. "I'm sorry. It's full," she lied.

"Full? Even the last waltz?" His face darkened.

"Yes." She wanted him to hurt the way she did. It was wrong, but she couldn't stop herself.

"But we always dance the last waltz together." He made no attempt to disguise his hurt.

She felt awful, but it didn't keep her from her own anger. "We also always go to dances together. Things change." She whirled around and walked away.

This time she knew where she was headed, straight for her father. Her parents had engaged the Taylors in conversation. Elizabeth wanted to roll her eyes. As if they don't spend enough time together as it is! But she knew it was only because of her anger with John that she felt that way. She approached the group, smiling.

"Hello, Dr. Taylor, Mrs. Taylor."

"Hello, Elizabeth. You're looking well," Mrs. Taylor replied.

"Looks are deceiving, Mrs. Taylor. It is this very reason I have sought out my father. I fear I have developed a headache and would like to return home."

He gazed at her, his eyes clouded with doubt.

She glanced past the Taylors and caught a glimpse of John and Diana conversing over punch, laughing together, enjoying each other's company, and a wave of nausea overcame her.

"My goodness, you do look ill," her mother said.

"We should see you home straight away," her father decided. "If you will excuse us," he said to the Taylors.

"I do not wish to spoil your evening nor steal you from such fine company. After all, I can make it home well enough in the carriage and have it sent back for you to return home at your convenience."

"Are you sure, dear? I'm not so certain we shouldn't go with you." Her mother's face twisted in concern.

"I'm sure, Mother," she confirmed. "Nanny will care for me once I get home." She was old enough to no longer need the services of their aging Nanny, but they kept her employed for Andrew's sake.

Her mother's features relaxed with that assurance.

"I'll walk you out," her father said.

She took her father's arm and allowed him lead her through collecting her wrap, saying her farewells to the host and hostess, and being loaded into the carriage.

"Now, in my medicine bag..." he began as she settled into the carriage.

"I know where to find what I need, Father. Thank you."

He smiled and patted her hand. "Feel better, darling."

The carriage ride home seemed to take forever as she was left alone with her thoughts of John and Diana. Once she arrived, she checked in on Andrew and the already sleeping Nanny then tucked herself into her own bed.

But it was no better. She tossed and turned, struggling to remain calm about what might be happening between John and Diana.

Even after she heard her parents arrive, sleep escaped her. For their sakes, she pretended to be asleep when her father came to check on her. And she waited until she heard them retire to their room before she slipped from her bed.

What could be the matter? Elizabeth had to admit that one thing disturbing her was what she felt for John. Had she been wrong this whole time? It took this whole thing with Diana for her to see that she cared for him. And not just as a friend, but far more deeply? She wanted to be the only one on his arm at a ball, or in his arms anywhere. Just the thought of his lips touching Diana's to kiss her goodnight drove Elizabeth to the edge to madness. This was unbearable!

I must go to him...tonight. She had to make it right. At least she had to apologize for lying to him, for hurting him. But she also needed to tell him what she was feeling. Even if he had long ago moved beyond any deeper feelings for her, she had to try.

Putting on one of her simpler dresses, she made her way down the stairs as she had so many times before, sneaking out to meet John, something they hadn't done in many years. She slipped out the door and couldn't help but run all the way to his house. Grabbing some sticks and pebbles, she started tossing them up against his window. Nothing. No light, no sign of life.

Was he still out with Diana? Walking her home? Walking to the park with her? Kissing her? The knot tightened in Elizabeth's stomach. Or was he just so mad at her, he refused to speak to her? Either way, Elizabeth wrapped her shawl tighter around herself and headed home, dejected.

As she rounded the last corner toward her home, she heard a ping-ping-ping. *Her eyes moved toward the spot below her bedroom window.*

There he was.

John stood at her window, throwing pebbles. She could scarcely believe it!

He whirled around.

"Elizabeth," he rushed to her, putting his hands on her arms. "You can't be out wandering the streets this late at night by yourself."

"We did it all the time as kids," she said defensively.

"That's when we were young and didn't know better. It's not safe for you to be out like this. If anything happened to you, I don't know what I'd do."

There was silence between them for a few moments.

"What are you doing here?" she asked as if he was the one being odd.

"I came to see if you were all right." His eyes were intense on hers; her knees became weak.

"I am well," she said, looking away. Why was she acting this way? Hadn't she just gone to find him to profess her feelings for him?

"No, you're not. Don't shut me out, Elizabeth. Tell me what's wrong."

He rarely used her full name. How to begin? What to say? *She didn't know. So instead, she blurted out, "Do you love her?"*

"Who?" His reply was short, sharp. As if he didn't know.

"Diana." Elizabeth almost couldn't get the word out, she was so charged with emotion.

He studied her face for a moment before answering her. "No."

"Good." She met his eyes then. And couldn't help the relief that washed over her.

"Is that what has you so upset? Diana? It was just one ball."

Elizabeth turned her face away from him, embarrassed.

"Besides," he said, using his fingertips to turn her face toward him.

"How can I be in love with anyone else? When I am completely, hopelessly in love with my best friend."

"Truly?" her voice laid bare the emotions swirling inside her.

"Truly." His gaze seemed to search into her soul. Then he leaned forward and captured her lips with his. The kiss was soft and sweet at first, but soon he pressed deeper.

When they broke apart, he leaned his forehead against hers.

"I love you, too," she said, breathless, as tears fell down her face.

"Always and forever?" He smiled with a little laugh.

"Always and forever." She smiled back.

Elizabeth bolted awake to find a concerned John by her bedside.

"What are you...how did you...?" Her mind whirled, full of questions.

"You've been calling for me for the last hour. No one could rouse you." Leaning over her, he pushed her hair off her forehead. A layer of sweat covered her.

Reaching for a cloth in the bowl of water near her bed, he began patting her face with it. This wasn't the task of a doctor, but of a nurse. He shouldn't be taking his time to see to her menial needs.

"I was so worried about you, Lizzie," he whispered, his eyes searching hers.

"John," she whispered back, "I remember. I remember everything."

He smiled down at her, and his eyes glistened with emotion.

"What are we going to do?" she mouthed.

"I don't know," he whispered back. "All that matters, Lizzie, is that we're together."

And what did Elizabeth have to fear? These were her friends. Would they turn on her now that her memory was back and she discovered she was from the other side of the war? She needed to realize this was a very real possibility.

John continued to stroke her hair and gaze upon her.

"I love you," she mouthed to him.

"Always and forever?" he whispered.

She nodded. "Always and forever."

Matthew had found himself in the hospital tent minutes before. Seeing Annabelle in distress, he knelt by her side.

"Annabelle," he laid a gentle hand on her shoulder. Should he attempt to wake her?

She groaned and turned her head away from him, muttering something in her sleep. His Pa had always said never to wake his sister who was known to wander the house in all manner of states in the middle of the night. Perhaps it wasn't wise to stir Annabelle now.

Still, he leaned in closer, breathing her name, "Annabelle."

Continuing to move in sleep, her mumbles became more audible. He hated watching her in such fits. Should he fetch the doctor? If she would just turn toward him again, he might be able to discern what she said.

In that moment, she blurted out a name. "John!"

His heart froze and he jerked his hands away from her. Who was this man? What was he to her? Some ghost from her past?

Determination filled him. He pressed his hand against her shoulder again, this time attempting to rouse her.

"Annabelle." If only she would give some indication that she heard him. That she knew he was there.

"John," she murmured in her fitful sleep. She cried out for this person.

And Matthew's heart ached.

Then he became aware that they were not alone. Yes, they were in the hospital surrounded by caregivers and patients, but it was more than that. Someone watched them. He gazed across the space. Everyone seemed intent on his or her work. Then he knew. Jerking around, he saw the prisoner. The man looked on, but not at Matthew, at Annabelle.

Matthew rose, placing himself between the prisoner and Annabelle.

The man's eyes drifted toward Matthew's. There was sadness in them. Almost as if he knew Annabelle. She had been taking him dinner. Perhaps he felt sorry for her fitful state.

Matthew cleared his throat. "You're a doctor, right?"

The prisoner nodded.

"Can you help her?"

As the man's eyes fell back on Annabelle's form, Matthew stepped out of the way. Should he be more cautious? Who was this man after all? Would he hurt Annabelle?

"I can try," was all the man said.

"Please." Matthew had to let him try. He allowed the Union soldier to pass by him and crouch by Annabelle's bed. But he stayed nearby, only a few feet away, watching carefully as the man examined her.

Suddenly she jerked awake. Matthew started to step forward, but stopped as the prisoner moved his hands over her hair in what could only be described as a caress. What was happening here?

And so he watched much of the exchange between them. His heart sinking as Annabelle not only accepted his attentions, but also returned them. While he couldn't hear what was said between them, he didn't have to. Their interaction said enough. At last, he couldn't watch any longer. He turned and left the hospital tent, crestfallen.

The time had come for her appointed visit with Jacob. Melanie had delayed for long enough and had run out of excuses. Rather, Daniel had stopped accepting them. They arranged to meet after lunch to walk to the hospital together. She had finished cleaning from the meal when she spotted Daniel approaching.

"Are you ready?" His gaze was soft upon her.

Still, Melanie's last interaction with Jacob flashed across her mind. "No."

It was an honest answer. She was fearful Jacob would take one look at her and order her to leave his presence again. No matter how much Daniel assured her that would not be the case.

Daniel lowered the angle of his face. She knew how he felt about her trepidation toward this meeting. And how determined he was.

"I can't shake this strange feeling," she said, putting her hands on her stomach. "I just know he's still cross with me. That he still blames me."

"Then we'll have to help him see differently." Daniel reached for her hand. "I'll be right there."

Sliding her hand into his, she allowed herself to sigh with the comfort, no matter how small, that brought her. Daniel was right. It was time. She had avoided Jacob for long enough and it wasn't fair to him. He truly did need his friends right now.

Daniel tugged at her, encouraging her to come from behind the dish bin.

She obeyed.

Then she allowed him to lead her through the camp toward the hospital. Neither released the other's hand as they walked. Nor did they speak again until they approached the large tent.

Daniel held up a hand for Melanie to go on in front of him.

She gave him a long look, pleading with him to not make her do this.

His eyes glistened. He was sympathetic, she knew, but his hand extending toward the interior of the tent told her that he was resolved.

Melanie stepped into the hospital, Daniel close behind her, and moved in the direction of Jacob's bed.

Jacob sat, eating his lunch. He looked toward her as she approached, setting his lunch to the side and shifting to sit a little straighter.

Once she reached her usual spot by his bed, she looked back to see that Daniel was no longer with her. He had stopped a few feet short of the bed. Close enough to offer support, but far enough to give her space and privacy.

Jacob swallowed hard. Was he trying to come up with the right words? Did he struggle the same as she?

Melanie remained silent.

"How've you been?" Jacob finally managed.

"I've been well." She didn't know what else to say.

A silence fell between them again.

"Melanie, I'm...so sorry...for the way I acted before. I was...I was a..."

She shook her head. "You were dealing with a lot."

He nodded. "I didn't mean to blame you." His voice was not much more than a whisper.

"Thank you." She took a seat next to his bed. "I was afraid you never wanted to see me again."

He lowered his head. "I know my words must have hurt you."

She nodded, a tear escaping. "I blamed myself. I wondered if only I could have done more, done better..."

He reached out and put a hand on hers. "There's nothing you could have done. I'm at peace with that. I want you to be, too."

"Maybe someday I will be."

He released her hand. "I hope so."

Elizabeth found Matthew by the stream. He sat on the hillside, plucking blades of grass, rubbing them between his fingers then discarding them. She watched him for a few moments. From all appearances, he was deep in thought. After some time, she decided to disturb his solitude and came closer, placing a hand on his shoulder.

Jerking at her touch, he turned. Seeing Elizabeth, he gave her a half smile, but his eyes were sad.

She sat beside him, shoulder to shoulder. He moved to scoot away. The movement was slight, but enough for her to notice.

"What's the matter?" This conversation had plagued her enough without more trouble being heaped onto it.

At first he didn't respond, looking away.

She laid a hand on his arm. "Talk to me."

He did look at her then, his eyes hard as steel. "I saw you with him in the hospital."

"Oh," she let her hand fall.

His eyes fixed on the ground again and he dropped the grass he had in his hands.

"I can explain." How much she dreaded this talk they would have to have. But have it they must. "I want to explain."

He didn't respond, simply looked toward the stream. Did he even want to hear it?

She moved her legs so that she sat cross-legged, her hands folded in her lap. How she had thought this would go, she wasn't sure, but jumping straight into it wasn't her plan. Perhaps it was for the best. "I have my memories back."

"And so what? Now it's just Union soldiers for you?" His jab was harsh and it hit its mark.

"No." She tried to keep her voice neutral. His comment stung. "It's just that Union soldier. He is my fiancé."

Matthew turned to look at her, eyes wide.

She understood. The odds were astronomically against it. The captured doctor returned to their unit to assist them would be the fiancé of the woman they had captured by accident. Elizabeth allowed several moments for him to process this information.

"It doesn't change what's happened between us," she said, hoping he believed her. Because what she felt for him was real. And what had happened between them mattered to her.

"Then why did I witness that reunion?" he challenged her.

"Because it does change where we go from here," she said sadly.

"I don't accept that. If you love me and I love you, why can't we be together?" He shifted to face her, reaching for her hands.

"It's not that simple, Matthew." She pulled her hands away. "Don't you think I wish it was?"

"I don't know what you wish."

She closed her eyes and fought tears at the harshness of his voice.

"There's more going on here than just the two of us," Elizabeth said, almost unable to force the words out. This was harder than she'd thought it would be.

"Only because you choose to let it be complicated."

"No, Matthew, it *is* complicated. There are more people involved. What I have with John is deep. We have a long history together."

"So, it's all about how long you've known each other. I lose out because of time."

Why did he have to make this so much harder? She knew the answer to her own question. Because his heart was involved.

"It's more than that. Love alone cannot survive when two people are standing on opposing principles. You and I don't see eye-to-eye on this war for one thing."

Matthew met her eyes then. "Be mindful, Elizabeth, what you say is treacherous. You have certain freedoms in a Confederate camp that perhaps you should no longer be afforded."

"Matthew, what are you saying?"

He stood.

"Matthew?"

Without anything further, he walked off.

What action might he take? How hurt was he? He seemed quite angry by what had happened between them. And she had not done a good job of communicating her thoughts and feelings. Would he go to the colonel? Would he do something to John? Nothing was certain.

One thing she did know—she had to get herself and John out of camp. How was she to accomplish this? Trying to clear her mind to think, she knew there would be enough obstacles without the added problems presented by whatever Matthew might do. But she couldn't afford to make guesses about that. No, she had to form a plan for John's escape. Now.

To get him out safely, they would have to subdue his guard and sneak out of the camp. Everything else they could worry about later. Timing was everything. By now, most of the soldiers were enjoying their evening rations and each other's company. So, once they passed the obstacle of the soldier guarding John, they would have little trouble fleeing the camp. She hoped. But she had never moved through camp at that hour thinking about how many soldiers she did or did not pass.

Elizabeth walked back to camp, uneasy as she entered the familiar grounds. As she passed people she knew, she exchanged nervous smiles, unaware of what they may or may not know. She became suspicious of everyone. The soldiers were making their way to where dinner rations were distributed.

Slipping back into the hospital, Elizabeth gathered what few personal possessions she acquired during her stay. She fought back tears as nearly all of them made her think of Matthew. Sneaking over to the laundry, she grabbed a confederate uniform that she prayed would fit John. Then she made her way to the prisoner's tent.

The guard stopped her upon approach, but she was ready with her story.

"The nurses have decided that the prisoner's uniform is no longer sanitary. It needs to be washed. But, I doubt that Union blue will come back from the laundry in one piece," she said with a smirk.

As usual, he showed little emotion, just shot her a skeptical look. That must be his job—to intimidate everyone. Evidently, it wasn't his job to determine how crazy the story sounded, because he let her pass.

Once in the tent, John rushed to her, gathered her in his arms, and kissed her the way she wanted him to in the hospital.

She responded, wrapping her arms around him and pulling him closer.

When they pulled apart, her head spun, dizzy from him.

"We have to leave at once!" she managed as she returned to her senses.

"We what?" he whispered.

"I told Matthew everything and it didn't go well. I don't know what he's going to do. I fear he might turn me in."

He nodded. "Then we must leave tonight."

She held up the Confederate uniform. "For you."

He took it from her and began unbuttoning his Union jacket.

She turned her back to him.

"I can't say that I ever thought I'd be happy to put on a Confederate uniform," John said as he pulled on the jacket.

Elizabeth laughed a little. "Desperate times..."

There was a rustle of clothing behind her and she imagined he was exchanging the pants of his uniform for the Confederate pants.

"All things considered, I'm at least glad to have some clean clothes."

"That uniform must have been through a lot," she mused. But it wasn't the uniform she thought of. She imagined what John endured since his capture. One day she would ask him, but now was not the time.

A tap on her shoulder interrupted her thoughts. She turned to see John, now clad in Confederate gray. She smiled, giving him the once over.

Both of their heads jerked toward the tent entrance as they heard muffled voices just outside.

Elizabeth was gripped with fear. They might have been able to take out one guard, but if there were more than one soldier out there, they were pretty much stuck. Had someone come to collect her?

The voices conversed. But try as she might, Elizabeth could not discern what was said.

Then a scuffle broke out. Elizabeth reached for John as he pulled her into his arms. After several seconds, everything was quiet. John maneuvered his body between Elizabeth and the opening, but she refused to be moved. She wanted to be by his side. They would face their destiny together.

Matthew burst into the tent.

What was his plan? Why had he subdued the guard?

A low grumble escaped from John's throat.

"What are you waiting for? Let's go!" Matthew held the tent flap open.

Elizabeth and John exchanged a look. But they didn't have the luxury of questioning whether or not they trusted Matthew, this was their chance. So they followed him. John moved first, keeping a hand on Elizabeth, drawing her closely behind himself. Would there be a company of soldiers with guns pointed at them?

Once they were outside, nothing but darkness greeted them. And the sight of the guard incapacitated on the ground.

Elizabeth looked over to meet Matthew's eyes, but his attention was focused elsewhere, checking the immediate area for any sign of movement. When he did turn back toward John and Elizabeth, it was to crouch down and grab the guard's weapon.

"Here," he said, handing it to John. "You know how to handle a weapon?"

John nodded. He must have received at least some rudimentary training along the way.

Elizabeth saw the glint of metal off Matthew's own gun shining in the moonlight as he moved around the side of the tent.

"This way." Matthew motioned for them to follow.

John indicated for Elizabeth to follow Matthew and that he would take up the rear. Moving through the camp without making a sound, they stayed close to the tents. Matthew maneuvered in such a way as to keep them away from any activity. It was a miracle, but they neared the edge of camp and had not been noticed.

A scream pierced the night, yelling that the prisoner had escaped.

Elizabeth's heart raced. What were they to do now? Could they outrun a group of armed soldiers? They needed a distraction.

"Run," Matthew told them. "Run for the trees." He pointed northwest. What was he planning to do?

"Come with us, Matthew," Elizabeth begged. How could he not come with them?

"I can't. Don't worry about me, Annabelle, I'll be fine."

She took a moment to embrace him. "I do love you, Matthew. Don't ever forget that." She pressed a quick kiss to his lips.

All too soon it was over and they parted ways. John pulled at her arm, urging her toward the tree line and Matthew ran in the opposite direction toward the stream. She knew she would never see him again.

CHAPTER EIGHT

VOWS

After a night of running, John began to tire. And Elizabeth started to slow. He did what he could to find places for them to stop and hide along the way to catch their breath. But they shouldn't try for long. The soldiers would catch them.

Neither of them were outdoorsmen however, and he worried if they were, in fact, moving in the right direction. Then the sun rose on the wrong side of the sky. John hung his head. They had been running farther south most of the night.

He turned toward Elizabeth, who leaned against a tree trunk, bent over with a hand on her stomach.

"I am so sorry!"

Elizabeth looked up at the coming dawn. But to her credit, she did not dismay. Rather she stepped over to him and placed a hand on his shoulder. "You didn't know. Besides, it may have saved our lives. I doubt those Confederate soldiers would have been looking for us farther south."

He smiled, warmth spreading through his chest. "That's one of the many things I love about you, Lizzie. You're always able to see the bright side." Leaning forward, he kissed the tip of her nose.

She returned his smile.

"But we'd better head north, now that we know." John motioned in that direction.

"I don't mean to complain," Elizabeth said, tugging on his arm. "But I don't think I can go much further without some rest and water."

Her eyes reflected how tired he felt. "Let's find a place to bed down for a little while."

They moved around the forest until he spotted a clearing that was suitably well-shaded. John sat on the grass, laying his gun on the ground. He must keep it no more than an arm's length away.

Bidding Elizabeth come toward him, he indicated the ground next to him. She sat beside him. But instead of stretching out, she caught his eyes. Why was she not lying down?

"Go ahead." He waved his hand. "I'll keep watch."

"You need rest as much as I do."

He lost himself in her eyes for a moment. How he had missed her! Reaching a hand across the space between them, he grazed the side of her face.

"I'll be all right. You rest."

"There cannot be such danger here that you cannot take a moment to sleep."

Her concern touched him. "All the same, I will keep watch. We cannot be too careful."

She closed her eyes and nodded, then stretched out beside him, giving him her back.

All was silent for several moments. Had she gone to sleep?

Then she stirred. Propping herself up on her elbow, she leaned back so that she could look at him over her shoulder.

"Something troubles you?"

"The ground is not the most comfortable surface."

"Says the woman who made a campsite her home." He smiled and looked down at his clasped hands. She was quite the little manipulator. When he glanced toward her again, she had the most innocent, pleading expression on her face. "All right. But only until you fall asleep."

John maneuvered his body so that he lay beside her, but on his back. She turned and snuggled up against his side, her head on his shoulder. Her silken hair against his jaw, her warm breath on his neck, it was enough to drive a man crazy. Wrapping a protective arm around her, he pulled her closer. But he dare not move any more.

No sooner had they stilled than he heard the pattern of Elizabeth's breathing alter. There was little doubt that she was deep in sleep.

There had not been much brightness or laughter in the Moore home since the last missive came concerning Benjamin. Henry's step picked up when he saw a letter in Jacob's handwriting. It had been too long since they'd heard from their younger son. They had begun to fear the worst. Martha could not handle any more bad news. So a sign of life from Jacob would be something that might perk up their spirits and give them hope.

Henry entered the solemn house and set his jacket and hat on the coat rack. He moved toward the parlor where he found his wife sewing and his daughter drawing. Ever since the news had come, Martha wanted Susan with her whenever possible. It seemed as if she were fearful to be alone.

"I have a letter from Jacob," he said, poking his head into their space.

Martha's head jerked up.

"Jacob! Oh, Father, do read it now," Susan pleaded. "I don't think I can wait until after dinner."

Martha's eyes begged the same.

"All right, darling." It was directed to his daughter, but said more for his wife. "But just this once."

He sat in his chair and Susan curled by his feet, but Martha stayed where she was.

"Dear Mother, Father, and Susan,

"I am sorry I haven't written for so long. There is no excuse for my delay in writing you other than my inability to come up the words. As you know, I was injured in battle. It is my left leg and the doctors and nurses have tried very hard to do what they can for me. There is a young woman here named Melanie who spends time with me every day cleaning my wound and keeping me company. I could not find the right way to tell you without worrying you. But I now have to tell you that they were not able to save my leg."

Henry paused and Martha gasped.

"What does that mean, Father?" Susan's eyes were wide.

He ignored her and continued reading. "Please do not be upset. I have come to be at peace with it. You should be glad to know it means I won't be fighting anymore and will be sent home soon. And I am eager to be home. War was not what I had expected and I cannot say I will remember my time here well. Except for the people I met. I miss you all, I miss home, and I look forward to being with you soon. Love, Jacob P.S. Thank you for the package. You don't know what it has meant to me. Both the treats and your letters.'"

Henry and his wife exchanged a look. Martha wiped away tears with her handkerchief. There was nothing he could say to make her feel any better. So he remained silent.

"Father, what's wrong with Jacob? Is he coming home?" Susan's questions came at him.

He did not want to answer her, but he couldn't put his daughter off. She needed answers. At least the best answers he could give her.

"Yes, dearest, he's coming home soon. Do you remember when I said he would be different when he came home?"

She nodded.

"Well, one way he is going to be different is that he won't have part of his leg anymore." He choked on the last words and tried to cover it up with a cough.

"What happened to it?" Her questions were so innocent. If only he could protect her from the hard things of this world. But life had dealt them a hard blow. Twice.

"There was an accident." His eyes moved from Susan's face to Martha's. She watched him, but continued to dab at her tears that now flowed freely.

"What kind of accident?"

"That's not important." He was determined that he would shield her from what atrocities he could. "What's important is that we love him just the same, right?"

"Of course, Father." Susan's words were confident, as if there was never a question about her love for her brother.

It brought a smile to his face. "Good. Because he needs to know we love him now more than ever."

Elizabeth awoke to the sound of birds chirping high above her. A glance skyward told her it was mid-day. Eyes turning toward John, she found him watching her. How long had he been awake? Had he been waiting on her? Letting her get as much rest as she needed? She sat up, looking down at him to thank him for his kindness. The grimace on his face gave her pause.

"What is it?"

"My arm." He sat up, rubbing the offended limb. "It was asleep and now there is blood flowing back into it. Not the most pleasant feeling."

"I'm sorry." Guilt stabbed at her. He didn't have to let her sleep so long.

"Don't be. I enjoyed our little nap." He reached over and cupped her face, drawing it closer to his for a gentle kiss. "Before we get started, I think we need to find some food and water."

Elizabeth nodded, her stomach rumbling at the mention of food.

"While you were sleeping, I heard the sounds of a stream coming from that direction." John indicated what Elizabeth guessed to be west.

Standing, Elizabeth stretched. Turning to help John up, she found him halfway to his feet, moving his arm around in its socket. He then reached for her hand and they made their way to the stream. Along the way, they took advantage of the berries and nuts they found to eat. It was not enough to fill their stomachs, but enough to sustain them.

At the water's edge, they drank their fill. Elizabeth wished they had something to gather water in so they could carry some along.

"I think we should follow the stream. As far as I can determine, this is north." He pointed upstream.

It was a sound plan.

"Ready?" He stood, having slaked his thirst. Holding out a hand to help her up, he seemed eager to press on.

She grabbed his hand and allowed him to pull her to her feet. "As ready as I can be."

He led the way along the stream's bank, and she fell into step beside him. They walked in silence for quite a while, concentrating on where their feet fell.

John broke the silence after some time. "How did you come to be at that camp?"

Elizabeth didn't want to answer, but she had to tell him the truth sometime. "I, um, I was captured from your camp."

"What?" John stopped.

"Yes, I hid from you as a sanitary assistant at your camp," Elizabeth said. Her face warmed. As much as she wanted to hide from him, she turned to face him, having moved a couple of steps ahead of him.

"But how?"

"I sneaked out of my parents' house the night you left and paid for passage on your train." She looked away. Why was this so hard to share with him?

"Elizabeth, you shouldn't have done that." John's eyes were dark.

She was uncomfortable with this side of him. Always had been. It was obvious he wasn't pleased with her.

"I had to sneak around and hide because I knew that's how you would feel. That's how my parents would feel. And maybe you're right." She let out a ragged breath.

"But why would you do such a thing?" His voice demanded an answer. Something she was all too ready to supply. It was time she was able to speak her peace.

"How can you ask me that? I did it because I love you! I couldn't stand being away from you, not knowing what might happen to you."

John stared at her, perhaps moved by her words, but still unconvinced.

"I knew the risk I took. Even the chance that you wouldn't understand. But I did what I had to. Can't you try to understand?"

He remained quiet for several seconds. She let him digest her words. When he finally spoke, it was to ask another question.

"How is it that you were captured?" He stepped toward her, closing the gap between them. His voice was softer, but she knew he had to know all of it.

She wanted to look away, to not see his reaction as she spoke, but she couldn't pull her eyes away from his. "It was the day of that first battle. When I found that you had gone to the front lines, I went looking for you. And I attempted to rescue a wounded soldier. I was mistaken for a soldier and shot and captured. Apparently I hit my head and lost my memory. For whatever reason, they had mercy on me." She didn't know why she didn't tell him that it was Matthew she had saved on the battlefield.

He nodded. His features still set and dark.

But she marveled again at the story. The fact that the Confederates had any consideration for her was truly astonishing. God's hand had been with her.

The lines on his face softened. "Whatever happened to you,

you're here with me now." He took her face in his hands. "And you're safe." He pressed a kiss to her lips.

She wrapped her arms around his midsection and relished the feeling of being with him again.

As they parted, John motioned for them to continue walking, hand in hand.

"What about you? What happened to you that day?" She needed to know, too.

He attempted to shrug it off. "When they captured me, I was sent away for interrogation. They tried to collect what information they could, which was nothing. I didn't know anything. Then they sent me back to the front lines to get some use of my skills as a physician."

She nodded. It was astounding that they had been separated and brought back together. How long would it have taken her to recover her memories, if ever, had he not come back to her?

Silence fell over them again.

Elizabeth spoke into the stillness. "Did you mean what you said that first day you came to camp?"

"What do you mean?" His brows came together.

"You said that you regretted not marrying me when you had the chance."

John nodded once. "Yes, I meant it and I still do." He paused. "Why?"

Elizabeth chose her words carefully. "It's just that, with all that's happened, I can't imagine going back to life as it was."

"No?" His voice was difficult to decipher. What was he thinking?

She continued anyway. "No. And one thing I can't imagine is being separated from you ever again."

He stopped walking. This caused her to stop and look back at him, curious after his thoughts.

"Then let's do it." There was no reservation in him.

"Do what?"

"Let's get married." He shifted his body to face her.

"What? Here?" She dropped his hand.

"Yes, right here."

"You're crazy." Stifling a laugh, she quirked an eyebrow at his ridiculous notion.

"Maybe I am, but I want to pledge my life to you." He took both of her hands in his.

She looked at him, weighing his words.

"I'll still promise you a church wedding, but let's share our hearts here and now."

"Like exchange vows?" She was becoming more perplexed by his suggestion.

"Exactly."

Turning his head this way and that, she followed his gaze to a grouping of wildflowers nearby. Holding up his index finger, he moved away from her and gathered a small bouquet's worth and brought them to her. She inhaled their fragrance, smiling at him. Then he reached for her hands again.

He stood for a moment, looking into her eyes. Then he cleared his throat and began, "I pledge to you my faithfulness, Elizabeth. You are my best friend and my soul mate. I pledge to you that I will love you every day of our lives together and do whatever I can to ensure that you will never know need or want for anything. If you will but pledge yourself to me, I will spend my life trying to make yours as beautiful as you have made mine."

She stared at him. How could she possibly respond to that? It was several moments before she found her voice. Swallowing, she then returned his vow with one of her own. "I pledge you my faithfulness. You are everything to me. My love, my friend, my confidante, my soul mate. You have made me so happy, and I know I will spend my life dedicated to your happiness. And I will love you forever. For as long as we both shall live."

John pulled her to himself for a long, meaningful kiss. She returned his fervor with her own, wrapping her arms around his neck, holding to him firmly. And she loved the way his arms came around her and enveloped her. Nothing could harm her here.

He continued to press kisses to her face while she remained in his embrace. She tilted her head back and his lips grazed the tender flesh of her neck. There was a tingling sensation that began where his skin made contact with hers, but it didn't stop there. It filled her body. Not wanting him to stop, she pushed a hand into his hair.

But he did end the contact of his lips with her skin, instead burying his face into her shoulder.

"Lizzie," he breathed. His voice was deep.

After some moments, John extricated himself and, pressing one more chaste kiss to her lips, drew back. "We should be on our way."

She nodded, dipping her head. It was mid-afternoon by now and night would be upon them before long.

As they continued to follow the stream, headed north, they traveled hand in hand as much as the landscape allowed them. They would release each other only in order to manage more difficult terrain. And they slipped between easy conversation and comfortable silences seamlessly as if they'd never been apart.

Afternoon faded into the earliest hours of evening. They had traveled a good distance along the stream without disturbance. But that was no longer to be the case. Up ahead, an older man fished with a young boy.

Elizabeth glanced at John. What were they going to do? Should they hide from this man? Or had they already been spotted?

The older man raised his arm in greeting.

There would be no hiding.

"Good day to you, sir," John said to the man and Elizabeth nodded toward him as they approached.

"And to you, soldier, ma'am," the man responded, pulling his line out of the water. "What brings you around these parts?"

What should they say? They couldn't share the truth.

John didn't skip a beat. "Left my regiment, with permission, to get my wife and bring her to our camp. We're in bad need of some womenfolk to launder and sew for us. My wife's happy to volunteer and I'm happy to have her."

Had John been thinking of this story already?

"How far away from your regiment are ya?" the kindly man asked.

"Another day's walk at least."

"So, you'll spend the night in the woods?" The man seemed rather concerned.

"Suppose we have to." John put an arm around Elizabeth. "But we don't mind."

"Nonsense, my good man. A loyal soldier like you? Y'all are welcome to come stay at my house. It's the least we can do."

Elizabeth looked at John, trying to keep her breathing even. How were they going to get out of this?

John, once again, didn't seem fazed. "Sir, your hospitality is much appreciated, but I'm afraid my wife and I, well, we could never repay such generosity."

The man didn't seem to notice the hesitation. "Never mind that. Besides, my son is a soldier same as you. If he were in your position, I'd like to think someone would do the same for him."

John and Elizabeth exchanged another look. How could they refuse without being outright rude? It wasn't possible.

"Thank you, sir, we accept your benevolent offer." It was Elizabeth who spoke up.

"George. George Davis."

"Excuse me?" Elizabeth asked, confused.

"That's my name. As opposed to 'sir'?" He smiled and winked at her.

Elizabeth's mouth curved into a smile.

"I'm John Smith and my wife's name is Elizabeth."

The man clapped a hand on the shoulder of the lad next to him. "And this here's my grandson Sam. What do you think?" he said, directing his attention to the young boy. "Are we ready to head back home?"

The young boy nodded, pulling his line out of the water.

John stepped forward to help them gather their fishing gear.

Once everything was packed and situated, they moved away from the stream. They hadn't walked long before their destination became visible. There in the distance was a structure that was little more than a white block. However, as they neared the building, Elizabeth saw that it was a massive plantation home. This was no farmer they had come across. He was the master of a plantation.

The house sat atop a slightly crested hilltop. Large fields of grass lead up to it with beautiful gardens of flowers wrapped around. Columns in front of the house rose to meet the upper level deck where she saw what seemed to be the lady of the house perched, calling down to one of the house servants in the front yard.

There appeared to be some amount of hustle and bustle as people went in and out, carrying out their various duties. Just beyond the house, planted fields stretched to the tree line, with crops just starting to sprout. The energy of this entire country estate was similar, and yet unique to the buzz she was used to sensing back in Boston. It seemed there were always people moving out and about when she and John would walk to the park or return from their fathers' practice. There seemed to be the same amount of energy here. It just had a different style and personality.

As they neared the house, their host waved to the lady of the house.

She waved back, a question in her eyes as she looked over his company.

"Look what I found! A bonafide Confederate soldier. He and his wife will bed down with us tonight," George told the woman.

She nodded, clearly used to her husband's flights of fancy. The woman waved in acknowledgment of her guests before turning to re-enter the house.

They climbed the few steps that would allow them to access the front entrance of the house that now loomed over them. In seconds they were inside the grand foyer. Their host busied himself setting down his fishing gear and divesting himself of his hat, handing it off to a servant who appeared out of nowhere to collect whatever the master chose to drop off.

Elizabeth corrected herself. These are not paid workmen. These are not servants. They were slaves.

A portly black woman made her way down the main staircase. She had a wide smile and happy eyes. And she seemed genuinely pleased to welcome them.

"John, Elizabeth, this is Gracie. She'll take care of you." He turned toward the slave woman. "Gracie, show them to the Rose Room."

"Yes'sa," she said, nodding. "This way, folks." She indicated that they should follow her up the stairs.

George took his leave of them and the room, heading on to the next thing, leaving them in Gracie's care.

John and Elizabeth followed Gracie up the stairs.

"Well now, y'all be stayin' the night here with us I hear," Gracie said.

"Your bo-, er, master is very kind to open his home to two traveling souls such as we," John spoke up, seeming to have the same trouble delineating between slave and servant.

"He is that," she said. "He be right down kind-hearted that Masta Davis. Sho nuff."

They had reached the top of the stairs and turned down a hall to the right. The hall had several doors on either side alluding to a number of rooms. They stopped at the second door on the left.

"This here's the Rose Room. It's Miz Lynette's favorite room."

She opened the door and stepped out of the way so they could enter.

It became obvious why it was called the Rose Room. The theme had overtaken the room. Wallpapered in tiny rosebuds, the bed pillows also had embroidered roses on them, and the vanity boasted a vase with fresh roses. A washbowl and pitcher set was also painted with roses.

The room was furnished with a double bed in the center and two nightstands, one on either side. There was also a vanity and chair on the wall near the door across the room from the fireplace, and a lone chair occupied what would otherwise be a barren corner of the room.

"It's lovely," Elizabeth exclaimed, hoping to appease the sentiments of the slave woman.

Gracie just nodded. It occurred to Elizabeth that perhaps this wasn't her cup of tea. If it were, it would certainly be in a rose print tea set.

"I'll leave y'all here to freshen up for supper," she said. "If y'all need anything, don't hesitate to call."

"Thank you," John said, then he seemed to remember his role, and added, "That will be all."

Gracie nodded and closed the door.

Elizabeth exchanged a disapproving look with John.

"I don't like it any more than you do, Lizzie." He stepped close to her and kept his voice low, "But we're playing a part. There are certain things these people will expect of us. Certain ways we're supposed to act."

Elizabeth looked away and toward the window. He was right, but that didn't mean she had to like it. Glancing back into his eyes, she saw that it pained him to disappoint her in any way. She knew he was only doing whatever he thought necessary to get them home safely. As she searched the room, her gaze fell on the bed. Her body was so tired and worn from being pushed these last couple of days.

Almost as if he could read her thoughts, John said, "I think we have enough time for you to lay down before dinner." He pulled her toward the spacious bed.

She looked longingly at the mattress, but resisted his tugging, glancing down at her dress. "I'm a mess."

John opened his mouth to say something when a knock on the door sounded through the room.

"Come in," he called.

The door opened to admit Gracie and she had clothing draped across her arms. "Miz Lynette thought you might need these while we get yer dress clean, Miss," Gracie said to Elizabeth, moving past them to lay the things on the bed.

As she laid them out, Elizabeth noted that one was a dress and the other a nightshift.

"Oh, I couldn't," was her immediate response.

"Well," Gracie said seriously, "Miz Lynette insisted I collect that dress of yers for cleanin' and she won't be too happy with me if I come back empty handed."

Elizabeth looked at her. Getting Gracie in trouble was the last thing she would want to do. And so she conceded, nodding to the woman.

Gracie came over to her and began unbuttoning her dress, though her dress buttoned down her front and she could have easily accessed the buttons herself. Instead of protesting, Elizabeth's eyes met John's as Gracie began to expose her chemise.

His face flushed and he turned his head as if he searched for something to focus on, but he was trapped in that corner of the room between the vanity and the bed. He seemed to have trouble gathering his wits. But once he did, he sat on the bed, back to her, and averted his gaze, acting interested in the embroidery on the pillows.

For her part, Gracie was too busy with her own work to have noticed that Elizabeth's supposed husband avoided looking at her in an under-dressed state.

Gracie removed the dress and Elizabeth stood, clad only in her chemise. "Miz Elizabeth, are you hot? You are flushed all over!"

"I think I am a little warm," Elizabeth lied. How could she explain the true source of her warmed skin?

Elizabeth prayed it would be over soon as Gracie helped her into the dinner gown and began buttoning the fabric closed. It wasn't that Elizabeth wasn't used to being helped into a gown, or even that she begrudged Gracie her job. No, her trepidations had everything to do with John's closeness while she was so exposed.

The sound of a bell ringing from somewhere in the house caused Elizabeth to jump.

"Oh, that's for me! It's Miz Lynette. I'll be back to finish as soon as I can," Gracie promised as she rushed out of the room after whatever life-and-death errand she was being called to. At least that's how she reacted to that bell.

They remained as they were for several minutes, quiet and still, waiting on Gracie to come and finish so that John could once again look at her. The minutes ticked by like hours.

"Oh, this is ridiculous," Elizabeth finally said. "John, you can finish buttoning me up. I'm decent enough."

He hesitated to turn, as if fearful of what he might see. At last, he turned his head to look at her and visibly relaxed. Did he think he would find her exposed?

"Would you?" she asked, turning.

As Elizabeth turned, John discovered that she was fully clothed only from the front. There was a deep 'v' open down her back where the buttons would normally hold the dress together. Only a few had been put through their holes. Her thin chemise, as well as her bare shoulder blades, were displayed before him. It was far from indecent; still he eyed the back of Elizabeth's head. Relief washed over him that she couldn't see his flushed face.

He stood and stepped toward her. Reaching out and touching the delicate fabric, his face warmed even more. And his fingers fumbled with the buttons more than he thought possible. It took some time and concentrated effort before he started to make progress. Eventually, he worked up past the top of her chemise and his hands grazed her bare back.

Goose flesh raised on his arms as a wave of electricity rushed through his body. But he focused on the task at hand and managed to push the last button through. He let out the breath he didn't realize he was holding.

"Thank you," Elizabeth said, turning.

He looked away, working to still his nerves and appear calm and collected as if nothing about it had fazed him.

"Why, John Taylor," she said. "As a doctor, I wouldn't expect you to be so easily spooked by the female form."

"What? I was just..." he started.

"I'm just teasing." She smiled. "You were a gentleman."

John let out another ragged sigh and smiled back at Elizabeth. Leave it to her to take an awkward moment and turn it into something lighthearted. It was one of the many things he loved about her.

The dinner bell rang, breaking the moment. John hoped to have as little contact as possible, but they would not be able to shirk having dinner with the family.

His eyes caught Elizabeth's. Did she share his nervousness about the evening ahead?

"How are we going to get through this one?" Elizabeth whispered.

"Together," he said, taking her hand in his.

Her mouth became a thin line, and her breathing was short and fast.

Pulling her toward his chest, he held her for a moment. "Think about what your mother would do." He kissed the top of her head.

She groaned.

He let out a little laugh. And when he pulled back, her features had softened into a slight smile. "Ready?"

She nodded.

Keeping her hand in his, he moved over toward the door. Opening it, he then led her into the hallway. She maneuvered her hand into the crook of his arm and they went down the stairs. Moments later, they joined the family in the parlor.

George appeared to be in deep conversation with his wife. In the corner of the room, the young boy, Sam, sat with a woman John could only guess was his mother. They played some manner of game. As their arrival was noticed, George broke off his conversation and stood, nodding toward them.

"I hope you found your accommodations adequate."

"Far more than adequate, Mr. Davis," John said with all sincerity. "My wife is quite eager for a good night's sleep on that fine mattress. I had to convince her to come down for dinner."

Elizabeth smiled broadly.

"She deserves it. What a brave woman to go traipsing through the countryside with her husband and join up with his regiment for more hardship and work."

"Thank you, sir," Elizabeth said, meeting his gaze. "But I simply wish to be with my husband and serve any way I can."

"I'm impressed your colonel gave you such reprieve to retrieve your wife. I haven't heard of such a thing," Mr. Davis said, his brows coming together.

"I had to but mention her cooking and cleaning skills. I also told him of her valuable assistance in the hospital on many occasions."

Mr. Davis's features did not give. Did he not believe John's story? "Hospital?"

"Did I not mention that I'm one of my unit's surgeons?"

The confusion on the man's face evaporated. "Oh. I thought you were one of the infantrymen. Never heard of a commanding officer giving his line men a furlough."

"Of course not. That must have sounded strange." The tension in the room eased.

Elizabeth let out a slight sigh.

"Dinner is served," the butler's voice interjected. The man must have entered the room at some point during their interchange.

Everyone looked toward Mr. Davis. Was he satisfied? Would the interrogation continue? John swallowed, but worked to keep his features even.

Mr. Davis stepped toward his wife and offered her his arm as if nothing was amiss. So everyone in the room proceeded toward the dining room. Once in the massive room, the butler motioned John and Elizabeth to their seats. No sooner were they seated then other servants started bringing out the serving dishes.

John's mouth watered at the smells that filled his nose. It had been too long since he had eaten well. The first course, a hearty stew, sat in front of him. He longed to grab the bowl up and drink down the wonderful concoction. But he resisted, forcing himself to take slow bites. And his concentration soon became divided.

"I can't tell you how much I appreciate your service, Doctor."

John nodded, his mouth full of vegetables from the stew.

"I would serve, if I could. But someone has to stay here and keep things in order."

"Of course. Someone has to care for the women and children in our stead." John glanced over at the Davis women and the young boy.

"God knows we need good men like you out there fighting, too. We can't let the Union think they can lord over us."

John nodded, but looked down at his empty bowl.

"It amazes me how much the Union thinks they can run things. I don't know what kind of situation you come from. But in the last year, the tariffs on everything we bought had tripled." Would this become a tirade? John started sweating.

"Yes sir, it...is rather amazing, isn't it?"

"How is my family supposed to run this farm with such ridiculous costs? We have been producing the biggest cash crop of cotton seen in the past ten years! Yet those conceited Yankees think we somehow owe them more of what we worked so hard to produce." Mr. Davis waved his spoon around as he spoke. He had drained his bowl, and signaled for the workers to bring the main course.

John gulped. Mr. Davis had been quiet for a handful of seconds. Did he wait for John to respond? Taking a long drink from his glass, he then proceeded. "How indeed?" John said, trying to sound outraged.

He noticed Elizabeth staring down at her plate.

Mr. Davis proceeded to eat what John believed to be an excellent meal. If only it wasn't spoiled by such a tense discussion.

"Who do those egotistical Yankee industrialists think they are, trying to insist we buy everything from them instead of the British? Not everything must come from the North." Mr. Davis shoved a fork full of vegetables in his mouth but his face was rather dour.

"Mr. Davis, might I say, this is an excellent meal," Elizabeth chimed in.

John appreciated the effort to shift the conversation.

She continued, "I wish I could cook this well."

"Thank you. We have one of the finest cooks in the area."

"Indeed, I almost feel like it's unfair to the other soldiers in my unit," John said, taking a bite of ham.

"I never pass up an opportunity to treat one of our loyal soldiers to something he deserves. Your commitment to fight for our way of life is something we should never forget." Mr. Davis raised his glass towards John. "We all have a part to play. This may not be the richest farm around, but we do our best to supply things that others need. You supply our troops with what I'm sure is the best medical care we could get. And my son, well he is out there just like you, protecting our rights and freedoms with his very life."

As Mr. Davis finished that last sentence, his gaze shifted towards the window. A moment ago, he seemed quite angry in his remarks, but his expression about his son showed that he was just a father who worried.

John was gripped. Did his own parents have this same distant look?

"Grandpa, do we have to talk about this?" came a younger voice from the other side of the table, breaking into John's own self-reflection.

"Listen, Sam, if you are going to run this farm one day, you need to understand how things work. It's important for you to realize there is more to farming than just planting seeds. We have to tend the fields, collect the harvest, and then bale it up. But it doesn't stop there. We have to get it to market at the port, and then deal with the brokers to get paid.

"Son, there are many things we must buy there, and we always look for the best deal to keep our costs down. If that means we buy British, so be it. Those Yankees insisting we pay them more taxes to get the same things we have always bought just isn't fair." Mr. Davis ate his last bite of ham, and motioned for the servants to start serving dessert.

John, counting the minutes, smiled weakly.

"You run a fine farm here, Mr. Davis," John said, again hoping to change the subject.

"I appreciate that, Doctor. My father was a small farmer, didn't have much. I worked to grow this place into something better, and my son has done even more. In fact, before war broke out, we worked to attain more land to the east. It appears our only option."

"Why is that?" John asked.

"About ten years ago, I had looked at selling this farm and taking everything we had out west to build a bigger estate and possibly a much larger farm. But those idiot politicians from the North decided to deny our property rights of taking our slaves with us. The idea that they can encroach upon our free rights is amazing."

John kicked himself for that last question. He attempted to rush through his dessert. It wasn't difficult. Had he ever had anything so delicious?

"Are you all right, soldier? You appear to be eating a bit quickly," Mr. Davis said.

"Sorry. I just get excited when I think too hard about the audacity of the North."

"I know what you mean." Mr. Davis grinned.

John glanced at Elizabeth, trying to read her opinion. He couldn't discern anything. Maybe that was a good thing. If he couldn't read her thoughts, perhaps Mr. Davis couldn't either.

"That was a fine meal..." John started to say.

"Indeed it was. Would you join me in the men's parlor for a cigar, Doctor?" Mr. Davis interrupted.

Everyone started to rise from the table.

"Sir, I think..." John looked at Elizabeth. How was he to avoid spending more time with the man?

Elizabeth shook her head. He would have to play along a bit more.

"I think that would be a fine idea. We don't get many cigars in the field," John said, surrendering to the situation. "But with your permission, I believe my wife would like to retire for the evening. Traveling on foot has been much more wearying on her than we had expected."

"By all means," Mr. Davis said. He stood and leaned toward his own wife.

John drew Elizabeth toward himself. What was safe to say in this company?

Her eyes were wide.

He leaned forward and kissed the side of her face, lingering there to whisper in her ear. "I'm sorry. I will join you soon."

Her hands squeezed his forearms and she pressed a light kiss to the side of his face before pulling away.

Mr. Davis approached as he and Elizabeth parted. The man was upon him in a moment, clapping a firm hand on his back and leading him toward the hall.

"You know, we get some of our best cigars from this French trader. We try to catch him every time we visit the market, but he isn't always there..."

Mr. Davis's voice boomed all the way down the hall. John would have to suffer more political ranting from their host. Elizabeth said a quick prayer for him. Then she nodded to the other women in the dining room before taking her leave and going upstairs. Back in the relative safety of the Rose Room, it was all she could do to resist collapsing on the bed. Instead, she deflated into the lone chair in the corner of the room.

Knock, knock, knock. Coming back to full awareness, she realized she had drifted off. How long had it been? Rubbing her eyes, she struggled to stand. *Knock, knock, knock.* Who was at the door? John?

"Come," she called as she managed to rise.

The door creaked open to reveal Gracie. Where was John? How late was it?

"I come to help with yer dress, Miz."

Elizabeth nodded. She remained silent as Gracie helped remove the gown and prepared her for bed. She hadn't noticed at first, but Gracie carried her dress. It had been washed. And the woman hung it over the fireplace to dry.

The woman was efficient in her work. Elizabeth was prepared for bed in short order. She thanked Gracie, who nodded and took her leave.

But Elizabeth wondered after John. How much longer would he be? Should she wait up for him? It was best she should. And so Elizabeth, clad in the fine nightshift, sat at the vanity to wait for John to appear. She watched the flame flicker on the oil lantern for a time. It was nice to blank out her thoughts and focus on the dancing of the single flame.

Her attention was eventually drawn to her reflection in the vanity's mirror. Must the stresses of the last few days be so obvious in her face? And her hair! It had been braided, but now as she took the braid down so that she could brush it out, she saw the true state of her locks. And it surprised her. With much effort, she removed the tangles. Once satisfied that her hair was as good as it could be under the circumstances, she braided it again and pinned it up.

By this time, the weariness of the day loomed over her, threatening to once again overtake her. But she was still determined to wait for John before bedding down for the night. Still, her head seemed heavy. So she rested it on her arms on the vanity. And her eyelids...they were heavy too. Maybe she could just close them for a minute...

"Elizabeth?" She startled. Had she dozed off yet again?

Now that she came around, she cringed, surprised he could have sneaked up on her. He smelled strongly of cigars and whiskey.

"It appears you survived Mr. Davis," she grimaced. "I guess there is one thing you said that was true. This trip has worn me out." Elizabeth reached out her arms for a slight stretch. "How long were you in the parlor?"

"About an hour. I am not usually so unwilling to share a cigar. But tonight? Just be glad you didn't have to put up with another hour's worth of talk." John pulled off his boots and jacket.

Elizabeth's face became serious. "I wish we didn't have to lie to them," she whispered.

"I know." John stepped over to where she sat, cupping the side of her face. "Me, too. But we don't have much of a choice." The weariness in her eyes must have been as apparent to him as they had been to her. "We need to get some rest."

Elizabeth glanced around the room and her eyes settled on the lone bed. "Are we going to share the bed?"

"I'll sleep on the floor," John said, yawning.

"No," she stopped him, as he grabbed a pillow from the bed. "It will be fine. We'll keep our clothes on and we'll be fine."

His gaze on her was skeptical, but he seemed too tired to argue. Having removed his jacket, he was in a long sleeve shirt with a slight V-neck opening. She climbed into bed and he tucked her in, while he chose to lie on top of the covers. He turned on his side to face her.

"You all right?" His voice was soft.

She nodded.

He reached up and moved a few stray hairs off her forehead. "It's been a long day. You need your rest."

She reached over and stroked his face. Her eyes caught his and held. Fingertips worked as if of their own accord, relishing the feel of his skin. And of his hands as they stroked her arms. It wasn't long before her hand wandered to the exposed area of his chest that the V afforded her. Smoothing her hand over the area, she felt this part of him that she had never touched before. His heart beating faster under her hand, and she heard his breath quicken.

Suddenly and without warning, he grabbed her hand to stop her. It was such a harsh gesture that she looked up at him. Had she gone too far?

"If you want a church wedding," he panted. "You are going to have to stop."

She nodded, feeling like a child being admonished for having her hand in the cookie jar.

"Lizzie," he said softly. "You didn't do anything wrong. A man only has so much restraint." He leaned over and kissed her soundly on the mouth. "I'm sorry, love, but I'm going to need to sleep on the floor." He grabbed his pillow and moved to sit up.

"Take one of the blankets," she said.

He nodded. "Thank you." He grabbed a blanket and moved to the floor.

They lay in their separate spaces in silence for several minutes.

She felt so foolish. There were unshed tears in her eyes. "John?"

"Yeah?" His voice was a whisper.

"I can't sleep." It was the truth. Her mind so full of guilt.

She heard him shift. "What's the matter, Lizzie?"

"I need you." It was all she could manage to get out.

"But..."

"What if I promise to keep my hands to myself? Could you maybe lay here with me until I go to sleep?" Maybe that would make things better.

Her plea was met with silence for a stretch of moments.

Then he spoke. "Of course."

He moved back onto the bed and enveloped her in his arms, holding her to himself.

True to her word, she kept her hands to herself this time and it wasn't long until she drifted off to sleep in her beloved's arms.

Daniel sat down to rest. The run this morning had been particularly grueling. He had his marching orders and didn't mind if their commander pushed them harder. They had slacked off since their last bought of fighting. But in these last few days they had seen a shift in the way the commander handled maneuvers. Though he hadn't known Jacob prior to that first battle, he felt his absence in the run this morning. Jacob had always stood out in that way. It saddened Daniel to remember this and think that Jacob would never run again.

Someone came up behind him, interrupting his thoughts. Turning, he saw Melanie crouch and lean on the tree he rested against. His heart skipped a beat. It didn't matter how much he tried to talk himself down from these feelings; they continued to flourish. He needed to get a handle on his heart lest he risk damaging it. Couldn't he see that she and Jacob cared for each other? Just the other day in the hospital told him as much—the way they interacted, the way they looked at each other.

"Hey," she started, almost whispering. "You look tired."

"I just ran six miles with all of this gear on." His voice came out in spurts, pants.

"Oh my. Why on earth would they have you do that?"

"To prepare for battle." He could see the concern in her eyes. "We march out tomorrow."

She fell quiet for several seconds, which was a bit unusual for her. It allowed him a moment to study her features. Not that he didn't have them memorized.

Chiding himself, he broke off his musings. "Did you need something?"

"I...um...just wanted to thank you for what you did for me yesterday." She placed a hand on his arm.

He nodded, his breath catching at the contact.

"You were right. Jacob apologized, and everything is fine now between us."

He looked at her and knew that even though her words spoke of everything being fine, that something was still off.

"And you? Is everything fine?" He needed to know that she was okay.

She took a moment before she answered. "It will be a while before I can accept that I did everything I could to save his leg."

Daniel nodded. He reached out and put a hand on hers.

She flipped her hand over so that their fingers intertwined.

Daniel's stomach did flip-flops.

"I will miss you, Daniel," Melanie said, her eyes serious. "You've been a good friend to me."

He squeezed her hand. "As have you."

She smiled at him and squeezed his hand back. "I have to get back to the laundry. I just sneaked away for a few moments when I saw you walk by."

He nodded. "If you must."

She released his hand and stood, walking back the direction she had come. And Daniel watched her go. Part of him wished he could have said so much more; part of him was glad that he had protected his heart. Either way, it was time for him to report for musket drills.

CHAPTER NINE
HONESTY

Elizabeth's eyes opened. How long had she slept? It must have been a whole month. Nothing ached as she came to consciousness, her body well cushioned by the fine mattress beneath her. Mattress? Where was she? Home? The bed was not familiar. Her and John's escape came rushing back to her memory. They were at the Davis's plantation home.

Stretching, she glanced around the room. She had fallen asleep in John's arms, yet he was not in the bed next to her as she woke. Turning onto her back, his form became clearer, silhouetted in the early morning light. He sat at the vanity, but faced her.

Should he be here with her in the morning? It seemed awkward. She reached to draw the covers higher, but remembered all they had been through and how they had committed to one another yesterday. Letting her hand fall to her chest, she met his gaze.

"I wondered when you would wake," John said, smiling.

She yawned and deepened her stretch. "I think I like falling asleep in your arms, John Taylor."

"Hey," he teased, moving to the sit on the edge of the bed, leaning over her. "That's Dr. John Taylor."

She smiled up at him. "My apologies."

"Just don't you forget it," he joked gently, stroking her hair.

"How long have you been watching me?" She sat up, eyes wide. This most certainly wasn't her home. They weren't safe here. Shouldn't they have been on the road by now?

"Maybe thirty minutes. You must have been exhausted. I couldn't bring myself to wake you."

Elizabeth slid out of the bed, opposite side of John. She turned on him. "John Taylor, that was foolish! We aren't visiting family. We should try and get out of here as soon as possible."

Grabbing her dress and chemise, Elizabeth turned her back to John. Throwing a glance over her shoulder to make sure John averted his eyes, she then pulled off the night shift and jerked on her chemise and dress, straightening things out as best she could.

Her simple frock was not made for a fine lady who had servants. The buttons were down the front. No need of assistance. For which she was grateful. As she buttoned her dress, she heard John shifting behind her. When she turned, she saw that he had risen and pulled on his jacket.

"I think if we continue to follow the stream, we'll find ourselves in Union territory perhaps tomorrow." His voice was muffled by his collar as he looked down to button the jacket.

Nodding, she closed her eyes. This would be another long day of walking. And she dreaded it. But they must. She would do everything she could to push on every step of the way. While the restful night's sleep on a comfortable bed had helped, it made her loathed to return to the mats on the ground. Yet that was the choice she had made.

John turned and their eyes met at last. Elizabeth read in his eyes some of the things she felt. It was not in her to survive another dinner conversation like the one last night. Could he? She doubted it. They had reached the limits of their ability to play these roles. It was likely their disguises wore thin as well. No, they best not stay one minute longer than necessary.

She prayed they could be on their way without further entanglements with the family. But could they avoid facing the family before leaving? It was doubtful.

Gathering everything they came with, which wasn't much, they made their way out of the room and down the stairs. It did not escape her notice as they took the stairs that John angled his torso a bit oddly. Was his back stiff from a night on the hardwood floors? Guilt washed over her.

Though he descended a bit slower than normal, it did not take long before they stood in the grand entryway without a soul in sight.

Elizabeth looked at the door. Dare they just slip out?

John's breathing quickened beside her. Was he thinking the same thing? He took her hand and, reaching toward the door's latch, stepped forward.

The *clip-clop* of shoes on the floor caused John to flinch. Elizabeth grabbed his arm. But still he reached. Could they disappear out the door before whomever stalked the halls saw them?

Elizabeth couldn't hear for the pounding of her heartbeat in her ears. She couldn't risk it. Pulling at John, she prevented his fingers from wrapping around the latch. But just so.

He glared at her.

She diverted her gaze toward the direction of the footfalls as the butler appeared.

Would they have made it? She and John would have to debate it. There would be no way to know. But she doubted it.

"What can I do fer y'all?" the man asked, dropping in a slight bow.

"We wish to speak with the master of the house."

The butler nodded and hurried off after his errand.

John's gaze turned once again toward the latch.

Elizabeth's hand gripped his upper arm. When he turned his head to meet her eyes, she shook her head.

Only seconds passed before Mr. Davis came toward them from the direction of the main parlor. "Well now, there are my guests. I hope you got some good rest. Things probably aren't quite that comfortable at the encampments."

John smiled. "No, sir, they never are. In fact, I feel as if I cheated my fellow men."

"I understand what you mean, son. But come. It's time for a good breakfast before you resume your hike back to your post." Davis took a step toward the dining room.

"I do appreciate your hospitality, putting myself and my wife up last night." John spoke up.

Mr. Davis turned, an eyebrow quirked as he met John's eyes.

John continued, "Especially after serving us a fine dinner. But I feel we must be on our way."

As Elizabeth held John's arm, it was as if every muscle in his body tensed. Elizabeth spoke up, "I think what my husband is saying, Mr. Davis, is that we don't want to overstay our welcome. When did your colonel expect us back?" Elizabeth turned back to John.

"I believe he wanted us back by noon. If I read the case clock outside correctly, we need to head out, or I'll get a good thrashing from my commanding officer."

Davis eyed the two of them, clearly disapproving of such haste. But when he spoke, it was with his genial, calm voice. "I never like to send a guest away without a meal. But I understand. Let me have our house cook fetch something for you to take." He waved at the butler, who went off down a hall to the right.

In a few minutes, he returned with some biscuits and a few pieces of bacon.

"This is too much. Your hospitality is much appreciated," John said, trying to shake Mr. Davis's hand while stuffing the food items into his knapsack.

The master of the house then ushered them toward the front door, a frown on his face. Their farewells were brief and, in no time, John and Elizabeth were outside, headed onto the main road. Half an hour down the road, they stopped to look back. Seeing no more sign of the plantation, Elizabeth breathed a huge sigh of relief.

"So, Mrs. Taylor, would you like a biscuit and a piece of bacon?" John joked.

"Why, yes, Mr. Taylor, I would enjoy that very much." She dipped into an exaggerated curtsy.

They stepped to the side of the dirt path and munched on a few of the foodstuffs for a light breakfast, saving some of the things for later. Then they continued down the road. Another half hour later, John decided it was time to get off the road and veer back toward the stream they had been following.

It wasn't too long before they were far enough from the road that they felt much safer, surrounded by woods. The fear of running into Confederate patrols visiting either the house or touring the roads was now behind them.

More daylight passed before they found the stream. They then turned right and began to follow its generally northern direction. After walking for half a day, taking only short breaks, they stopped to take a rest. Elizabeth collapsed next to a large rock, leaning against it.

John walked closer to the stream, and knelt beside it. He pulled something out of his knapsack. What was it? She craned her neck to see, but with his back turned to her, she couldn't get a good view. As he walked toward her, however, she discerned that he had a teacup filled with water. Strange. It had escaped her notice before that he carried a teacup. Still, she drained the cup and handed it back to him. Then she caught a glimpse of the markings on the cup. Little rose buds. He didn't. He couldn't have.

"John! You stole that cup from their house. I can't believe..."

"I know. I didn't want to, but when I saw it sitting on the vanity, I thought it would be useful. So I stowed it before you awoke."

How could he? What was he becoming? What else would he do, all for the sake of trying to get them back in one piece?

"John, I don't like that we are having to lie and steal to get back. It's one thing to steal a uniform to escape a Confederate camp, but preying upon that nice family seems a bit much. Look at us. Look at how we have lied and stolen."

"Lizzie, I agree. If we hadn't run into Mr. Davis and his grandson, we wouldn't have done any of this. But we were caught and had to bluff our way through. Don't worry. I am not turning into some highwayman planning to rob another traveler." John's eyes were shining and she saw sincerity in them. And the way his mouth twisted told her that he had regret for his actions.

He went back to the stream and gathered another cup of water for himself. They sat in their separate places, each thinking about the things they had done to get where they were. And so there remained a silence between them for several moments.

"We'd better get moving again." John stood and moved toward Elizabeth. "We don't have a lot of daylight left. Let's see how far we can get."

Elizabeth nodded. She was ready to create distance between herself and everything else, even though her legs fought her.

They resumed their walking, trudging through the woods, following the winding stream. The sun crawled across the sky, causing the short shadows of the trees to grow longer. Elizabeth grew more tired with each passing minute. As they trekked along the stream, the surrounding land became rockier. And they found themselves going downhill, hitting sections that required them to climb down boulders.

As the day moved on, clouds began building. While this provided welcome relief from the sun that had been beating down upon them, John's worry became evident.

"Lizzie, I think we may be in for a storm tonight."

Elizabeth stopped and looked at the sky.

As they kept climbing downhill, the clouds seemed to be getting thicker. The wind had already picked up its pace.

"John, I don't like this. What are we going to do?" She had endured much and had been willing to take on any number of hardships, but sleeping in the cold rain in the middle of the night wasn't one of them.

John looked back to answer her question. "We need to find shelter. These boulders keep getting bigger. Maybe if we look for some outcropping, we can avoid the rain there."

Just as he said those words, Elizabeth looked forward and saw that he neared a ledge at least ten feet up from the ground below.

"John!" She called out just as he turned and noticed it too. He stopped, holding out his arms so Elizabeth wouldn't accidentally walk past him.

"Watch out, Lizzie!" he said as he tried to look over the edge.

Glancing to the left and to the right, John headed off to the right and worked out a path to get around the drop off. He helped Elizabeth follow. At the bottom, there appeared to be a giant ledge that stretched on for several feet. Not far off, Elizabeth could see the stream, crashing over the edge at one spot.

As John continued to search, he signaled for Elizabeth to follow him.

She did so, walking below the ledge, trying to avoid slipping on the loose rock. As she approached John, she saw that he had found a big, worn out area underneath the ledge. It appeared to go back about fifteen feet.

John looked at it with an approving nod. "I think we should try and camp out here. It may give us some protection from the wind."

A loud boom of thunder shot through the air.

"Quick, get under!" John yelled.

Rain started to fall.

Elizabeth rushed under the overhang, John close behind her. They were both well enough underneath before the heavens opened and it began to pour. The wind picked up and blew in on them, but it wasn't horrendous. At least they were dry, for the most part.

After John ensured that she was safely tucked into the cave-like structure, he walked to the edge, looking out. What was he watching for? An animal?

Though they had escaped getting drenched, Elizabeth's clothes were damp in places. And as the wind blew in on her, it brought a chill. Soon enough she was shivering. Wrapping her arms around herself and sinking to the ground, she made herself as small as possible. Still, the wind seemed to blow through her. Her teeth began to chatter.

"John!" she called. She could barely hear her own voice over the rushing of the falling rain. "John!"

After some moments of calling for him, he turned. As his eyes landed on her figure, he made his way to her. He crouched down next to her and gathered her to himself, wrapping his arms around her. "My goodness, Lizzie! You're freezing. I didn't know."

The warmth of his body soaked into hers. And she clung to him, her teeth no longer chattering.

"You know, I wish that instead of a cup, I had found a box of matches." John chuckled.

She buried her face in his shoulder, continuing to shiver. Was it only from the chill in the air? Or was her fear getting the better of her?

Turning her face to expose her mouth so she might speak, she whispered into the crook of his neck. "John, we're going to make it home, right?"

He hugged her to himself. "You bet. As long as we stay together, we can do anything."

She leaned into him, relishing the closeness and the scent of him. How she had missed this the many weeks they were apart. Except... except she'd had amnesia and hadn't remembered him at all. Except that Matthew had been holding her closely. How was she ever to tell him? How was she ever going to make it right? She stiffened in John's arms.

"What's the matter?" John spoke into her hair.

"It's nothing," she said. She couldn't delve into it now. Not with him.

He craned his neck to look at her face. "It's not nothing, Lizzie, you're crying," he said, moving a hand to wipe away an errant tear.

She remained silent.

"Lizzie, why won't you talk to me?"

She shook her head, clinging to his jacket, trying once again to bury her face in his chest.

"This isn't because I stole the cup, is it? Lizzie, I'll find a way to..."

She shook her head again. "No," she said, her voice quiet. "I know you were only doing what you had to do."

John was silent for several seconds. He was probably wracking his brain, trying to search out what disturbed her so. Why couldn't she just tell him?

"Is this about that man from the Confederate camp? The one who helped us escape?"

She was silent and still.

John knew he was right. What John had seen of the two of them had been enough to incite his protective, jealous urges. Had there been more? There must have been for it to disturb Elizabeth so. And what he didn't know started to scare him.

"Lizzie, don't shut me out. You can tell me anything," he said more confidently than he felt. But he was sure that nothing she said would change how he felt about her. They belonged together and they would be together. Always and forever, right?

"Matthew," she said after some time, lifting her face to look at him. "His name is Matthew. Was Matthew..." Her eyes drifted.

"Matthew," John said, hoping to get her back on the subject.

Elizabeth's gaze returned to John's face and she continued after a moment. "You have to understand that my memory was gone. I had no recollection of you or what existed between us. My life was a blank."

John's nod was slow. He became more nervous as she spoke, but he tried to keep his face neutral.

"Matthew was so kind." Her gaze drifted to somewhere beyond John, as if she looked out into the distance. "Something just developed between us. The day you came to the camp, he had just asked me to marry him."

"What?" John cleared his throat. He didn't want to keep her from talking. So he remained calm. "What did you say?"

How had their relationship developed that far? And so quickly? How deeply was she involved with this man? Had they said things, done things...? His stomach turned. He couldn't think like that.

"I said no." Her eyes refocused on him.

John breathed a sigh of relief.

"Were you in love with him?" He had to know.

Elizabeth looked into his eyes. "Yes."

John nodded, stricken by her answer, numbed. He looked away.

Elizabeth reached out her hands, placing them on either side of his face and turned his head to face her. "But I chose you. I might have loved Matthew for a time, but you are my life. I belong with you." She maneuvered her face upward to kiss him.

He tightened his arms around her, holding her more closely and deepening the kiss. There were no more words. While he knew he would hurt for a time, he knew that she had chosen him. And that they would get through this because they belonged together.

She, too, held on to him with all that was in her. While a part of her did still care for Matthew, she knew she loved this man in her arms with reckless abandon.

Dinner was over and Daniel headed back to his tent. He would march out in the morning. So he intended to get as much rest as that mat on the ground could afford him. It was good that he would leave in the morning. The part of him that wanted to make some sort of profession to Melanie seemed to be getting louder by the second. And he feared he was on the verge of spilling his guts to her. That was the last thing he should do, right? Great. Now he questioned even that.

He continued to move through the camp toward his tent, nodding to the various soldiers he passed along the way.

Pit-Pat-Pit-Pat. Light footfalls sounded behind him. Someone followed him. Someone smaller. Turning his head to look over his shoulder, he saw a flash of red-blonde hair. Melanie! What was she running from? Spinning around to see, he searched for her pursuer. His body ready to leap into action.

As he turned, however, she slowed and closed the distance between them.

"Daniel," she said breathlessly.

"Melanie, what's the matter?" He continued to search behind her for some unseen attacker.

"I...I just..." She still tried to catch her breath.

"Take your time." He put a hand on her shoulder to still her.

Her eyes spoke her gratitude as she put a hand on her stomach.

"I just couldn't let you leave without telling you how much you mean to me. I was first thinking 'I need to wait and let him make the first move,' but then I was thinking, 'What if he dies in this battle and he never knows? Is it worth it to me that I waited for you to make the first move if I never got to tell you?' And I thought 'No, I'll never be able to live with myself'..."

"Whoa, slow down. What are you saying?" He became more confused by the second.

"I care for you, Daniel, so much. And I needed for you to know that. It's okay if you don't feel the same. I understand. I just wanted you to know that I..."

Daniel's lips met hers. He had been taken aback by her confession. It made his head swim. Then she kept talking and he couldn't think straight. The only thing he could think to do was to kiss her. So that's what he did.

As they parted, she looked into his eyes. Did she want for some reassurance of his feelings?

"I care for you too, Melanie. You're all I think about. And I'm sorry I didn't tell you first. I guess I..."

She reached for the sides of his face and pulled his lips to hers for another kiss.

When their lips parted this time, he embraced her, holding her to himself and pressing kisses into her hair.

After several long moments, Daniel spoke up. "Tell me I'm not dreaming."

She pinched him.

"Ow! I said 'tell me'!"

She pulled back only enough to look into his face. "At least now you know for sure."

He pressed a kiss to her mouth again, a softer, more gentle kiss than before. "Yes, now I know."

"I could stay like this forever," Melanie said, snuggling up to his chest again.

"I know," he kissed the top of her head. "So could I, dearest Melanie. But it's almost curfew."

Melanie groaned. "I don't want to let you go. Because that means it's time to sleep and when I wake in the morning you'll be gone. Perhaps forever."

"But we'll forever have this moment. I will hold it here." He placed a hand over his heart. "And cherish it every moment of my life."

She nodded. "As will I."

He captured her lips again for one last kiss, holding her as close as he dared. And when it was over, it was he who insisted she turn and walk away. As he watched her go, a name drifted into his consciousness. A name he had neglected to think about at any point in this whole encounter. Jacob.

And Daniel's heart sank as he thought of Jacob.

The next morning, Elizabeth woke earlier than usual. Sleeping under a rock ledge with blowing wind wasn't the most comfortable experience. It wasn't long after the rays of daylight had emerged the next morning that the two of them stirred.

"You know, I think getting up early every morning back at camp has gotten me used to early risings," Elizabeth observed out loud.

"It's not quite like it was in Boston. But you're right, Lizzie, this would have been harder back when we first shipped out." John rose to his feet. "It's not coffee, but let's get a drink from the stream. I think we have a couple more biscuits for breakfast. I'm hoping it isn't too much farther. Maybe today, maybe tomorrow."

John journeyed over to the stream and collected water for Elizabeth. Bringing it back to her, he encouraged her to drink her fill. He returned to the stream and filled it as many times as he thought necessary.

Elizabeth drank from the cup and started gnawing on her biscuit. It didn't taste quite as good as it did when it was hot. But it settled the growling in her stomach. They were careful not to linger too long after finishing what foodstuffs they had.

They started to move down the foothills. As they progressed throughout the morning, trying to keep in general sight of the stream, the rocks seemed to be getting smaller, and the slope of the hills smoothed out. Then John determined it was time for a break. And Elizabeth was grateful for it.

"I'm going to get some more water. That was a rough walk," John said.

"Yeah. I used leg muscles I didn't know I had." Elizabeth leaned back against a tree.

After John returned, he handed the cup to Elizabeth.

"I wanted to say, Lizzie, that I hope I didn't make you feel bad last night. I realize that you were in a tricky situation with your amnesia and all, and..." John started to stumble over his words.

"What I'm trying to say is, I'm glad you shared with me what happened. I appreciate that you trust me."

"You deserve as much, if not more. I'm glad Matthew decided to help us in the end. I was so worried when he stormed off. I sincerely hope he was able to escape. He did help me through a tough situation," Elizabeth said, signaling not love for Matthew, but instead honest hope.

"I hope he makes it, too. Maybe he'll head out west and find a new life there," John said with true conviction. It was a good place for them to settle with the Matthew situation. Perhaps that was all that needed to be said.

The break was over sooner than Elizabeth would have liked. Her legs muscles were sore and her feet ached. Still, they continued for several hours more. John stopped them for more breaks, but he could not disguise that their situation grew that much tougher. They had finished off whatever biscuits they had at breakfast. And though they felt hungry, Elizabeth preferred that to having to feign being Confederates and stay in another plantation.

At one point, as they stumbled along in the afternoon, John raised his hand and looked back at Elizabeth, signaling for her to stop. He glanced around then motioned for Elizabeth to come up next to him. As she did so, John directed her attention to the dirt, pointing out footprints.

"Those look like boots from soldiers," John whispered.

The tracks traveled all the way to the stream.

"Those might be from soldiers fetching water. Let's see where they lead. But keep your head down," he continued in a quiet voice.

Elizabeth nodded. They crouched down, and started walking away from the stream, tracking the prints. Eventually, the trail became impossible to follow as they approach the edge of the forest and saw an open field. John stood behind a tree, and pointed at the next one over as a place for Elizabeth to see as well. Her eyes scanned the field and the small hill that rose up further away.

"I don't see any troops, do you?" John asked.

"No, but something is familiar," Elizabeth responded. Something nagged at her. She couldn't put her finger on it. Suddenly she realized what it was. "John, that hill. I remember that hill. It's the one I used to sit on and sketch in the morning before my duties." Elizabeth raced out into the open field.

John chased after her. "What are you doing?"

"This is where our camp used to be. It's moved, but I remember that hill. On one of the first days, I was up there and noticed you," Elizabeth said excitedly.

John's face lit up. "I remember that day. That was you?"

"I managed to enlist help that got us out of a Confederate camp, so don't you start sassing me, John Taylor." Elizabeth's tone was strict, but she hoped her eyes betrayed her joke.

Smiling at her quick comment, John remarked, "Lizzie, you'll make a great mother some day. Come on. Let's check things out. Who knows? Maybe we can find a scrap of leftover food."

They found where the camp had been centered, where latrines had been dug, and saw signs where tents used to be pitched, but there wasn't much of anything left behind they could eat.

"Drat! I wasn't hoping to find a slab of bacon and a pan. Just a piece of hard tack would have been nice."

Elizabeth felt his frustration. They were so near, and yet so far.

"What are we going to do now?" She looked up at him. He had brought them this far.

"We need to search around and figure out which way they moved." John's eyes scanned the horizons around them. "You know, when I was looking over there," John continued, pointing to the left, "I think I may have seen more foot prints. It's hard to tell, but let's check it out."

John headed that direction, and Elizabeth followed. They didn't find decisive footprints, but they did spot a set of wagon tracks headed off to the east, definitely away from the camp, so they decided to follow.

They continued hiking for the rest of the day, watching as the sun started to get closer and closer to the horizon. The shadows grew longer, and Elizabeth began to realize they were now missing something important. The stream!

No food...no water. Would they make it? But she chased those terrifying thoughts from her mind. She had to trust John.

"Don't worry, Lizzie, I'm sure we'll catch up to them in plenty of time," John said. Had he read her mind?

An hour more and the sun set. They had just reached a small ridge and could see the sun settle in as the moon began to rise.

"We'll stop here. It shouldn't be too far to walk in the morning." John stopped and settled down next to a tree.

Elizabeth sat down beside him and wondered after an evening routine. There was no food or water to consume and she was exhausted. Perhaps settling in to sleep was best. So she leaned into John's side, enjoying the simple feel as he wrapped his arm around her, pulling her ever closer.

As the night came upon them, John snuggled Lizzie. He had pushed her hard today and she was tired. It did feel strange to just stop and bed down, but what else was there for them? So he decided to entertain her the way he always had—with his cases.

Wanting to give her something else to think about so she wouldn't worry, he started to tell her about some of the cases he had dealt with while working in the Confederate hospital. John had hardly finished his first case, when he heard her heavy breathing. It truly had been a long day.

John had a harder time sleeping. He felt deeply responsible to get Elizabeth back safe. Not only did he feel the need to get her back to Union territory, but back to her parents. If something happened to her now, he could never live with himself. She had proven herself extraordinary in some of the most dire circumstances, but he told himself that she had been lucky. And luck was something that tended to run out at the worst possible moments.

As the sun had set, and a partial moon came out, he noticed in the far distance some slight twinkling. It was difficult to make out. John squinted, but it didn't help. Are those campfires? He tried to judge the distance, and decided it was too far to travel now. Besides they needed their rest, and he just couldn't bring himself to wake Elizabeth. If they started early enough, they'd probably make it by mid-morning.

And so, with that new information to give him peace, John fell asleep, too.

"Lizzie." John stirred her, a gentle shake bringing her around to consciousness. "I saw campfires last night. Maybe from our unit."

She opened her eyes lazily. "What?"

"I saw campfires last night. I'm sure we can get there in a few hours."

She yawned and stretched, chasing sleep from her limbs.

John stood and helped Elizabeth to her feet. "You ready?"

Elizabeth nodded and they moved on. Her body ached still from the previous days' walks, but she dared not utter a complaint. Not that John wouldn't understand. She didn't want to burden him any further. They were both tired, worn out, hungry, and thirsty. If a few hours of walking would solve those problems, she would push her protesting muscles a little longer.

As determined as she was, however, her mind-over-matter strategy started wearing thin a couple of hours into their journey and she found it harder to push herself. But John urged her ever onward.

At one point he paused to scan the horizon. It was the one time she got ahead of him.

"We're almost there, Lizzie. It won't be long until we're…"

Bang! Elizabeth stopped in her tracks, ducking as much as she could in an open field. Where could it have come from? She scanned the area for the source of the sound. "Should we take cover?"

There was no answer.

She turned.

A large pool of red formed on the upper right portion of John's uniform.

"John, no!" she screamed as she eased him down to the ground. She put pressure on the wound with her hands.

John moved his lips to speak.

"Shhh. Don't try to talk. You'll be fine," she said to herself more than to him. "Somebody help me!" she screamed.

Union soldiers stepped out of the underbrush, guns drawn and aimed at her.

"We are on your side," she screamed at them. "Help us!"

"Why is he in a Confederate uniform?" one man questioned her, his gruff voice demanding an answer.

"Because we were prisoners of war and that's how we escaped. This is Dr. John Taylor. He's been missing from the 16th Regiment."

"That camp is not far. There's a hospital there."

"Did you hear that, John?" She looked down at him.

He was unconscious.

She checked his pulse—faint.

He was barely breathing.

"No, John, no," she yelled as tears poured down her face. "You can't leave. Stay with me!"

One of the soldiers pulled her off John, and the other two lifted him. She wanted to fight the soldier that held her, but it was no use. So she buried her face in his chest, sobbing as the other two carried John away. Eventually, she calmed enough for the soldier to lead her in the direction they had taken John.

They may have walked for minutes or hours. Elizabeth did not know. In a daze, the time stretched out and became exaggerated in her mind. As soon as they arrived, Elizabeth rushed for the hospital and tried to squeeze her way to John's side, past the nurses who already bustled around him. She hadn't noticed Dr. Smith until she heard his booming voice.

"Could someone please remove this young lady? She doesn't need to see this."

"No," she protested as a nurse stepped to her, placing a hand on her arm.

"Miss, it would be better for everyone if you wait outside."

"But John needs me," she argued, fighting the nurse's hands.

"I understand, but the doctor needs to work. He's doing everything he can to save Dr. Taylor's life and he doesn't need any distractions." The woman motioned for another nurse to help her.

Now there were two nurses, one grasping each of Elizabeth's arms and ushering her out of the surgical suite. Once outside, they were met by Melanie, who indicated she would take Elizabeth from there. They released her arms and Melanie took hold of her forearms, pulling her further away from the hospital.

"Elizabeth, you're alive!"

"I need to get to John," she tried to push past her.

Melanie moved her grip until she had a hold of Elizabeth's upper arms. "You can't go in there. You know that."

"No, I don't." Elizabeth tried to wriggle free.

"Yes, you do," Melanie said firmly.

Elizabeth was surprised by Melanie's grip. Try as she might, she couldn't struggle free. She gave up and half collapsed into Melanie's arms. "I'm so afraid!"

"I know you are, but he's strong. He'll make it." Melanie patted Elizabeth's back.

"How can you be sure?" Elizabeth sniffed. She didn't want to fall apart, but her whole world seemed to be crumbling.

"We have to have faith that he'll pull through."

Elizabeth nodded.

"Let's get you cleaned up." Melanie directed Elizabeth away from the hospital and toward the women's tents.

"No," Elizabeth renewed her protests. "I have to be here when he wakes up, I…"

"He'll be in surgery for a while," Melanie reasoned with her. "You don't want him to see you the first time after surgery all covered with blood, do you?"

Elizabeth looked down at herself. She was a mess. Her dress was bloodstained and dirty, her face and hands were dirt-marred and blood-streaked. So when Melanie went to lead her away again, she didn't protest.

Melanie took her first to their tent to grab one of her dresses for Elizabeth and some soap. Then she walked to the stream, stopping to recruit another woman for some assistance. They scrubbed every inch of Elizabeth's skin clean of dirt and blood before drying her off and redressing her.

Elizabeth, for her part, did as she was told.

Every once in a while, she would wonder after her beloved and ask, "John?"

And Melanie would assure her that he was in surgery and that the doctors were doing everything they could.

Melanie and the other woman then led Elizabeth back to Melanie's tent and laid her down on her old mat to rest. Just then Sarah came in. She indicated for Melanie to step outside.

"He's out of surgery, but it's still not good."

"What should we tell her?"

"Let her rest for now. When she wakes, tell her he's alive."

Abigail pulled herself out of bed. Her maidservant had brought her some tea, but had placed it by her chair. Yes, it probably wasn't wise for her to take her tea in the bed, though she loathed to slip out from underneath the covers. Stepping onto her feet at this hour of the day always felt a little odd. Almost as if her legs didn't want to support her.

Making her way to her sitting area, she grazed the curtain with her shoulder. The light of the noon sun burst into the room through the slit created. Abigail jerked away from the window dressings.

Finally sinking into her sitting chair, she sighed. How could it be that the trip from the bed to the chair had cost her so much energy? She reached for the tea, sipping the warm liquid, allowing it to soothe her throat.

Thundering footfalls on the stairs gave her pause. And cause for alarm. She opened her mouth to call for the maidservant. Was there an intruder in the house? Surely none of the staff would be rushing about so. The loud thumps drew closer to her room and she attempted to scream, but nothing came forth.

The door to her room flung open. And Thomas walked in, heaving, bearing a paper in his hand. His eyes were wide and wild.

"She's alive," he said, closing the distance between them and falling to a knee in front her.

"Alive?" Abigail found her voice. Had she heard him correctly?

"Yes! Alive and well."

She didn't have to ask who. Or when. Or why. Abigail shrieked for joy, tears falling as she reached for her husband to embrace him.

He lingered in her embrace, attempting to catch his breath. "I received a letter today."

She pulled away and sat back in her chair, hand over her heart, which beat faster than she thought possible. "Read it."

He opened the folds of paper and began to read.

"'Dear Sir and Madam,

"I apologize that you are hearing from me again rather than your own daughter. But there is news I thought you would want as soon as possible. Elizabeth has returned to us! She is in good health. She had been captured by Confederate troops and was being held in one of their camps. But she escaped with the help of one of our doctors, Dr. John Taylor, who had also been captured. I assure you that all is indeed well and she will write to you soon. Regards, Melanie'"

"She was captured with John?"

"As it would seem." Thomas met her gaze.

"So all this time...they've been together?" Her voice trailed off. It was not a question.

"And he helped get her back to safety."

All was happiness and joy for they and their friends. Their children were alive, well, and together.

The doorbell rang, interrupting her thoughts.

Thomas looked toward the door. "That will be Franklin and Charlotte. Would you like to dress?"

Abigail nodded.

Thomas leaned forward and pressed a kiss to the side of her face.

She smiled at him. Their daughter was alive. The world was right again.

Thomas made his way down the stairs.

Soon after a maidservant came to assist Abigail in preparing herself for company.

But Abigail's mind was elsewhere. It seemed as if she could fly! Her daughter was whole and well. And they had renewed hope of bringing her home. If she was with John, he would find a way to get her back to Boston. She was sure of it.

CHAPTER TEN
WOUNDS

Jacob sat on the edge of his hospital cot gathering a few things and putting them in the crate his family had sent him. The time for him to be transported back to the train and returned to Boston was fast approaching. He had grown eager to be home again, but he loathed leaving Melanie. How could he tell her? Figuring himself too timid to take the direct approach, he had not yet said anything. But as time passed that seemed the only way it was going to happen. The right moment just wasn't presenting itself.

It wasn't for lack of opportunity. Melanie continued to visit him daily. She came to check on him and bring him the camp news. These last couple of days, she seemed sad. Daniel had gone back out to fight, and he knew that Daniel and Melanie had developed a friendship. And Daniel was one of the soldiers who had yet to return. Perhaps that made her sad. He had not yet ventured to ask.

Even now, she was overdue for their visit. He watched the tent opening. It was all for naught. Willing her presence no more produced her than his attempts at pulling a rabbit from his hat after seeing a magic show when he was ten. Yet he kept his eyes on the entrance to the hospital.

Several more minutes, perhaps a half hour even, passed before she appeared. She moved to his bedside, pouring him more water before greeting him. Melanie neither explained nor apologized for being late, she just started chatting.

"How are you feeling today?" She handed him the glass.

"I am well, and you?"

She nodded.

He watched her as she moved around his bed fluffing pillows, straightening sheets and his bedside table, before finally taking her seat.

"Are you?"

She looked at him, eyebrow raised.

He gathered the courage to broach the subject he had avoided. "You haven't seemed yourself these last couple of days. Is something the matter?"

She continued to meet his gaze for several seconds, as if gauging her response. "I'm just worried about the soldiers gone to battle is all."

"And Daniel in particular?" he guessed.

"Yes." There was a hesitation in her voice. "He has become a good friend to me."

Jacob nodded.

A silence fell between them.

Jacob spoke into it. "Melanie, there's something I've been wanting to talk with you about." He shifted to sit straighter.

She raised her other eyebrow.

"I know my time at camp is short. And while I am excited about going home, I also know I'm going to miss some of the people here."

"I can understand that. With what we've all been through together, it's like a second family. It will be bittersweet whenever it's time for me to move on from this camp," she chattered on.

"Yes, of course." He stopped her, his voice coming out a bit harsher than he'd intended. "But, what I mean to say is that there is one person I will miss more than all the others. Someone who has become quite important to me, someone I care for."

"Oh?" Melanie's eyes were on him then.

"It's you, Melanie. I think...that is, I've come to...I truly..." he closed his eyes and took a deep breath. "That is, I think I love you."

Melanie took a deep breath, allowing the long pause to hang in the air.

"Jacob, I love you, too." She took his hand in hers. "But, not in the way that you want me to."

He looked at her. What could she mean?

"There are different kinds of love, Jacob. And the love I have for you is the kind of love friends have for each other. It is deep and meaningful, but not, I fear, what you are hoping for."

Jacob looked down at her hand holding his, not able to meet her gaze.

"One day," she continued, "You will meet someone who does feel that way about you and you'll understand."

Jacob pulled his hand away. "No, I won't. Look at me." He motioned in the direction of his amputated leg.

"I am looking at you. And I see an intelligent, warm, caring, handsome young man that any girl would be crazy to pass up."

His eyes met hers again. Did she have to be so kind? This would be a lot easier if she would just turn him down and walk away.

"Trust me, Jacob." She squeezed his hand again.

She waited for him to say something, but in his hurt, he had nothing to give.

"I'm going to go for now. But I'll stop by tomorrow."

He nodded.

With some reluctance, she extricated her hand from his and moved away from his bed. Giving him a long look, she then turned and left the hospital.

Jacob leaned back in his bed, hand over his eyes, wishing he hadn't said anything at all.

Stirring and coming around to full consciousness, Elizabeth blinked her eyes open. Where was she? Boston? A Confederate camp? A plantation house? Her back ached as she sat upright. She had been leaning over onto a cot. Stretching out her back, she gazed down at the resting face of her beloved. John. Yes, they were back behind Union lines in their own camp. And John had been in and out of consciousness, mostly out, these last few days as the nurses and doctors continued to work on him. They never stopped reminding her it was out of their hands, that they were doing everything they could to save John's life. Only time would tell.

Elizabeth ran a hand over her hair. She didn't like the odds they were giving John. And she didn't like being so helpless. Still, she did what she could, keeping to his side. His bouts of consciousness thus far had been utilized to consume water and broth for his strength. He said precious little, and nothing coherent. But she waited.

Melanie volunteered to stay by his side from time to time if Elizabeth would go back to their tent for a nap. It took some work, but she reasoned to Elizabeth that it did John no good for her to become sleep deprived. Yes, Melanie could be quite convincing when she wanted to be.

Turning her head, Elizabeth looked for what might have roused her, her thoughts first on John. She leaned over, as she often did, and clasping his fingers in hers, pressed a kiss to his strong hand. His breathing changed and he shifted.

"John?" She pulled back from his hand so she could move closer to his face, running her hand over his forehead, brushing his hair back.

He blinked his eyes open. It took him a while to focus, but he did seem to look at her face. "Elizabeth?" he croaked.

"Yes, John, I'm here," she said, a tear escaping her eye. She was thrilled to hear him say her name. This was surely a good sign.

His eyes lingered on hers for a few moments.

"Water," he managed.

She turned toward the pitcher they kept by his bed and filled a small cup. With gentle hands, she held his head up, bringing the brim of the cup to his lips.

He lay back and his lids slid closed. Then his eyes flew open and he tried to sit up.

Elizabeth attempted to still him.

"Are we out of danger?" His eyes were wide.

"Yes, we are behind Union lines and in our old camp. Dr. Smith and Dr. Young have been taking care of you."

"What happened to me?" He looked at the bandage on his shoulder and chest.

"You were shot." It was hard for her to speak the words.

He grimaced as if he were just then feeling the pain.

"Dr. Smith and Dr. Young have done a good job. You gave us quite a scare, but I think it's a good sign that you seem to be yourself again."

He nodded, agreeing with her.

"Would you like me to find one of the doctors for you?" She started to stand.

"No." He reached out to still her. "Stay with me."

She nodded, sitting again.

He closed his eyes and settled.

"How do you feel?" She ran her fingers through his hair.

"Like I've been dragged through a field by a team of horses."

"That rough?"

He nodded again.

Elizabeth spotted a nurse passing nearby.

"Excuse me, nurse?"

The young woman stopped.

"Would you see if one of the doctors is available to speak with Dr. Taylor?"

The young woman nodded and moved on after her errand.

"There, John, you'll have all of your questions answered."

He was unmoving. She couldn't discern his chest rising and falling. Her heart stopped.

"John?" she placed her hands on his arm, shaking him.

"What?" he jerked awake.

She hugged him as best she could in the bed. "For a moment, I thought I'd lost you!"

"I'll take this wake up over the screaming and shaking any day."

When she pulled back, his eyes were serious on her face. And she felt tears escaping her eyes. As they began to fall, he used the pad of his thumb to clear them. "It's all right. I am well."

"No, you're not, John," was all she managed before she pulled away. It was no use. Why weigh him down with her worries? With how difficult and scary her life had been these last several days? Even when she closed her eyes, she saw the movement of his breathing. And she couldn't escape the fear. What if he stopped? What if the end came? What would she do then?

"Elizabeth, don't pull away from me. Talk to me."

"It's not fair to burden you."

"I want to share your burden. Remember what we said? Together through everything? Don't shut me out."

"Your prognosis hasn't been good, John. I have been here, by your side, day after day, night after night, waiting for you to wake or waiting for you to die, knowing that each breath could be your last."

His eyes glazed over. "I can't imagine how horrible that must have been."

More tears came. "It was horrible, John. It was a nightmare I couldn't wake up from."

He took her hand in his. "I'm here now and I'm not going anywhere."

She smiled at his efforts, but the truth was that he might not be out of danger yet.

Movement behind her drew her attention.

Dr. Smith walked toward them.

Elizabeth had no desire to hear the whole story again, nor did she want Dr. Smith to see her cry yet again. Grabbing the water pitcher, she said, "Looks like we need a refill."

"What? Let a nurse take care of that, Lizzie."

"Nonsense. Besides, Dr. Smith is here to keep you company. And far be it from me to become the third wheel," she smiled and stood, not giving John further opportunity to protest. She moved away just as Dr. Smith greeted John.

Elizabeth stepped out of the hospital tent and moved toward the stream. Why should it be so strange to be back in the Union camp? This should feel like home, and it did to some extent, but the Confederate camp had been like home, too. Why was this so strange to her? So difficult? There were people here who made her feel cared for and missed, like her tent mates. Was that home?

Passing the laundry, she nodded at Melanie who worked to clean uniforms. As Melanie looked up, Elizabeth saw that she had been crying. And Elizabeth paused.

"Melanie, what's troubling you?" She veered off course and stepped closer to the wash bin.

Melanie rubbed her eyes with the back of her hand. "It's nothing."

"Don't tell me that," Elizabeth scolded gently. "I see that something is upsetting you."

"It's just that..." Melanie started then seemed to think better of it. "No, you have enough on your shoulders without my problems too." She pulled the pants out of the wash and hung them.

Elizabeth came around the bin and placed a hand on her arm. "Please. You've been so supportive for me. Let me at least be an ear for you."

Melanie studied her for a handful of seconds, and Elizabeth doubted she had convinced her friend. And then Melanie teared up again and started talking.

"I've made a real mess of things."

"I'm sure that's not true. Tell me what happened."

"It's Jacob. The boy I told you about that had to have his leg amputated?"

Elizabeth nodded.

"He told me he was in love with me."

Elizabeth felt her eyes widen, but she tried to keep her face neutral.

"And so I had to tell him I wasn't in love with him. But you should have seen his face. It hurt him!"

"I know it feels like it's your fault, but it's not."

"It's not?" Melanie sniffled.

Elizabeth shook her head. "No. Matters of the heart are nearly always difficult, and as long as you're honest, you have nothing to be ashamed of."

Melanie nodded, but tears came anew and she put the back of her hand on her mouth to keep from sobbing.

"Tell me."

"There is a man I care for deeply. He went off to battle several days ago and hasn't returned."

"Oh, Melanie!" Elizabeth hugged her friend. As she pulled back, she continued, "I know your heart is aching and fears the worst, but listen, you know for a fact that some of the men have to stay behind sometimes to hold the line. Trust. Have faith."

Nodding again, Melanie calmed and gained control of her emotions.

"So when you have those fears, maybe write him a letter, even just a few lines, and imagine how happy he will be to get the letters when he returns."

"Thank you," Melanie said, wiping away the last remnants of her tears.

"Of course."

"Oh, look at me. I must be a sight! And I must seem so silly to you."

"Not at all. You seem like a girl who's in love."

Melanie smiled at her. Then sighed. "What I truly am is a girl who will get in a heap of trouble if these uniforms aren't cleaned and drying within the hour."

Elizabeth looked at the pile, too. "I'd best let you get to it."

Melanie moved back to the wash bin, placing another pair of pants into the water as Elizabeth grabbed her pitcher and moved off in the direction of the stream. She glanced back at Melanie when she heard humming. There was a smile on her face. Elizabeth could only imagine that Melanie was thinking of her beau.

Daniel watched the scenery around him. He was battle-weary and ready for a good night's rest on his mat. Had he truly just thought that? His body ached from being on alert for so long, but he'd gained a renewed sense of energy when they had been relieved of their stations. The battle was long over, but some of the men stayed behind to reinforce the line.

Camping under the stars was not nearly as glamorous as it had been when he was a kid. Especially when you had to take turns on watch, knowing that when you did sleep, you put your life in someone else's hands. It didn't take more than one night for that to wear thin.

All of it was behind him as he returned to camp. And to Melanie. Thoughts of her had been what pulled him through on many a lonely night watch when his body begged for sleep. Visions of her helped him persevere when he wanted to give up on those long days on his belly on a dirt mound, ever watchful for Confederates. Remembering the feel of her lips on his kept him going through the whole ordeal. It gave him the determination to press on that he might see her again, that he might hold her again. And now that day had come.

By now, they were able to see the camp on the horizon and his step quickened. The other men with him followed suit. Whether they took their cue from him or had their own reasons to hasten their return to camp, Daniel did not know. His body begged him to take it easy, but he ignored it, his thoughts only of Melanie's face when he walked into camp. Would she be expecting him? Were the women of the camp privy to the change in orders? He doubted it. What a delightful surprise it would be.

It was only a matter of minutes before they jogged into camp. The men dispersed upon setting foot in camp, each off to find his friends or loved ones to show himself unharmed. Daniel had no idea where to find Melanie. First, he walked to her tent. Empty. Next, he wandered over to the hospital, peeking in. He saw Jacob's cot from where he stood, but Melanie was not there with him. Making his way over to the women's area, he checked the laundry and cooking stations.

As he turned to move on, a loud shriek let out behind him.

He spun toward the sound.

There she was. Her eyes wide, her hands covering her mouth, a basketful of clothes dropped at her feet.

"It's you," she cried, rushing to him, throwing herself into his arms, and knocking him over with the force of her body hitting his.

He had the forethought to wrap his arms around her as they toppled, taking the brunt of the fall. It knocked the wind out of him. But he didn't care.

"Yes, it's me," he said, gasping for air. He tried to maneuver their bodies so they were at least on their sides.

But Melanie wasn't budging. Instead she pressed her lips to his, uncaring that they lay on the ground.

He accepted her kiss, returning her passion with his own.

Once they broke apart, his hands were on both sides of her face and he stroked her hair.

"Dearest Melanie, I have so longed to hold you, to kiss you, these long days that I have been away. But I have to request we do this from a different position, my love."

She looked down at him for a moment. Only then seeming to realize that he struggled to breathe. "Of course." Rising to her feet, she reached down to help him up.

Once he was on his feet, he gathered her in his arms again. "Tell me you missed me one ounce as much as I missed you," he said, playing with the fabric of her sleeve.

"Tell you? Can you not see it in my eyes?"

He looked into her green orbs and saw the emotion there and the unshed tears that were threatening to spill. "I can," he said softly. He kissed the tip of her nose.

They gazed deeply into each other's eyes.

"I hope those clothes weren't important." Daniel smiled.

Melanie glanced at the pile of clothes, now spilled out onto the ground. "Oh, no!" she kneeled beside them. "These were clean."

Daniel crouched next to her and picked up a shirt. "They only landed on the grass. I think they're fine."

Melanie snatched it out of his hands and examined the shirt. "I suppose so. I just can't believe I would be so thoughtless."

"Hey," Daniel reached out and touched the side of her face. "Don't be so hard on yourself. Besides," he joked. "I'm a pretty big deal."

She paused collecting the clothes to give him a smirk.

"Let me help you there." He reached to pick up some of the clothes.

Once they had collected them, Melanie stood with the basket, facing him. "Thank you. Even though I am so glad to see you, I'm on laundry duty today and I need to get back to my post and finish."

Daniel nodded, disappointed. "Meet you later for dinner? I'll save you a seat."

"You'd better," Melanie said, taking a few steps backwards in the direction of the laundry bin before turning around.

Daniel watched her go. And he knew his heart was hopelessly lost to her.

When John took a turn for the better, it seemed as if all the darkness had passed. He continued to improve until his prognosis became a full recovery. No one was happier than Elizabeth as no one had spent more time praying or nursing him than she. Eventually, the doctors recommended John take short walks around the camp for fresh air and exercise. Elizabeth volunteered to ensure he didn't overdo it.

Walking arm in arm, they would make their way down to the stream each day. These days, John said he felt a need to be near the stream, a need that Elizabeth understood. As it turned out, if they had followed the stream, it would've brought them to the camp. While they walked, Elizabeth thought about their journey and how the stream sustained them and guided them, but neither said a word about it. There were plenty of other topics to cover.

Elizabeth shared the silly camp gossip, not that either of them cared two snits about it. Other topics often covered were John's recovery and Elizabeth's duties around the camp. Then it would be time to walk back to the hospital. But today, John stopped Elizabeth when she made a move to stand.

"Can we sit for a little while longer?" He continued to gaze at the movement of the water.

"Sure." She readjusted her skirt to sit on the ground again.

"I was thinking. The wagon is prepared to take the amputees to catch the train to Boston. I'm doing well enough that I think you should join them."

"What are you saying, John?" Her eyes widened. What was he thinking?

"I'm saying that I think it's time for you to go home," he said, turning to face her. "To relieve yourself of all this hardship and danger. I would go, but I have to fulfill my tour of duty."

"Then I'm not going anywhere. I stay with you." As if to emphasize her point, she hooked both of her arms through his. He had the ability, if he so chose, to go to the colonel and have her shipped back to Boston with or without her consent.

"Now you're just being stubborn," he grumbled.

"John Taylor, how dare you?" She loosened her grip on his arm and shifted until she created some distance between them. "And after all I've been through."

He propped his arms up on his knees, glancing over and catching her eyes. "I'm sorry you feel that way, Lizzie, but that's how I feel. You are not some farmer's wife, you belong in Boston with your parents." His voice was raised. He never raised his voice at her.

"What does it matter what my station in life is?" Her response was sharp.

"Women of your station do not get involved in war this way."

"I'm not just a city girl wearing a pair of soldier's boots." Her eyes narrowed. "I'm doing what I can to contribute here. Just like you, I'm making a difference for these men."

His voice softened. "Lizzie, think of your parents. They are worried sick about you!"

She deflated somewhat. "I know. I feel terrible for what I've put them through."

"And what about me? I have a duty to protect you. What kind of man would I be to allow you to remain in harm's way?"

That lit a fire in her. "The kind that has come to understand that we face these obstacles together. Did our trials getting to this point teach you nothing?"

He was silent for a moment.

She had him.

As he pinched the bridge of his nose, she wondered if he felt a headache coming on.

"Lizzie, please understand that I am trying to do what's best for you."

Her voice calmed. "I know you are. And I need you to understand that what's best for me is to be with you. It's always been us. I don't know what it is to not be us."

He met her eyes again, gazing deeply into them. Could he see into her very soul?

After some moments of silence, he spoke, "Then, Lizzie, let's be us. But not like this. For real."

"What do you mean?"

He leaned toward her, his face inches from hers. "Marry me. That's one of my conditions."

She beamed and threw herself into his arms. "Of course I'll marry you, John Taylor!"

He let out a stifled groan and she realized she pressed on his wounded shoulder.

"Oh, sorry." She eased off.

"My second condition is that you promise me you will never run out on a battlefield again."

"But what if you..."

"Never. I cannot do my job if I am always worried after you."

She met his gaze and then, reluctantly, nodded.

"And my third condition..." His eyes lit up as he gazed at her. He took her hand in his.

"What?" She leaned into him.

"Love me." He bent his head toward hers, his lips so close. "Always and forever."

"Always and forever." She closed the distance between them.

Jacob had been traveling for days. First, in the rather uncomfortable wagon. His joints still ached from the jostling his body had been through. Next, he was transported on the train. That had afforded him a much smoother ride, but it had been just as crowded as the small wagon. Unfortunately, on the train, he was no longer only with his comrades, his fellow amputees. Other passengers from the general public surrounded him as well. And these passengers stared.

They tried to pretend that they didn't, but Jacob sensed their eyes on him. Every single second. A few men were bold enough to thank him for his service and congratulate him on a job well done. *I obviously didn't do a good enough job,* he would think to himself. *I lost my leg.* But he responded to these well-meaning comments with a polite smile and a 'thank you.'

One thing was for certain, he'd had enough of the general population long before he saw the familiar sights of Boston. Was this a taste of what was to come? Would he always be a freak in the eyes of some and forever marked as simply a soldier in the eyes of others?

After what happened with Melanie, Jacob had been all too eager to return home. But now he would give anything to be back at camp. He wished he could replay his farewell with Melanie and Daniel. Maybe it would go differently. It had been so tense.

He only added to the tension as he held on to his hurt and wounded pride. Those were two people he always imagined he would stay in touch with. However, after that farewell, there was no certainty as to where they stood. Why couldn't he have let go of his anger and hurt? Treated them like the friends they were? How he wished for a second chance!

In his musings, he almost missed the announcement that they approached Boston. He looked out the window and began to pick out familiar sights. Blinking back tears at the realization that he was home, he tried to gather his wits. Minutes later they pulled into the station.

Jacob waited for the other passengers around him to get up, collect their things, and move on before he could get up. He needed the extra space to stand, however awkwardly, with his crutch. Grabbing his pack, he slung it over his shoulder, careful to balance it. Then he moved to exit the train. Having done some walking around the camp with the crutch, he had gained some confidence. But it was still a new skill. So things like getting down off a raised train took time and concentration lest he lose his balance and fall, making a real spectacle of himself.

Not long after his foot hit the platform, he heard a familiar voice. "Jacob!"

Glancing in the direction of the voice, he saw his family and friends standing several feet away. Some of them held American flags. He raised his hand to wave at them, suddenly embarrassed about his leg.

Jacob's parents and sister moved toward him. His little sister reached him first. She threw her arms around his midsection. His parents were seconds behind her and embraced him as best they could with Susan in the way.

"Jacob, you're home," his father said.

His mother tried to speak, but it came out as little whimpers.

Even in the embrace, Jacob felt that she sobbed.

Susan pulled away to look at Mother. "Mommy, don't be sad. Jacob's home."

Father looked down at Jacob's sister. "Oh, Susan, Mommy isn't sad. Those are happy tears."

As his father gazed at Susan, Jacob saw tears escaping his eyes. Jacob was moved as well. At last, he was surrounded by people that saw him as Jacob first above anything else, apart from his injury or his status as a soldier.

So he pressed a kiss to his mother's face, his sister's hair, and even to the side of his father's face. Then he waved his friends to come closer.

There, among the faces, was a pair of bright blue eyes. Clara? Had she truly cared to be at his homecoming? Their eyes met and her lips curved into a timid smile. He returned it. And his heart skipped a beat.

"I'm home." He sighed. "I'm finally home."

Somewhere else, farther west, Matthew stepped off another train and into a new life. Had he truly left the other behind? A lost love, a narrow escape, and now a man on the run. What did life hold for him? He gazed at the mountains in the distance, and the ache in his heart seemed to lessen if only slightly. Perhaps this could be home.

People milled about him, passing him by. Then he got a firm bump from behind. Turning, he was prepared to fend off any manner of attack, but found himself looking down into a pair of hazel eyes.

"Pardon me, sir," the woman said, straightening her posture. "But should you be standing on the platform when everyone is trying to get off the train?"

"I believe, ma'am," he said, trying to keep the irritation out of his voice. "That you should watch where you are going."

Her eyes widened as she glared at him. "Well, I never!"

Gathering her bag closer to herself, she raised her nose in the air, and moved off toward the building labeled "Boarding House."

And he watched her go, noting the swish of her skirts and the way her brown curls bounced as she walked. The corner of his mouth tugged upward. Yes, he could grow to like it here.

Elizabeth tried to sit still while at least three women pulled at her in different places. But it didn't bother her. This was her wedding day! The women all wanted her to be perfect for John, so she gave them a lot of leeway. They had been so generous to her in preparation for this day.

She had always dreamed of getting married in John's favorite color, blue, but had decided that, if at all possible, she wanted to wear a purple dress in remembrance of all of the fallen soldiers. All the women went into their bags and there was, indeed, one woman who had a purple dress. The best seamstress in the camp volunteered to take some of the lace off Elizabeth's nightshift and adorn the dress as she made the necessary alterations so it would fit Elizabeth. Even now, the women pulled up her hair and brought forth what selection of jewelry existed in the camp.

"These are my grandmother's pearls. Would you let them be your something old?" one of the women said.

Elizabeth smiled and nodded, leaning her head forward so that the older woman could fasten them behind her neck.

"And I have your something borrowed," another woman said as she handed her a handkerchief.

"Where am I going to find something new in this camp?" Elizabeth eyed the women around her.

Melanie walked up, hand behind her back. "No worries. I've got just the thing." She pulled out a beautiful bouquet of wildflowers. "Freshly picked. And there are bluebells in there. So they can be your something blue, too."

"Thank you." She smiled up at her friend. "Am I ready?" she asked the congregation of women as she stood.

There were more than a few tears as the women en masse nodded their heads.

Elizabeth looked at Melanie. "Ready?"

She nodded.

"See you all at the ceremony," Elizabeth called back to the women as they moved on in the opposite direction.

Elizabeth and Melanie walked toward the hospital to find Dr. Smith. Because Elizabeth's father wasn't there to give her away, they'd asked Dr. Smith if he would do the honors. It took them several minutes to reach the hospital tent from the women's area. As they neared, they spotted Dr. Smith standing near the entrance.

"My stars," he said as Elizabeth round the corner. "You look like an angel."

Her face warmed and she smiled at him.

He offered her his arm and she slid her hand into the crook of his elbow. They then headed toward the open field designated as the site for the wedding.

Elizabeth and John had wanted to exchange vows at the spot by the stream where he had proposed, but everyone in camp wanted to attend the wedding and it was decided that a forested area just wasn't conducive to a crowd. So they were to be wed in the adjacent field.

The short walk from the hospital seemed to take forever. How long had it been since she had laid eyes on her beloved? But soon enough, the tents gave way to the open field and she saw the gathering crowd.

They milled about, waiting for her. The mass of bodies prevented her from seeing John until they parted, creating an aisle for her. Only then could she see him, standing so proud in his uniform. Her heart pounded when she caught sight of her husband-to-be. John seemed as cool and collected as ever. How did he do that? John's head was turned down toward the ground. But soon enough his eyes came up to meet hers.

She would give anything to be able to capture the expression on his face when first he saw her that day. But no sketchbook would do it justice. So she would just have to lock it away in her heart.

Melanie, her maid of honor, went down the makeshift aisle first. Then it was time. And she froze.

Dr. Smith stepped forward, but she couldn't make her feet obey. He put a hand on her arm as if to get her attention. Still, she could not make herself budge. Looking at the crowd, she thought about how all these people would be so disappointed. Then she caught sight of John and felt her body relax.

Exchanging a look with Dr. Smith, she smiled and nodded, and stepped forward. As they made their way down the aisle, drawing ever closer to John, she saw that he was indeed a mess of emotion, not nearly as collected as she had first assumed.

When Dr. Smith handed her off to John, she felt his need to be near her.

"You are breathtaking today," he whispered.

"For you," she whispered back.

He squeezed her hand.

They turned their attention to the chaplain.

"Dearly beloved, we are gathered here in the sight of God and in the presence of these witnesses, to join John Taylor and Elizabeth Thompson in holy matrimony, which is an honorable estate, instituted of God in the time of man's innocence, signifying to us the mystical union which is between Christ and His Church. It is therefore not to be entered into lightly or inadvisably, but reverently, discreetly, and in the fear of God.

"I charge you both as you stand in the presence of God, to remember that true love and loyalty alone will avail as the foundation of a happy home. No other human ties are more tender, no vows more sacred, than those you are about to assume. You are entering into the holy estate which is the deepest mystery of experience, and which is the very sacrament of divine love.

"Are you prepared to make your vows?"

John and Elizabeth both nodded. And so they repeated after the chaplain.

"I, John, take thee, Elizabeth, to be my wedded wife, to have and to hold from this day forward, for better for worse, for richer for poorer, in sickness and in health, to love and to cherish, till death us do part, according to God's holy ordinance."

"I, Elizabeth, take thee, John, to be my wedded husband, to have and to hold from this day forward, for better for worse, for richer for poorer, in sickness and in health, to love and to cherish, till death us do part, according to God's holy ordinance."

"Forasmuch as John and Elizabeth have consented in holy wedlock, and have pledged their troth; by the authority committed unto me as a chaplain of the U.S. Army, I now declare you husband and wife according to the ordinance of God, and the laws of the United States, in the name of the Father, and of the Son, and of the Holy Spirit, Amen.

"You may kiss your bride."

John leaned in, putting his hands on either side of Elizabeth's face, and met her lips for a kiss to seal their union. As he pulled away, he wiped her tears with his thumbs before he took her hands in his.

"And now it is my happy privilege to congratulate Dr. and Mrs. John Taylor!"

A cheer sounded from the crowd and soldiers from either side of the aisle stepped forward to raise their sabers in the air, making an arch for them.

John held out his arm. Elizabeth took it and allowed him to lead her under the arch. Once they were through, the sabers were re-sheathed. John and Elizabeth gazed at one another and sighed. They had done it. They had actually gotten married!

But what was to be done from here? Elizabeth knew there were no plans beyond the ceremony. In their haste to make wedding preparations, they had not sought out the colonel in time to secure alternate bedding provisions so that they might stay together after the wedding. Just yesterday, when John went to the colonel he discovered that nothing could be done on such short notice. They would be consigned to their separate accommodations tonight.

Melanie stepped into their path. "Let me be the first to say 'Congratulations'!" She reached out to hug Elizabeth. "I'm also supposed to tell you that the women have planned a wedding supper. It won't be anything fancy, but I think it will be great."

"I know it will be," Elizabeth said, so touched by the thoughtfulness. Did their generosity know no bounds?

Everyone, it seemed, approached them to offer their congratulations and wish them a long and happy marriage. John and Elizabeth received each person graciously, grateful for their family away from home. Once all the guests made their way by and they were alone, John turned to her.

"Shall we make our way to dinner?" John squeezed the hand he had not released since the ceremony began.

Elizabeth shook her head. "Not yet. I want to spend a few more minutes just being Mrs. John Taylor." She wrapped her arms around his neck.

"Oh?" John had a mischievous smile on his face as he splayed his hands across her back.

She hugged him close to herself, her face in the crook of his neck. "We have waited so long for this, I can't believe we did it."

John rubbed her back. "I know. But we did. And we'll return to Boston as man and wife when this is all over."

Elizabeth was struck with that thought. "John, what about our parents? How could I have forgotten to write and…"

He held up a hand. "Already taken care of."

She smiled. Of course he would think of that.

He tucked that stubborn, errant curl behind her ear. "You are so beautiful, Lizzie. You take my breath away."

Her face warmed as she leaned into his embrace once again. "And I truly am, now and always, your Lizzie."

After several seconds, John turned his head to whisper in her ear. "I think we'd better head toward the party or I fear we might miss it."

Elizabeth pulled back reluctantly and nodded. She wrapped her arms around one of his and let him lead her toward the dining area.

The women of the camp had indeed outdone themselves. Among the other camp staples, they made a rare treat — warm biscuits. One of the men brought out his fiddle and there was dancing around the fire in celebration of the blessed event. A special evening everyone took part in.

The war was forgotten for the moment, the threat of battle no longer looming. Rather, the music and food filled everyone's senses for this evening. This respite, however, would end as curfew neared.

Elizabeth loathed parting with John and retiring to her own tent. She caught John's eye and knew he thought the same thing. But what else could be done?

Melanie stepped up to Elizabeth and took her hands. "There's one more surprise. One I can't take all the credit for. That is, I had something to do with it, but there was also Dr. Smith and the colonel…"

"What is it, Melanie?" Elizabeth laughed.

Melanie looked at Daniel. "I think we should blindfold them."

Daniel agreed and so they went about blindfolding John and Elizabeth.

"This had better be worth it," John muttered.

"If I know Melanie, it will be," Elizabeth assured him.

They allowed themselves to be led through the camp. Elizabeth became clueless as to where in camp they were after just a few steps and a couple of turns. It wasn't long before they stopped. Melanie told them to wait a moment. Then Elizabeth felt someone working the blindfold tie. And then she could see.

"Ta-da!" Melanie shouted.

Before her stood a tent, one of the larger ones. The flaps were open and a lantern illuminated the inside. Elizabeth didn't understand.

"We can't accept this," John said. "It's too generous."

Accept this? This tent was for them? Just for them? Elizabeth had assumed they'd be staying in their regular accommodations for a while, perhaps until they went home. She'd never imagined that they'd be given a tent in the family section of camp, much less a spacious tent like this.

"It's too much," Elizabeth echoed John's protest.

"Nonsense. After all you've been through? After all you've sacrificed? No one thinks it's too much. Besides, the colonel approved it, so it's done."

"I don't know what to say." Elizabeth couldn't tear her eyes away. She couldn't imagine that this would be her new home. Her first home with John, the place where they would first live as man and wife.

"You could say 'thank you'," Melanie teased.

"Thank you, a million times over!" Elizabeth exclaimed, pulling her gaze from the tent to look at her friend.

"Yes, thank you," John added.

A sly grin crossed Melanie's face. "Daniel and I don't wish to keep you up any longer, so..."

She let her sentence trail off.

"Lizzie, you've had a long day. I'll go with Melanie to collect your bag and then get mine."

"No need," Melanie said. "I..."

"Now, stop right there," John said. "I cannot let you collect our bags. I'm perfectly willing and able to do that."

"What I was going to say is that I...that is we...already did that. Your bags, both of them, are already in your tent."

"Oh," John said. "Well, we owe you another 'thank you'."

"It was nothing."

"It means everything to us that you went to all this trouble."

Melanie just smiled. "I think it's getting close to curfew, so we'd best be on our way."

Elizabeth went to Melanie and grabbed her in a fierce hug. "Thank you, dearest friend. Thank you."

Melanie hugged her back.

Once Elizabeth released her, Daniel took Melanie's hand and they walked off into the moonlight, disappearing around a couple of tents as they made their way back to their side of camp.

John came up behind Elizabeth, putting his hands on her shoulders and pressing a kiss to the side of her face. "Want to go inside?"

She looked over her shoulder at him and nodded.

He took her hand.

Once they were inside the tent, Elizabeth got a better look at what had been set up for them. Melanie and whoever else had been involved in this surprise had been busy collecting every extra sleeping mat they could find. The bed was a series of sleeping mats built up to create a makeshift double bed that was maybe three or four inches deep. Compared to sleeping on one thin mat on the ground, this bed looked luxurious.

They had found a small table to serve as a nightstand, currently serving as a stand for the lantern. Their bags were stashed in the opposite corner. And a new nightshift for Elizabeth lay on the bed. Someone had forfeited her nightshift to provide Elizabeth with one after hers had been sacrificed for her wedding dress. Truly, the women in this camp had been too generous.

John was behind her. His arms wrapped around her. "Would you like to get dressed for bed?"

She felt a rush of nervousness. Since they had expected to spend their wedding night separated, she hadn't prepared herself for this part. But it was John. He was as familiar to her as her own reflection and closer to her than any other. She trusted him implicitly.

Turning in his arms, she pressed her lips to his. The kiss they shared felt different than any other. It became hungry, a kiss that wanted more and anticipated more to come.

"Let me get the light," John said, his voice full of emotion.

She released him long enough for him to put out the light.

He maintained contact by holding her hand. And then he felt his way back to her embrace. As their eyes adjusted to the dark, they fumbled their way onto the makeshift bed, still locked in each other's embrace.

John pressed tender kisses to Elizabeth's face, lips, and neck while she held him close.

"John," she said, softly.

"Yes?" he breathed.

"Promise me it will always be like this. That we will always be like this."

"Always," he said, kissing her deeply. "Always and forever."

EPILOGUE

"Elizabeth? Elizabeth Thompson...er...Taylor? Is that you?"

Elizabeth turned to see a beaming red-haired beauty making her way through the crowd.

"Melanie, how good to see you!"

"And my goodness, look at you! I had heard, but seeing is believing."

Elizabeth placed a hand on the swell of her belly, nodding. "We're so excited. Won't be long."

"What are you hoping for?" Melanie's face broke out with a smile.

"Oh, I just want a healthy baby."

"And I want a little girl with blonde curls like her mother," John said, coming up behind Elizabeth. "I found us some seats."

"Look, John, it's Melanie. Do you remember her? From the 16th Regiment?"

"I think so. It's good to see you are doing so well. And your husband, is he..."

Elizabeth elbowed him. "John," she admonished, "Melanie isn't..."

"Actually, he was just grabbing my wrap from the carriage."

Elizabeth raised an eyebrow.

"Here he is now." A young man came over to Melanie and handed her a shawl. "Daniel, I'd like you to meet my good friend Elizabeth and her husband John. Both from the 16th Regiment."

"Ah, I was a soldier there myself. Doctor, is it?"

"Why, yes sir, it is."

"I definitely remember you."

"I'm so sorry that I can't place you."

"It's all right. There were many soldiers, but only three doctors."

The music indicated that the ceremony would begin in moments.

"We'd best get to our seats," Elizabeth said. "Care to join us?"

"Of course." Melanie hooked Daniel's arm.

Once they were all comfortably seated and the congregation settled, the wedding ceremony began. Melanie kept her eyes peeled for her dear friend and when he appeared she knew she had never seen him so handsome as he was for this most special occasion. She watched his face even as his bride, a beautiful brunette, appeared. And his reaction was priceless.

But she had known he would one day meet a special woman who would love him the way he deserved to be loved. And that was why Melanie was here today. To celebrate her dearest friend, Jacob Moore's, wedding.

Keep reading for a preview of the first book in the Cripple Creek Series!

Thank you, dear reader, for for reading along with me! If you enjoyed this story, I would sincerely appreciate if you would submit a review. It would mean so much to me!

The stagecoach moved along, bumping and rocking as it went. Trees and other green scenery whisked by the window. Views of mountains and open plains were visible from the seat of the coach, vistas familiar to its occupant. Katherine Matthews was coming home. She returned to Cripple Creek, no longer the scared, unsure teenager who had left to further her education so many years ago with hopes and dreams of a new life in a new place. No, she had matured into a confident young woman who had grown in stature and in beauty. Her hair was no longer the mousy color she always hated, for it had deepened into the same beautiful chestnut brown she had always admired in her mother's appearance. She'd grown out of her awkward teenage features, and was now well regarded among her peers as a rather handsome woman.

Returning to Cripple Creek brought many rather-mixed emotions to the surface. Imagine, one of her first postings would be at the same schoolhouse where she received her educational start. When her mother wrote to her of the interim need, she was glad to help out. What an odd coincidence that the letter would find her, too, in transition. Would this turn into a permanent placement? Did she want it to?

The mountain scenery became more recognizable, and she thought back on her childhood. There were so many happy times here. Unbidden, her mind wandered to the day of the great tragedy that had marred her spirit—the day Ellie Mae died.

Even all these years later, she carried the scar in her heart. The events of that day had left her broken. Why must thoughts of Ellie Mac plague her so? And all the more as her return became imminent? She shivered as the images from her nightmares the previous evening flitted across her mind. They would not stop. These same visions visited her in sleep night after night. All the more frequently these last weeks.

Closing her eyes, the hazy images took form and became memory. It was as if no time had passed. She and Ellie, walking through the schoolyard just as they did every other day . . .

Hooking arms with Ellie Mae, Katherine stepped out of the schoolhouse and into the yard. A rather large group of students gathered off to the right near the old tree. It didn't bother Katherine. She turned her attention toward the path that would lead home.

"What do you think they're up to?" Ellie Mae whispered.

Katherine glanced in that direction and noticed Betsy Callaway at the center, flapping her jaws. Why would anyone listen to anything she said? But they did. The class at large seemed to adore Betsy. It didn't make sense. Clenching her teeth, Katherine grabbed for Ellie Mae's hand. "Whatever it is, we don't want to be involved." She pulled Ellie Mae along as she walked on, trying to pass the gathering.

"I know Miss Matthews couldn't do it," Betsy said loudly.

Katherine froze in her tracks. What had she just said?

The crowd of students parted and glared at Katherine and Ellie Mae.

"Let's keep going," Ellie Mae pleaded, tugging on Katherine's hand.

She should listen to Ellie Mae and not become a part of whatever game Betsy played. But she could not let Betsy get the best of her. What would everyone think of her?

So, she turned to face her accuser. There stood Betsy with Wyatt Sullivan, the most popular boy in school, right beside her. Betsy's blonde pigtails, tied back with perfect pink ribbons, shone in the sun. Her dress was no less perfect, pink with just the right amount of lace and even a slight puff to the sleeves.

"Do what, pray tell?" Katherine shot back. Her heart beat furiously in her chest.

"Go down through the mine shaft." Betsy folded her arms in front of her chest and raised an eyebrow.

Katherine's heart skipped a beat then, but she tried not to show her fear.

Ellie Mae's grip tightened on her hand.

"I assure you, Miss Callaway, it's not that I can't do it. It's simply that I have better things to do than to be traipsing about a mine shaft." She turned to leave and hoped that would be enough to silence Betsy.

"Prove it." Betsy's voice rang out after her.

Katherine's eyes slid closed. Was there any way around this? "I have nothing to prove to you," she called back over her shoulder.

"Fraidycat!" Betsy laughed.

The other students joined in.

Katherine's face burned. A fire had been lit within her. She was not afraid of anything! Releasing Ellie Mae's hand, she then whirled around. "I am not afraid!"

"There's only one way we'll believe that." Betsy's hands moved from her chest to her hips.

There was no way this would be a one-way challenge. "Are you going?" Katherine poked her chin out, putting her own hands on her hips, attempting to puff up her chest as much as she could.

"Of course," Betsy said, though her voice caught.

"Then, let's go." Katherine grabbed after Ellie Mae's hand and headed out in the direction of the old mine shaft. She hoped Ellie Mae didn't feel how her palms had started to sweat. Perspiration covered her whole body. How was she to keep up this façade?

The group of students followed, a din of voices behind. As they neared the cavernous opening, they became quiet as they halted several feet short of the forbidden place.

Wyatt pushed through the crowd once they had stopped. "Now, girls, this is foolishness. Talking about it is one thing, but you're not actually going down there, are you?"

Katherine glanced at the mine opening. It looked dark and ominous. Not what she *wanted to see. Then she eyed Betsy. She had everything—the popularity, the most handsome boy in school … But she would not have Katherine's pride, too. "I am."*

"Then I am, too." Betsy stared at Katherine, matching her glare through slitted eyes.

"Kath-rine," Ellie whispered, tugging on her hand.

Katherine looked over at her friend. Ellie's eyes begged her not to go. Katherine wondered again at the danger. Her friend had every right to be concerned, she supposed. But it would not last. Betsy would go but a few steps in and give up. Katherine was sure of it. So, she would not be dissuaded.

Wyatt's eyes moved from one girl to the other. A couple of years older than the girls at their thirteen years, he stood a good head taller than Katherine. At last, he threw his hands up in the air. "Then I'm going too."

"And so am I," came Ellie Mae's quiet response.

Katherine leaned toward her friend. "Ellie, you don't have to go." Her eyes held Ellie's. What was she going to do? She couldn't take Ellie into that place. But something had eased in her when Ellie Mae volunteered to go. Was it selfish of her to want her friend to accompany her?

"Yes, I do." Her voice was firm, though her chin quivered. "I'm sticking with you."

A bump in the trail jolted Katherine from her reverie. The scenery outside became blurred. Or was it her? Touching her face, she felt moisture. She wiped at the tears. This would not do! Whatever happened when she returned, Katherine was determined she would face it with as much bravery as she could muster.

To read more, find *Hope in Cripple Creek* here:

https://saraturnquist.com/hope-in-cripple-creek/

ACKNOWLEDGMENTS

There are so many things I am grateful for and so many people in my life who contribute in so many ways. It is just not possible to thank everyone who touches my life in a real way. But I want to take a moment and acknowledge the people whose contributions had a more direct impact on this book.

I want to thank my editor, Julie Sherwood, for making this book what it could be. Her input was both valuable and necessary. I also want to thank my irreplaceable beta readers Christina Horton, Stacy Schoenwetter, and Hillary Harvey, without whom this book would not be possible. Their insight and encouragement have added so much and pushed me through so many tough spots. As well, my writing mentor, Hannah Conway, deserves acknowledgement for pouring into me everything she can. And I want to give a shout out to my critique group members whose honest feedback and support are priceless!

I also want to thank the amazing cover artist, Cora Graphics, who is just phenomenal. I am impressed by both her talent and how easy she is to work with.

My photographer, Rachel Bull, is also one of the most talented people I know. I am grateful for her work as well.

For my sister, you make me want to be better. For my parents, you make me feel so good to have achieved this dream of writing. And for my husband and kids, you give me every reason to smile.

ABOUT THE AUTHOR

Sara is a coffee lovin', word slinging, Historical Romance author whose super power is converting caffeine into novels. She loves those odd little tidbits of history that are stranger than fiction. That's what inspires her. Well, that and a good love story.

But of all the love stories she knows, hers is her favorite. She lives happily with her own Prince Charming and their gaggle of minions. Three to be exact. They sure know how to distract a writer! But, alas, the stories must be written, even if it must happen in the wee hours of the morning.

Sara is an avid reader and enjoys reading and writing clean Historical Romance when she's not traveling.

Please follow along with her journey through her newsletter at: http://saraturnquist.com/list

Happy Reading!

facebook.com/AuthorSaraRTurnquist

instagram.com/sararturnquist

x.com/sararturnquist

youtube.com/@SaraRTurnquist

pinterest.com/sararturnquist